CEDRIC
THE
DEMONIC
KNIGHT

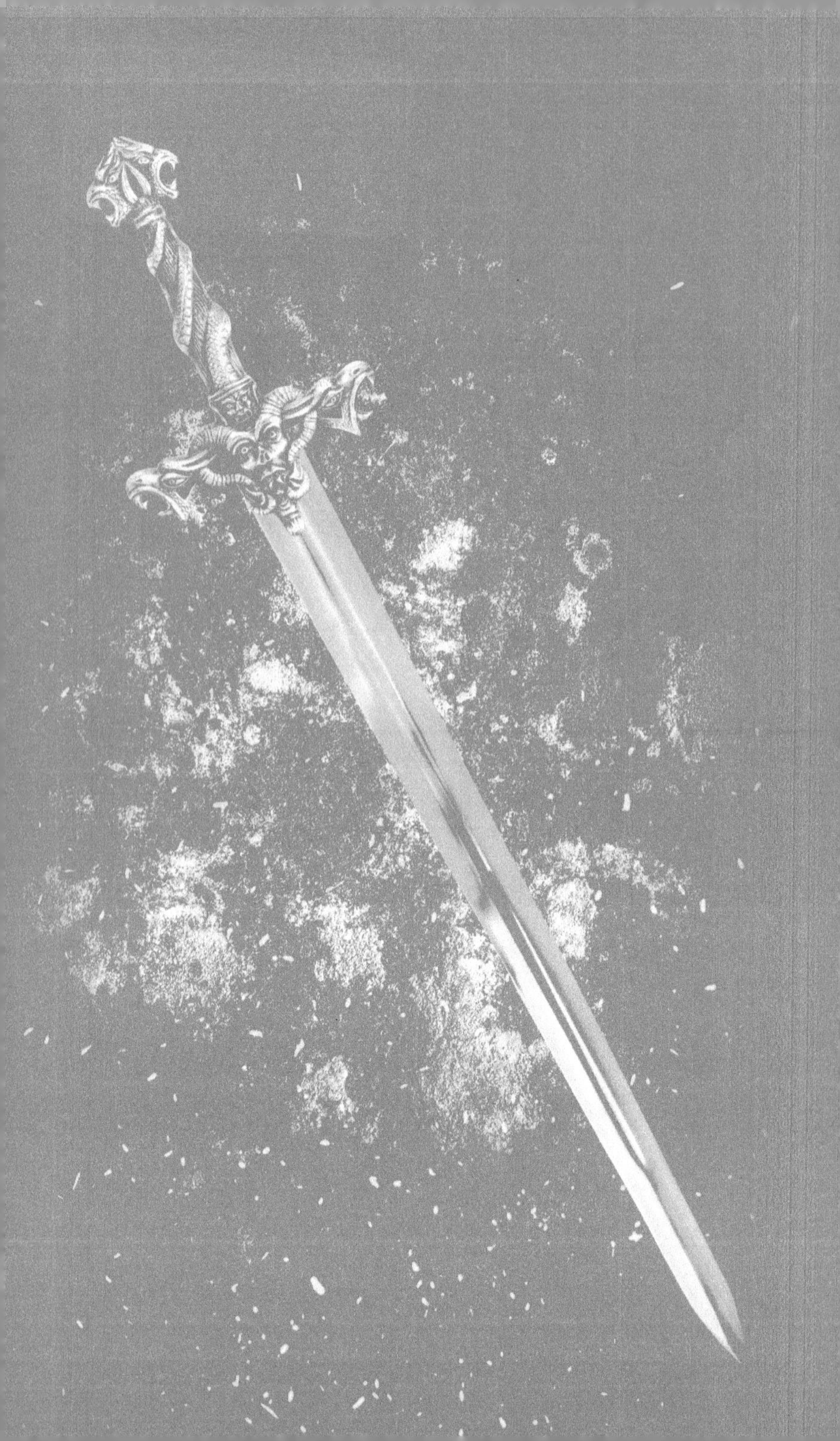

THE CEDRIC SERIES

CEDRIC THE DEMONIC KNIGHT

AWARD-WINNING AUTHOR
VALERIE WILLIS

4 Horsemen
Publications, Inc.

Published By: 4 Horsemen Publications, Inc.

4 Horsemen Publications, Inc.
PO Box 417
Sylva, NC 28779
4horsemenpublications.com
info@4horsemenpublications.com

Cover & Typesetting by Valerie Willis
Edited by Nick Savage

Paperback ISBN-13: 978-1-64450-086-6
Hardcover ISBN-13: 978-1-64450-270-9
Audiobook ISBN-13: 978-1-64450-037-8
Ebook ISBN-13: 978-1-64450-038-5

Dedication

This book is dedicated to my amazing husband. Without his patience and encouragement, none of this would have existed.

I Love You, Mr. Justin Willis.

TABLE OF CONTENTS

DEDICATION V

PREFACE. IX

ACKNOWLEDGMENTS XIII

CHAPTER 1
Present Day 1

CHAPTER 2
Cedric's story the 12th Century 5

CHAPTER 3
The Tournament 10

CHAPTER 4
Bait. 16

CHAPTER 5
Cursed Woods, Cursed Village. 23

CHAPTER 6
Hellhounds 32

CHAPTER 7
Shade for a Horse 42

CHAPTER 8
Shaman in the Woods. 49

CHAPTER 9
Venoms, Poisons, & Toxins 56

CHAPTER 10
A Cure. 63

CHAPTER 11
Desire 72

CHAPTER 12
Haunting Dreams. 81

CHAPTER 13
Lillith's Rage 88

CHAPTER 14
Morrighan's Chimeras. 100

CHAPTER 15
Badbh the Battle Goddess 108
CHAPTER 16
Legend of the Moroi 119
CHAPTER 17
The Hunt 134
CHAPTER 18
Romasanta: Father of Werewolves 145
CHAPTER 19
Army versus the Pack 155
CHAPTER 20
King Incubus Boto 164
CHAPTER 21
The Curse 174
CHAPTER 22
Rusty's Bar, Present Day 180
CHAPTER 23
The Sultan's Request 184
CHAPTER 24
The Sisters Arrive 195
CHAPTER 25
Merlin's Demise 201
CHAPTER 26
A Curse Broken 210

READY FOR BOOK TWO? 211
Romasanta: Father of Werewolves is waiting for you. 211

ABOUT THE AUTHOR 213
BOOK CLUB DISCUSSION QUESTIONS 217

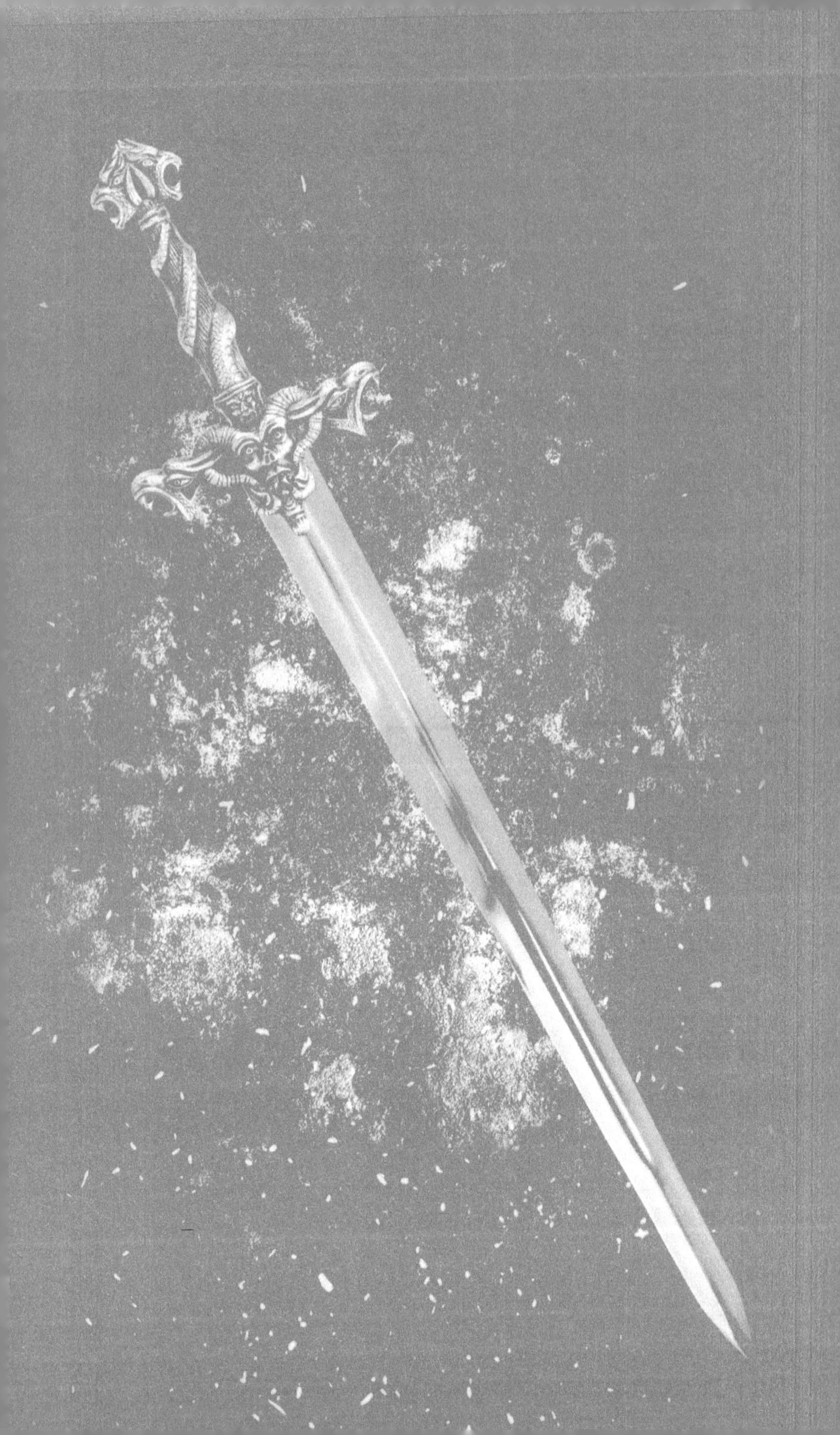

PREFACE

It was brought to my attention that I should take a moment to talk to the readers and fans of *The Cedric Series.*

I wish to share my inspirations for writing this story. This will explain a lot about how I came about creating these amazing ideas, characters, creatures, and events as a fictional work with heavy fantasy and romance elements in the mix. If one really wanted to drag out all its genres, I could label this a historical fiction, mythology, or even an occult and paranormal series. So far, fantasy romance has done this work the most justice for my readers' expectations.

Historical fiction can be applied to several parts throughout the series, whether it's a scene, event, or even a reflection of a character and their on-goings. What do I mean by this? Well, a lot of you might get the Vladimir Tepes, or Vlad the Impaler references, but it dove deeper than that. King Frederic was the First King of Germans and the lepers in those times did indeed have to ring bells and seek refuge in colonies, Cerdanya was a real trade town, and so on. There are a ton of subtle hints here and there because I wanted to bring the unseen, untold side of the history during the Medieval Times to a tangible state.

As far as the mythology side of this series, I wanted to teach you all my versions of forgotten lore, legends, and mythology. I did my best to not use anything that was newer than the 12th century as I dug deep. Some of the concepts woven in with my own perception were hard to obtain and justify. There was a lot of book buying, digging through a Medieval-age bestiary, and though I scoured the internet, it failed me often in my journey for research. As I created and developed each character, I did my best to tie them into one or more myths so that I may weave a wondrous story without limits. At the same time, I wanted some of you to get caught in a conversation or to be sitting in class and have that moment of, "Oh! I know how this myth goes!"

Let me enlighten you all on some of the tales, history, legends, and myths stitched into some of these amazing characters you have experienced so far:

- Cedric takes after a very forgotten and neglected epic legend from the Medieval Times of the Russian knight hero, Ilya Muromets. Search him, check it out, and feel free to compare what you unknowingly learned about this amazing legend. You'll be excited to see a red-haired knight on a black horse as one of the images in the mix. Included in this were some really obscure Romanian beliefs involving early vampire-like stories. The off-shoots involving the strigoi showed less fear toward these vampire creatures, but held a tone of sorrow and remorse. People who became these creatures had not finished living their lives (Including not ever getting married) and met the insane stipulations to come back as one of the undying. Truly interesting, and I can only hope to capture that same empathetic tone I had discovered in my digging.

- Barushka combines a few tales as well, starting with his name drawn from the Russian knight hero tales. Other than that, I focused heavily on the shag foal lores. I was intrigued by the first few variants I stumbled on and found that the internet proved void of information. Amazingly, the hairy phantom horse tales started so long ago. There was no exact date as to when they began. The folklore was mysteriously always there. Adding to my wonder about this lore was the fact I stumbled on a 1927 naturalist journal that devoted a section to them. Even this far forward, it was believed it may be an undiscovered species of horse! Despite that, the one thing I saw reflected in all the writing was that a shag foal approaches lone travelers and scares them so much that they run off to their deaths. Never once did the research say the horse actively killed someone.

- Morrighan, Badbh, and Nemaine were derived from the tales involving the evil sorcerer Calatin. This was an older tale involving them that did not mix the three as one entity. There are no words to describe my frustration and disappointment at how many times Badbh and Nemaine were labeled as alternative names for Morrighan.

Especially when the story of the Legendary Cuchulainn made it clear that they were three sisters, each with unique powers. Seeing that Badbh and Morrighan had earned the title of goddess at some point through the passing of time, I felt the need to give Nemaine her own placement as a goddess as well.

- Romasanta is the most complex of all my characters. His name is taken from a man in history who is not as common as he once was, Manuel Blanco Romasanta. He was the first serial killer to be trailed and as you read book two of the Cedric Series, you will see a lot of that history drawn upon. Feeding off the tragic aura, I pulled in both werewolf and wolf-related myths and lores, wanting to show a more accurate flow through a single entity. It was my intention to bring in familiar aspects and add in the historically forgotten complications that modern book culture has failed to take into account. Those well-versed in mythology will be able to pick out elements on their own, but the amount of lore here is wide. Tales of Apollo and Daphne, Pan and Pitip, Fenrir, versipellis, Romanian beliefs of vampires were caused by a werewolf, Wolf of the Cemetery from Haiti, Romulus and Remus, and so on. There are deep seeds that I only give you teasers of the mythology that is mentioned here.

- As for the monsters, you can say thank you to the Medieval Bestiaries. There are so many wild and crazy creatures in these that are no longer touched that I wanted to bring them to life again. Orms, Jidra, and Aitvaras were a few of the frightening things that travelers spoke of and warned each other about in their explorations. I can only imagine what they may have been based on, but there is a great sense of pride I take in including such monsters in my story. Granted, I have not followed their descriptions exactly and have embellished them with my own imagination, but I hope they make my stories more memorable.

In the end, I encourage my thirsty readers to explore what you've read in my *Cedric Series*. Search the names, look deeper into the scenes, places, and events, and discover these in more detail. My goal is to introduce you to the forgotten lores and history while adding my own perspective and imagination into the mix. May this tale make its mark in your heart and open your world to the legacy our ancestors once talked about over the dinner table so long ago!

Happy reading and discovery!

Valerie Willis

ACKNOWLEDGMENTS

I would like to take a moment to say Thank You to a large number of friends and family who have encouraged, assisted, and cheered me on in my endeavors of writing this piece and the many that will follow it. I love you guys and this was only possible through you all!

- Justin, my amazing Mr. Fixitall!
- Levi, my awesome little man who put up with my distraction!
- Shannon, my writing and art buddy and more importantly consultant!
- Jennifer and Jessie for their edits and enthusiasm!
- To the Kristin's for idea support and hardcore edits!
- Kris for making the intro stronger and pulling it together!
- Erin and her reading buddy, willing to choose my rough as their reading project!
- Alejandro and Hector for nagging me during the writing process!
- Jack and Josh for their stern insight for the beginning of the story!
- Kesa for getting me over some huge writing mountains!
- Stephanie for being the first to read the story in the rough!
- The Alliance of Worldbuilders gang for teaching me so much!
- To the "Shadow Legion" for sparking my want to write again a few years ago!

And, thank you to everyone else for letting me hound you all about helping me read and edit this monster epic story!

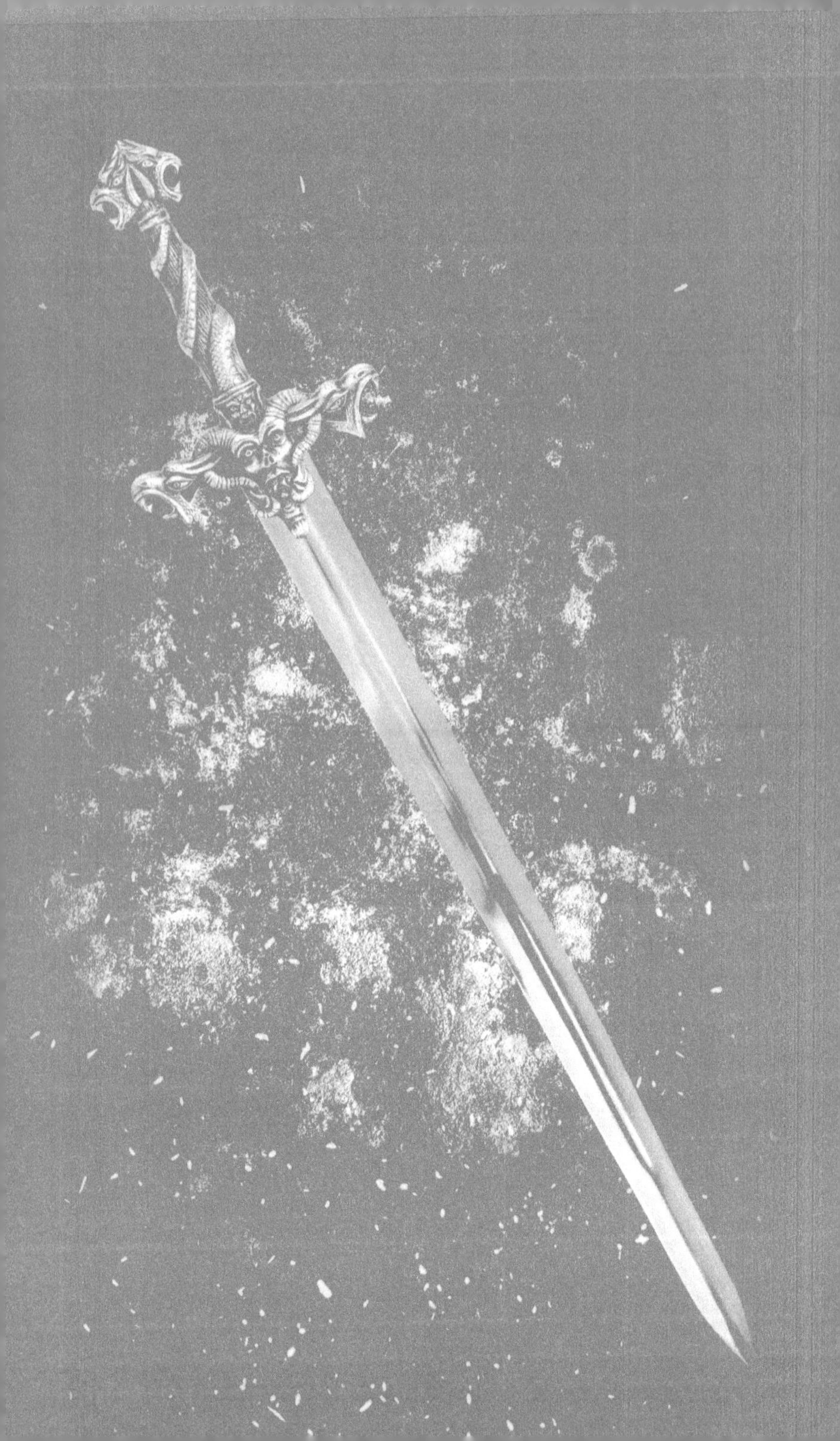

CHAPTER 1

PRESENT DAY

It was another dead Thursday night at the smoke-filled hole-in-the-wall bar, Rusty's. The bartender set out to look busy, vigorously scrubbing the bar top, waiting for the regulars to drag in. There was a wet musk scent in the air. Besides the homeless man in the back booth, there was not a soul in the joint. Most of the people rolled in closer to midnight after their late shifts and were gone within an hour. Startled by the bell on the door, the bartender failed to see someone settle into the chair nearest him.

Perhaps he was daydreaming again, but it was rather early for this particular customer to be here tonight. The regular appeared across from him as if he had been there all evening. He never saw the man come or go, ever. The customer did not give out his name and it was rare for the man to talk. He was just the "silent patron" over the past three months since he started coming in on Thursdays. At least he tipped well, paid in cash, and always ordered vodka on the rocks, top-shelf stuff. The bartender started making the drink without having to ask.

"Evening." A deep stern voice flowed from the lips of the regular. He was a broad-shouldered man and wore a hooded sweatshirt and baseball cap, the brim low, hiding the expression on his face. "Slow night?"

"It's Thursday," Tony, the bartender, replied, relieved that the man at the bar was willing to talk for a change. "Here you go, one Goose on the rocks. Besides, you've been here every Thursday. It's always slow."

The bartender slid the glass toward his customer, who met him halfway. There was a slight pause, as Tony could not help but stare at the man's left hand as it glided the drink away. He was missing his ring finger and curiosity was itching at the back of Tony's mind once more. Tonight, he decided to investigate the story behind the man's missing digit.

"I just have to ask. How did you lose your finger?" He gave the mysterious customer a conversational grin. "Was it work-related? I get some good stories from a lot of the guys about how their wedding bands saved their lives and cost them their fingers."

"No." The man took a sip from his drink and gently placed it back down. "I refuse to let it grow back... That's the only reason why it's still missing."

"What?" A sickening weight of dread came over Tony as he realized something was not natural in the man's tone of voice. The other servers were right; something was very creepy about the Thursday night regular with the missing finger. This had to be a sick joke. He wasn't serious, right? "You what?"

"I refuse to let it grow back." Holding up his left hand, he raised his head, covering his expression except for one gleaming green eye that stared menacingly at Tony where the finger had once been. "When I find her again, I'll allow it to come back. I know she is still out there. She is alive, but just out of my reach. I feel her even after all these centuries."

"What are you?" Paling, Tony's life drained from him. His instincts screaming, he reasoned against them. This was not your typical drunk off the streets, or was he? He finally stuttered his decision. "Y-You must be d-drunk."

"I am nothing for you to be afraid of." Tony could now see the strong jawline and grave expression the stranger had on his face as he spoke. Finishing his vodka, the green-eyed man slid the glass back to him, beckoning for another. "The others make you work tonight because they can't stand being in the same room as me. Shocked you're still alive, in fact. You are the only human in the entire lot of bartenders that work here. Normally they would have taken advantage, but then again, there is a good reason as to why they haven't yet."

"What are you talking about?" Tony's body moved automatically, bartending on its own. Shaking, he refilled the glass and reluctantly slid it back to his now frightening customer. "Cut it out. You're go-going to spook me away, too, you know?"

"Forgive me." His grin revealed wolf-like fangs as he scoffed to himself. "Call me Cedric. I am no enemy to you, just looking for someone to talk to, that's all. I have spent a lot of time alone with only my thoughts for company. Sometimes it's nice to talk with another person, instead of being trapped in one's own thoughts…"

"Ced-Cedric." Stammering, Tony was ready to melt where he stood, but something about Cedric made his curiosity override the fear clawing at him. A cold sweat sent chills across his back, his hands gripping the edge of the cooler of beer, afraid of his own questions. "How do you know about the other bartenders? What on earth did you say to spook them?"

"They are all female, yes?" He paused mid-sip while staring into the bartender's eyes, realizing he'd failed to explain the significance of this fact. "Female vampires have an easier time than the males in regard to hiding that they are not human. They can control their bloodlust much better and tend to inherit and master illusion-based traits more often. Anyhow, they could smell my blood and knew something was not right. It's like mice serving drinks to a hungry cat, or worse, a starving lion."

"Vampires?" Feeling silly for letting himself get so worked up over a fairytale, Tony began to rationalize the story. Nodding, he gave Cedric a dismissive smile, "That's cute. Yes, women are like vampires."

"You don't believe me? Well, I suppose not in today's world." Cedric took a sip of his drink again. "Let me tell you a story, then, perhaps we can be friends? I do miss having someone to talk to…"

"I don't know, Cedric. You're a little out of my league at this rate." Praying he had not offended him, Tony topped off Cedric's glass, eyeing the missing finger once more. "You can call me Tony."

"Well, Tony, I'll make it a Thursday ritual to tell you my story. I have nothing else to do while I wait. It's been far too long since I last indulged in another's company." Cedric let out a heavy sigh. His eyes grew dull, as if looking far into the past as he spoke on. "My best friend, he passed away not too long ago. The old dog lived far too long for his kind, but I was glad to have someone like that to help me during those hard times. Good friends are hard to come by, especially in my case. He was all I had after I lost my girl…"

"So sorry to hear that." Tony watched as Cedric's green eyes became vacant for several minutes; the weight of pain and sorrow was unmistakable in his gaze. "It's never good to lose a close friend, or your girl."

"Where to start?" The shine returned to Cedric's eyes as he finished another glass of vodka and nodded for his refill. "How about the first night I saw her? It's only appropriate. Like the poet said so many years ago; 'whoever loved that loved not at first sight'..."

"Yes, tell me about this girl of yours." Tony eagerly refilled the glass, waiting to hear what kind of story this was going to be...

CHAPTER 2

CEDRIC'S STORY THE 12TH CENTURY

A scream broke the cold air, shattering the calm. A villager scrambled to keep his footing over the wet cobblestones, fleeing the castle's stables. He failed to cry for help as he struggled to control his tongue. Swallowing, he shrieked the reason behind his fear.

"Werewolf! Werewolf!"

Not far from the battered man stood a massive hulk of fur. Baring its teeth, the werewolf displayed jaws large enough to chomp any man in half, drool dripping across the ground. The damp night made the inner castle courtyard seem empty in the full moon as it peeked over the towers. The villager slipped, taking a hard fall onto the road, gripping his bloody side where the beast had torn into him earlier.

"Be still." The thunderous voice rumbled from the werewolf's chest as it stalked closer. The muscled monster's saliva dripped heavily, like rain at the villager's feet. "I am in no mood to chase something so small."

"Help!" was all he could manage before coughing consumed him.

"Go on, cry for help." The werewolf crouched, laughing in a roar. "Cry out in pain and fear! No one can save you! They have all locked their doors and windows! No nobleman is going to crawl out of his bed to save a man who is nothing but stable scum! What a shame!"

"What of a lord, then?" The villager's heart skipped to hear someone else besides the beast before him, hope flooding his emotions.

The monster's laughter stopped, ears folding back on his head as it turned toward the direction of the questioner.

"Who are you, pest?" Growling, the werewolf returned to all fours, his tail whipping from side to side.

"I am Lord Cedric." Cedric's green eyes flashed from where he crouched on the ground next to the castle walls. He slowly stood, grinning, showing he was tall, broad, and fearless against the werewolf that stood before him. "I thought you were going to hide all night. It's a shame that you are only a street dog. I can see why Romasanta left you behind."

"Quiet you!" Barking and growling, foam dripped from the were-wolf's mouth. "You have no business speaking my master's name! I shall devour you for such insolence!"

"I am afraid you are the meal tonight." Drawing his sword Cedric sighed, his black-tipped, blood-red hair shifting in a gust of wind. "You are very naïve to think you are the predator here, mutt."

The werewolf's yellow eyes widened. Crouching, he took a more offensive stance. "The demonic knight who feeds on his own kind, I have heard of you! You're an abomination upon this Earth! I shall eat you here and end your suffering as a living being."

"I'd like to see you try." He held his sword loosely in his right hand and nodded, daring the creature to come for him.

The bulk of fur was instantly on the spot where Cedric stood. With equal speed and grace, Cedric placed a hand on top of the massive wolf's head, redirecting the pre-emptive attack. Using this connection for leverage, he propelled himself over the beast with a flip and landed without faltering. Enraged at the defensive maneuver, the werewolf spun around, swinging his claw with all his weight. There was a loud clanking as sword and claw met in front of Cedric's face. The muscles in the monster's shoulders twitched. Jerking, Cedric leaped back. He had gained enough distance in time to see the massive jaws snap shut where his head had been a moment ago. The stench of the werewolf's breath hung in Cedric's nose; it was too close. Snorting, their vindictive dance continued, both of them fueling their untold desires for vengeance. A grin and sparkle grew in his green eyes. The beast's panting became more apparent. The werewolf's movements began slowing with each pounce.

"You're old! I can never tell under all that fur until I start fighting, but you are already a tired old man!" Cedric jumped back, making room between them. He was allowing the old demon a moment to catch his breath as he glared back at him, growling. "You've eluded me for a few nights. I suppose even a veteran falls victim to the hunger at a full moon."

"Yes, even an old salt has no willpower against the ways of demon blood." His ears pricked forward and a toothy grin spread across his canine face. "How does one fight a cry of bloodlust with the mixed blood of many demons?"

"Unlike you, I do not feed on pawns such as humans. My lust requires stronger bloods that hold power within and it only yearns for quality, not limitless quantity. Gluttony is a sin, you know?" Placing his sword in its scabbard, Cedric straightened into a more relaxed pose. "I do not care for half-bloods very often. On the other hand, the older the half-blood, the better the meal he is. You should be a decent snack for me within castle walls."

"Speak for yourself; you're my meal!" Racing toward him, the pounding of the werewolf's weight reverberated through the cobblestones at Cedric's feet. "You should have never sheathed your sword, pest!"

"Fool!" Cedric's voice boomed, a yelping sound escaping the great wolf; crackling bones filled the air.

Cedric had brought the large beast's attack to an abrupt halt. The beast's arm was broken and he could feel a sharp pain stabbing into his neck. He had fallen for Cedric's ploy. The sword had merely been a distraction, which had allowed the demon at his neck to toy with his food. He winced as Cedric's fangs dug deeper into him; each suckle pulled his soul further from him. A deep sigh escaped the massive chest. The last of his life drained away into the darkness of death. Finally, his soul would be at rest after living beyond his means. Perhaps falling prey to the demonic knight had been a blessing in disguise.

Cedric released his hold from the now cold heap of fur, spitting blood across the ground as he looked at the corpse with disdain. "What a waste of my time; he was near death and had very little life force to offer me..."

"Pl-please mister, I... let me live, my lord. I will tell no one!" The villager, still bleeding, had crawled to Cedric's boots.

Smooth as silk, Cedric pulled his sword and severed the man's head. A pot crashed down from a nearby balcony. He had come through that way, but had seen no sign of anyone. Surprised, he stared wide-eyed at the young girl frozen in fear against her balcony door. He realized that he'd neither heard nor smelled her approach as he kept his intense eye contact with her. That was the first time he laid eyes on Angeline. Her big brown eyes wide, she could not break from his gaze.

Cedric scoffed, annoyed he would have to use the other abilities of his blood right, but he had no choice in the matter. Leaping up to the balcony, a feat no mere mortal could have accomplished, he stood towering over her, their eyes locked into an endless bond.

"Be still my pet." His whisper was tender, as if spoken from a lover.

He used what the myths called the incubine stare. The unbreakable stare allowed an incubus to ensnare their victims, tricking them into "falling in love" or even lulling them to sleep. It was usually not a dependable ability with full-blooded demons, since their powers that created an intoxicating level of sexual arousal would take hold by this point. In his case, it never failed him due to the vampiric mix in his blood. His voice came as a low, tender rumble for a whisper as he spoke to her in a songlike tone. Her fear fell away as he opened the door behind her. As he sang, she followed without hesitation.

> *"Don't fret, my dear,*
> *Come to me, close here.*
> *Go back to sleep, now love,*
> *I am now here, my dove.*
> *Pay no mind to the demons below,*
> *My eyes and heart you now follow.*
> *Come, my pet, lay your head down,*
> *And in dreams, you now drown."*

With the last note, he managed to lay her in bed. Her room was large and expensively furnished. A banked fire holding a low flame kept the room warm. A log fell apart into coals, popping and crackling. Curious, he sat in the embroidered chair placed in a dark corner of her chamber. Looking her over for a moment, he took in her cotton gown, thin and translucent with elegant lace flowers along its hem. She was clearly a daughter of a nobleman, a lady of the court. Unlike the stable trash painting the cobblestones crimson, her death would cause alarm. Still, he could use this to his advantage. King Frederick insisted if he, Lord Cedric, won the tournament tomorrow that he could have his pick of the ladies. In this case, he knew who he would choose to marry: this girl he had caught in his stare.

It was exhausting playing the games of the lady and knight, and he was glad to be putting an end to it at last.

She was fairly plain, and he could detect a hint of the farms in her scent. He assumed she was here to make her richer cousin stand out further. Despite what the world thought, he found himself staring deeply at her. She was far more beautiful than the background purpose given to her by the nobles. Her hair was long and thick, chestnut in color, while her skin was peachy and sun-kissed. The lips on her sleeping face folded out like the wide petals of a rose. She was lucky that she had gotten to her age untouched. With her voluptuous hips and the muscling in her arms and legs, she was a pleasant sight. She would have made for a good fight to any that may have tried to force themselves on her. A scowl came across his face. He cursed his incubine blood and the uncanny awareness it gave him of both age and sexual status.

A malicious grin crawled across his lips. Indeed, she would be a fitting mate for a short time and a better lure for bigger prey on his journeys. Yes, he would use this girl to attract his prey.

Bait.

CHAPTER 3

THE TOURNAMENT

"Hear ye! Hear ye!" Trumpets sounded and the bustling of the noblemen and peasants filled the arena. "Clear the arena! Your King, King Frederick the Fair, approaches! The tournament will be starting!"

Yelps, whistles, and gasps rang out. The arena for the tournament emptied quickly as the king and queen stood before their chairs. Noblemen and their daughters rushed to get seats as close to the king as they could. Ladies of the court had chairs below the royal family so that the men competing in the tournament could see every lady of his majesty's court. One by one, knights and mercenaries of high skills came out when announced. A knight gave his lady a flower; another gave a napkin with their family seal, while the others simply took a chance to kiss a soft hand. Lastly, they called out the man in whose honor the tournament was being held.

"Now enters our champion against the demons and the dark in this world, Lord Cedric of the House of Romulus, last of the Romulus line. We gather today to witness your skills and talents firsthand! First, King of the Germans, King Frederick, wishes for you to take the hand of one of his ladies of the court! Upon the chance that you defeat our own kingdom's finest warriors and knights, this shall be your prize!"

The crowd roared with delight as Cedric bowed, one knee to the ground, toward the king, and more importantly, to the ladies who watched, blushing. All the Ladies, but one, were red-cheeked from his stare. His grin faltered as his green eyes locked onto the frightened brown ones. The sweat on her brow and paling complexion told him all he needed to know. For some reason, she remembered him. It was the first time in over a hundred years that he had seen anyone break from the spell and its memory-altering effects. He would have no time to toy with his competitors. It was unclear if she thought of last night's events as a vivid nightmare or reality. Sighing a curse under his breath, he managed to grin again as he stood.

Out of the five total fighters, he and the ogre-sized brute were the only ones without a helmet and ensemble of metal. Though, unlike his giant cohort, he depended heavily on his agility and dexterity to win his battles. He was far stronger than the men next to him, but he was partial to the dance of swordplay. The smallest knight was wearing more armor than necessary for his size, and with the array of daggers in his belt, it was clear he favored close combat. On the opposite end of the lineup was the oldest competitor in brightly reflective armor. He dismissed the old man and shifted his attention to the mountain of flesh next to him. Sweat poured from the mildly obese brute. He would prove harder to take down without exposing his true strength to the observing audience. The last knight was a mercenary knight of average appeal. He wore his family seal with pride, but the armor he wore looked poorly maintained and ill-fitting for this tournament.

Again, his smirk failed as his eyes fell back on the girl. She visibly flinched as their eyes met and his jaw twitched in annoyance. While he was distracted by the lady's fearful stare, the ogre-of-a-man took advantage and swung his two-handed mace and slammed it into Cedric's shield. Thrown like a doll, he landed on the arena floor in a cloud of dust. The onlookers shouted and laughed at the feat. They cheered on the larger man for taking the first strike in the game and on Lord Cedric. Cedric huffed, tossing the bent shield to the ground as he brushed the dust from his pants. He would have to abandon his shield far sooner than he had initially planned.

"Whoa!" Cedric shouted. A shorter opponent made a swing, and he simply sidestepped for the miss. "I haven't drawn my sword yet. What dishonorable twits you all are."

The smaller knight retreated to give his larger companion another chance to challenge Cedric. Yanking his sword from its sheath, he blocked another blow from the massive mace with his blade. Cedric's feet slid, pushed back by the sheer force. This man clearly had some experience in small demon hunting. A shimmer came to Cedric's green eyes and his grin grew wide. He flawlessly back flipped to gain some distance in order to catch a better glimpse of the four men, two of them clearly braver than the others. The audience whistled and clapped at the acrobatic stunt.

Taking an offensive stance, he flicked two fingers, beckoning the brute to come. As if a dog called by its master, the large brute charged toward Cedric, mace readied for another try. Crouching low to meet his approach, Cedric waited for the swing. Elegantly, he leaped above the ground-skimming swing, and with massive strength, Cedric hammered the hilt of his sword into the back of the ogre-like man's head. There were gasps hovering in the air as all watched the large bulk frozen for a moment. Cedric walked past the man and focused on the other competitors, while everyone watched the brute's eyes roll back. He fell forward, knocked out in a dust plume on the arena floor.

The squirrel-of-a-knight came from behind the impeding paladin-armored guardsmen, anger seething from him as he closed in for a second attack. He aimed high at Cedric, who swiftly dropped to the ground and swung his leg around, knocking the mousy man off his feet. The roar of laughter that followed fed Cedric's ego as he dashed forward, locking his sword with the claymore of the mercenary guardsmen who had patiently waited for his turn. He was too slow for Cedric's taste, and after exchanging several ear-shattering blows from both knights' swords, Cedric managed to get behind the man. With a wicked kick to the lower back, Cedric brought the guardsmen to his knees and one swift knock of the hilt dropped him to the floor.

Two down and two to go.

Irritated by the rat-sized knight, he finally exchanged blows again after the second retreat. On the third hit, Cedric's strength and force knocked the man's sword free from his hands. Seeing that the knight was too stunned to react, Cedric took the opportunity and landed a punch through the haphazardly open helm. Like a miniature tree, the squirrel fell back on his heels, out cold.

One left.

"Ah! This is more like it!" Cedric twisted his sword about as he approached the last opponent. "I take it you prefer the one-on-one battle?"

"I am much older, and content to wait, but yes. I do savor the one-on-one battle." Unlike his fellows sprawled on the ground, this knight had lighter armor and his weapons of choice seemed to be two short swords.

"I must admit, after watching how quickly you dispatched the others, I am a bit wary, Lord Cedric. There is a reason everyone calls you the Demonic Knight. You fight like a demon, that's for sure."

"Keh." Cedric paused, admiring the sense of honor the man had toward his own skills. "It is hard to gauge one's skills with such clumsy opponents."

"Let me be the judge of that." The knight charged forward, his blades extended out behind him as he raced toward Cedric, who stood unmoving.

For an older warrior, he was as fast as the small knight. Cedric slid backward, missing the first swipe of a blade, and almost failed to gauge the second swing that followed it. Much to Cedric's surprise, the knight dropped, knocking Cedric's legs out from under him with a skilled kick. Reacting on instinct, he managed to firmly land a hand on the ground and flip himself upright, saving himself another bath in the dusty dirt. It appeared he had misjudged the range of skills that this aging fighter possessed. Again, he came at Cedric, and Cedric blocked the dual onslaught of the two short blades as efficiently as he could. Sweat crawled down Cedric's cheek as he guessed which swings to dodge or block with the sword. This knight clearly devoted himself to mastering the technique of hiding his second blade behind the other, a talent rarely seen in the kingdom.

Once more, Cedric caught a glimpse of the young girl's watery brown eyes. A stinging sensation sliced across his abdomen and he pushed himself back to gain distance. Rubbing a hand across the cut, he could feel that it was a skillfully shallow wound. The old knight was breathing hard from his efforts, a smile across his face as sweat dripped from his chin. Cedric scoffed in annoyance, spitting at the ground as his anger seeped forward.

How annoying. I hate using any of the incubine skills. They always do this to me! So damn distracting!

With uncanny speed, Cedric closed the gap between him and the knight.

Startled by the increase in skill, the knight faltered. He yelped, dropping one of his short blades as Cedric knocked him off his feet in a tackling motion. There was no mercy in Cedric's next move, a punch directed at the man's face. A crunching sound could be heard, crisp and clear. He had broken the knight's nose and the audience was quiet after this last defeat. Cedric snorted in dissatisfaction as he walked toward the king and kneeled before him. After a short pause, the arena filled with cheers and laughter. Under his fake smile, Cedric was fuming. He hated the very idea that a human girl distracted him and a human warrior landed a cut on him.

She will be bait, nothing more.

"Lord Cedric, our Demonic Knight! The savior of the lands!" King Frederick liked keeping the crowd shouting. "I now ask you, please choose a lady from my court for your own bride! May you live long and prosperous! May the House of Romulus stand strong in future generations!"

With that, he stood to look at the selection of women the king was offering to him. It was appalling to see the unpleasant choices that the court allowed in the ranks. His eyes fell upon the prettiest of them all, a petite blonde-haired woman. Her body was curvy with milky skin. She batted her large blue eyes at him to acknowledge his stare.

This was the girl they wanted me to choose. The one they have gone overboard on to make her standout.

Shaking behind the blonde-haired lady was the girl from last night. Clearly, she was the bland background for a songbird despite being taller; the brown-haired girl was without a doubt from the farms. It was a tad excessive considering that none of the other girls could come close to outshining their shorter cousin.

"Your Majesty, I choose that one." Cedric pointed in their direction.

"A fine choice! Cassandra is our best lady of the court!" The blonde-haired woman squealed happily, clapping her hands. "She is our most beautifu—"

"Not her, the lovely lady behind her." He was trying to hide his annoyance at the assumption. "The taller girl, with the rosy lips and hair so long that it would put the princess's to shame. I want her to be mine."

"B-But she is only a cousin! From the farms!" A nobleman pushed himself forward, gripping the taller girl's arm. "You cannot be serious, my lord!"

"Come now, Lord Cedric!" Even the King seemed ruffled by the selection made.

Someone had paid well for his daughter to be the pick of the litter today.

The king bellowed on. "Cassandra is a far better choice! She has been at the top of the court since she was a small girl here in my kingdom."

"Your Majesty," He kneeled, being as dramatic as possible while giving the king and his court the gravest stare he could muster. "You must understand. I do not wish to marry a lady as fragile as she! I travel across the land, taking paths that no one else would dare to brave, hunting demons, as you all know. What I need is a lady who can stand tall by my side! If she is from the farms, as you have said, then my heart yearns more so to have her as mine!"

Gasps and uncomfortable shifting could be heard from the audience as stares were exchanged. The nobleman's paled face revealed that he had failed to consider the conditions his daughter would be living in with such a person. The king stroked his beard, staring down at Cedric from his pedestal. Cassandra began crying as he heard her whispering urgently to her father, frightened now by the very idea of traveling in such peril. The taller girl still had her gaze on him. She had not dropped her eyes from him the entire time since he had entered the arena. His blood boiled as he felt himself enjoying the deep stare of her eyes on him as her bottom lip quivered like a leaf in the wind. Anger only steamed up one word in his thoughts.

Bait.

"But, Sire, if you insist, I could take Cassandra as you wish." A smirk snaked across his mouth as he shot a mischievous grin at the panicked blonde, sending her into a bigger fuss.

"No!" The nobleman, stunned by his own response, stumbled on his next few words. "Angeline is a fine girl! She comes from a small village and is a very skilled archer! She can out-shoot any man here, and has done so many times. It would do me proud for you to take my niece over my own daughter! If you desire her more so, she is yours."

"Very well!" The king smiled at the change of plans. "Angeline is a strong and well-mannered girl. She is fit for travel and danger, unlike the other ladies here. She is yours, Lord Cedric."

"Thank you, King Frederick!" Cedric tilted his head, avoiding the panicked look on Angeline's face as large tears streaked down her cheeks. "Please have your men ready my horse, and a horse for my lady. I must be off as soon as possible."

You'll be gone soon enough, my pet.

CHAPTER 4

BAIT

"Are you going to speak at all, girl?" They had traveled for several hours and she'd remained silent through everything. "You are stuck with me, my pet. You can free your tongue. Hell, you can even spit venom at me if it would take that look off your face."

"My name's Angeline." Her face flushed as she huffed at him from her horse. "I was told by my uncle and the king to hold my tongue in fear that I would anger you."

"My! A lively one!" He chuckled as he looked back at her. When he saw her cheeks reddening again, he could only assume that he was nothing but a man from a nightmare. "Red suits you, my lady."

"Ugh!" Her eyes darted away from his gaze.

The path they were following came to the edge of a clearing. Pulling back on his reins, he brought both their horses to a halt. Glancing back toward Angeline, he saw she was watching his every move. The fear faded sometime during the ride, and she now gave him a hardened look. Grinning, he pulled himself off his horse and walked both mounts over to a dead tree, hitching them to it. It was amusing to see how hard she avoided his stare as he gave her a hand off her horse.

"We'll camp here." Pushing her along, she noticed he was putting an abnormal amount of distance between them and the horses. "You can get the camp started. Clear this spot of rocks and limbs; I'll grab the packs."

"Fine." Hiking her long skirts up, she made quick work of clearing the campsite. "I will need to find more travel-worthy clothes soon, Lord Cedric. I wish not to slow you down in your travels. I prefer to be free of skirts if you would allow me to be."

"Don't worry, pet. We will be traveling through the cursed woods to a village there." Circling back, he pulled all the bags and packs off the two horses and returned, offering them to her. "If a dress does not suit you, then you shall pick out something more proper to meet your needs. I do not care what you wear, just as long as you do not slow me down."

"Thank you, my lord." Cedric smirked at her as she took the packs from him. Angeline laid out the campfire and sleeping spots without any further instruction from him. "You have camped out before I see."

"I used to live in the village we are going to, Raven's Den. I traveled with my father many times to sell goods at the castle and to see our cousins." She bit her bottom lip, annoyed that he continued to stand there, watching her do all the work. "Do you not have other business to tend to, perhaps food for the fire? I see you packed nothing to eat. For someone who travels often, that seems naïve."

"I am already at work for food. Don't you worry your pretty little head about that, pet." He walked past her and toward another tree. "Now excuse me while I take a piss."

Angeline's face mottled. Raised on a farm, she couldn't help but scoff at the fact his lordship was rather bold for someone of his rank. In all her years at the castle, not even a peasant had dared to spit in front of a lady of the court, let alone relieve himself. It was exasperating to keep her back to him. He was right behind her doing his business while she was trying to gather wood. Dropping what little she had in a pile, she decided it would have to wait. He was in the way and she was in no mood to go too far from the camp. She watched as the horses started fussing and fidgeting at their hitching tree. Her eyes caught a strange movement from the tree. Once more, the bare tree shuddered and one horse screamed, pulling its reins tight as it backed away.

"There it is." Cedric finished and turned around to walk back to the horses. "Stay back."

"What is going on?" Swallowing her nervousness, she watched the dead tree quiver again as more screams came from the horses. "What is happening?"

"Dinner." Scoffing, he stopped halfway; the horses were frantic and trying to tug free, biting at their reins.

Despite the distance, Angeline could see the whites of the eyes of the horses that were now pawing at the tree. They were desperate and frightened beyond anything she had ever seen. One horse managed to break free and sped off down the trail, leaving its companion screaming and bucking. The other horse was fighting to free itself, but all it managed to do was create raw spots from its harness that dripped blood down its cheek. The bright red lines glistened in the sunlight as the struggle continued. A rumbling was coming from the ground as the dead tree started to grow taller, as if it were a weed pulled up by an unseen hand. The horse was still bucking and squealing, becoming more frantic as foam dripped from its mouth, eyes wild with fear. In horror, Angeline watched as the ground exploded and the horse was pulled high in the air.

The dead tree was the horn on the nose of a sand orm. It was a massive serpent with scales running down into the ground that imitated the look of an earthworm. Smooth and the color of the surrounding soil, she marveled over its size as she caught glimpses of a treelike fin that ran the beast's length. Once more, the ground trembled under her feet. The mammoth orm snatched the horse, dangling from its nose-horn, into its mouth. Its gaping jaws were large enough to hold three horses, with plenty of room left over for their riders. She slid to her knees in awe as she watched the massive creature eat. The horse's screams were quickly muffled by its jaws, despite the lack of any teeth beyond its hard, boulder-lined lips. Her ears met with a mixture of crackling and popping. She couldn't decipher if what she heard was the bones of the horse or simply the stony collision of the monster's jaws.

Lord Cedric was unmoved. The orm turned its enormous head to face Cedric, a low groan rippling from it as it did so. Trees and bushes shifted and moved just behind it and down the trail. The entire forest snaked back and forth like waves on the ocean connected to this monster that towered over them like a small mountain. There had been rumors of whole forests changing, but seeing an orm so close explained how everything in an area could move. Its back fin was the forest, and with a shudder, it could shift and change acres of what could be mistaken as legitimate trees and underbrush.

"Whoa!" Cedric spat. "You're much bigger than I thought."

Snorting dust clouds from its nostrils, it moaned louder in response. The orm's reply sounded like boulders falling. Vibrations rattled through the ground, aiming to shake the air from Cedric's lungs. The plant-like fin rattled, sending a flurry of birds from their misplaced nests left behind on a demon's back. Two glowing eyes opened to peer down at who dared to stand against such power. With another shake of its woodland appendage, the orm came crashing down toward Cedric. An explosion of soil and rocks flew up and past the tallest of trees.

The roaring of the ground muted Angeline as she started to scream. The rolling cloud of dirt blocked out the sun and overwhelmed all her senses. Her shrieking burst into coughing as she gagged on a lungful of wet soil; rocks fell from the darkened sky. Crawling across the shaking ground, she desperately sought one of the sleeping bags or any cloth to help her breathe. Wheezing harder, she ripped her skirt, covering her mouth and nose. Her eyes stung from the debris. She could barely see her own hands in the darkness, let alone tell if the orm was closer or farther away. The ground shook violently again, the sun a distant memory in all the chaos and hell that swallowed her now. She scrambled backward, but a hand pushed against the middle of her back and she froze. The earthquake battle faded away as silence took hold.

"Stop moving." Cedric's whispering lips caressed her ear. Chills ran down her spine and through her limbs. "It can't see you, but it can feel anything move on the ground. Even when the blasted thing is moving around, it can pick out a grasshopper among all of this."

Her stinging eyes fought to open against the dust. She could only focus on—Fangs! Lord Cedric's pristine lips were embellished with the fangs from her nightmare. Fear stricken, she shuddered as muddy tears began to run down her soil-covered cheeks. With no willpower left to scream, all she could do was sob hysterically. Her gaze was fixated on the fangs framing the corners of his mouth. Cedric's lips were moving, but the dread had washed away his words.

"Come on." Snarling at her, Cedric's green eyes shone through the shadowy cloud of dirt, pulling her eyes from his mouth. "Keep it together, pet. I have no time to baby you. Stay here and do not move. Cry all you want, but do not move from here or risk being eaten."

Dashing away, he left her there in the unknown. She heard another deafening crash as more dirt and rocks fell about her like hail. Her body would not move despite her mental pleas to her legs to run away. In her mind, and with every painful blink, all she could see were the green eyes of the demon named Cedric. Shoving her face into the piece of cloth, she continued sobbing, no longer concerned with the rumbling and raining soil. Nightmares about this strange lord were coming true with each passing second. She had been married off to the devil himself, with no hope to ever be free of the hell she now called her life.

Seeing nothing past her cloth, she eventually realized the only wailing she heard was her own. It was unclear when the ground had stopped moving, but she was reluctant to look. Most of the dirt made its way back to earth as her eyes focused through the muddled daylight, and then she gasped. The orm's massive head lay close to her, close enough that the smell that greeted her nose was a mixture of mud and blood. Catching sight of what was left of a mangled horse's leg, her eyes jerked upward, caught by the color green. Cedric was kneeling on the top of the carcass, mouth bloodied as he exchanged glares with her.

Breaking the stare, Cedric went back to the task he was working on. Orms, much like dragons, dracs, or wyverns, were massive and held a great range of power. Cedric had found the life force from one of these creatures was indeed larger, their souls filling their bodies. On physically massive prey, the task of feeding was daunting, almost endless for him. He found himself growing perturbed by Angeline's stare as she continued her mournful weeping. Refusing to lock eyes, he focused on pulling the power out as efficiently as he could. There was little time left to separate the departing soul and its power from the dying body.

Distracting incubine blood, you dare interfere in my feedings as well. She is bait. I will not take her if that is all you desire. I do not desire the flesh of a human girl, even in the manners of incubine power gain. You insult me. I will not bend to your will.

Finishing his meal, he stood. The ground all around them was brown and littered with rocks and roots. Angeline was still gawking at him, sitting in the same spot, her muddy tears painting her cheeks and her figure caked in soil. Spitting the last of the foul-tasting blood from his mouth, he rubbed his lips clean of any bloodstains that smeared them. Content that she would not be moving anytime soon, he leaped down behind the orm out of her sight. It wasn't long before he came back with two rabbits in hand, but she had passed out. Grunting, he flopped her over his left shoulder and started to follow what was left of the old trail. The destruction left behind from the orm was stunning. Glancing over the wasteland, he smirked. This trail would be unpassable for those coming behind them. Gouges and holes would prove impossible for even the most agile of horses to jump or skirt around. Nothing more than a muddy crevice with a decaying orm and open sky remained. Heading through some trees and into the forest, he found the other side of the trail.

Crackling and a loud pop brought her from her restless sleep. The smell of soil was faint, but the stronger scent of succulent meat found its hold on her grumbling stomach. Opening her eyes, she found herself on a rolled-out sleeping bag, in front of a campfire that was dancing around two rabbit carcasses. Holding her breath and her apprehension, she sat up only to see Cedric sitting on a stump on the other side of the orange wall of flames. Flashes of a blood-covered face, wolf-like fangs, and feral green eyes flooded her mind. This was a beast, not a man, which sat across from her.

"Figured you would be hungry by now." His stare was intense, but his voice was much softer. She marveled over how powerful those emerald daggers gripped her, making her feel excited and terrified, agony and desire. "And we are far from the orm. That carcass will be attracting every manner of scavenger in this area for weeks to come."

"Wh-What are you?" Chills shook her as she caught a glimpse of contempt in his face. "No man could have killed an orm. It is rare for an army to take one down, and the size, I..."

"I am no man, if that is what you are asking." The muscles in his jaw twitched. "The forest is safe, thanks to my leftovers. There's a creek just past the trees behind you. Go wash up, you smell like you rolled in a dung heap."

She looked back through the bushes, her ears catching the faint trickling sound of water, but she hesitated. "I don't understand. You could have left me for dead, why didn't you?"

"It would look badly if I lost my new wife right after leaving the castle." The words stung as she looked at his cold, hard expression and his tone shifted to match. "I am sure you've caught wind of some rumors about me. This was a chance to quell any doubts about my humanity. Now wash up. You're insulting my nostrils and a disgrace to your title, Lady Angeline."

Scrambling to her feet, she walked away from the warmth of the fire and closer to the sound of the creek. No matter how hard she fought back the stinging in her throat, she found herself sobbing once more. There was no comfort in hugging her arms as she stopped next to the rocky circle of water. It swirled gently in a round pool before continuing farther down its narrow pathway. She noticed something folded on a nearby rock not far from where she stood. Kneeling as her eyes adjusted to the dark, it became clear that he had laid clothes out for her.

Soaking in the gentle rush of the water, the soil sloughed off with each wipe. Her concerns were far from the details of reassuring herself that she had freed her hair of every root and smudge of mud. Her life, her destiny, it all seemed so unfair. Tough times were all she had known and now she faced a far worse future than the horrible fortunes from her past. Married to the devil himself, she could only abandon all hope.

Chapter 5

Cursed Woods, Cursed Village

"Why are we headed to Raven's Den?" They were an hour's walk from her childhood village when the thought crossed her mind. "What business does a demon have there?"

"I am sure you have noticed..." Cedric stopped and she halted, staring at the back of his long red hair. "No one has come to trade at the castle from here in weeks. Rumors that the village has been bestowed with a curse have started to be whispered between the merchants passing through town. Word of an orm blocking the path spread like wildfire as travelers were spooked away or witnessed shifting of the trees in the area. Since we confirmed there was an orm, there must be something bigger going on in your little village, my pet."

"You are going to see if a demon has claimed my village, then?" Her voice was disheartening as she rubbed her arm. "That's why you look like a hero. You feed on demons, who feed on us. Showing up in time is easy for you. You take your fill and it just so happens to destroy the beast plaguing the town and spooks others away for a time."

"Did that take you long to figure out?" A warm breeze ruffled the leaves and blew past. "I hate to tell you, precious, but the wind tells me Raven's Den may be no more. The closer we get, the more I can smell rotting flesh. There are signs of a pack of hellhounds near as well."

"No." Angeline's denial escaped as a weak whisper.

Cedric continued walking and she followed without hesitation. Staring at her feet, her thoughts revolved around the faces she knew and her father. He was old and feeble; raising her alone after her mother died in childbirth, he did what he could for her. Raven's Den was one of the small villages that had been around for decades, but was now fading away as more and more of the newer generations left, never to return. It was unclear what the agreement was between her father and uncle, but somehow he managed to give her the chance to be a lady of the court with hopes of marrying into a better life. Unfortunately, she was now the lady of the Lord Cedric, a demonic thing with no respect for the lives of other living beings.

If Raven's Den was attacked, they would have been wiped out in seconds, whether it was demons, beasts, or bandits. It was nothing more than a farm run by the elderly the last time she visited. Some of the houses stood empty, abandoned by the last of their occupants, hoping for something better. Lost in her thoughts, she failed to notice that Cedric had stopped again. She rammed into his back, falling back onto her buttocks.

"Watch it!" He hissed as he kneeled down next to her, signaling for her to stay quiet. "Something isn't right."

He furrowed his brow, staring ahead. Turning her attention in that direction, she could see Raven's Den, nestled in the shade of the towering trees. From where she sat on the ground, everything looked normal. She could see someone plowing up new rows for seasonal plants, and an older woman was walking down the main path with a large basket of flowers. It looked like an average day; no one appeared fearful or upset from where they sat on the road. Narrowing her eyes, she tried to focus on individual people, but they were still too far away. When she failed to recognize someone, her brow knotted in confusion when she noticed there were too many villagers. Two herdsmen were standing at the front fence like guards, but their bodily movements seemed wrong. Watching the activity within the sleepy village, she became aware of an eerie silence. There were no bird calls and the main path was missing the usual herd of goats and flock of chickens, making her shudder. There were people tending to a cow that seemed nervous and kicking, and farther down the fence line, more guardsmen.

"Who are those men at the front fence? I do not know them." Looking over at Cedric, she was hoping he could see further. "There are far too many people to be just the occupants of Raven's Den and the animals are nervous. At this time of day, we usually let the animals graze in the field there."

"Those men are dead." Rubbing his nose, Cedric tried to alleviate the smell as he spat at her feet, grimacing. Catching her eyes again with a rigid look on his face, he helped her stand. "I smell some sort of magic in the air, but I don't recognize it. It seems there are living people among the undead ones, but I have never come across anything like this before. Not sure what will happen when we approach."

"Undead? Wait, approach?" Angeline questioned as Cedric thrust her in front of him. His hand gripped the material at the back of her shirt, pushing her forward. "Wait! What are you doing?"

"You live here, don't you?" Her heels slid as she failed to stop her descent toward the two men wielding spears. "Just go tell them that. Ask for a relative or something."

"My Lor—Cedric! You can't!" Her shouting caught the guardsmen's attention. "Let go! I don't want to die!"

"Stop making a show of it, pet!" Shoving her off balance, she fell to the ground, her chin bouncing off the ground and rattling her teeth. "You are so difficult. Do you think I would bother to give you to them with me right behind you? How incompetent do I look?"

"You're a wicked thing!" Tears rolling down her cheeks, she picked herself up. "You! You demon, you!"

"Halt!"

Following the spearhead down to its owner, she gasped, sucking in a stench, a flavor of decay and rot. More tears filled her eyes as her shaking lips whimpered at what she saw there. "Undead."

"Hey now!" Cedric smirked, throwing his hands up, pulling the tension to him. "I heard the village was cursed. I suppose I can confirm the rumors are true. I am Lord Cedric, the local demon hunter. Perhaps you have heard of the Demonic Knight?"

"Cedric, the heir to the House of Romulus?" Cedric's smile fell, his jaw twitching as the unnatural voice of the zombie continued. "The old witch told us of you. Angeline and you are allowed to enter. We have a task for you, my lord."

"How do you know my name?" Angeline's stomach lurched as she watched his silent zombie companion pick maggots from his arm, flicking them out on the ground, where they wiggled further. "How does a dead man know my name?"

"Please follow me," replied the first zombie as he motioned with his decrepit hand for them to do as he asked. Cedric brushed past, his shoulder smacking Angeline's arm, making her stumble. "My name is Josef.

I used to be a sheepherder here before I died a very long time ago. All the undead you see here have been brought back with a single purpose, to defend the village against the attacking hellhounds that have come recently. Not even I knew about the protection spell that the old witch cast on Raven's Den. It was a form of thanks for allowing her to live out the rest of her life among us. My ancestors knowingly took her in, treating her no differently than a neighbor or family."

Regaining her balance, not wishing to be close to the worm-infested undead man, Angeline picked up her pace, staying close behind Cedric. At least there was no dread of falling flesh or bugs coming from him. Shuddering, she looked about her old home. There were no signs of her father out in the backfields. Instead, her eyes fell upon several undead doing their normal chores and work. Her eyes widened in shock as she recognized her deceased grandfather and saw his unhinged jaw; her eyes focused back at her feet. It was much safer to look at the ground. She decided she'd rather not know if she could recognize anyone from her past in their new broken, rotted forms. Rubbing her throat was becoming a habit while listening to Josef's dry, eerie rasping. Each syllable sounded agonizing, as if speaking forced the air from his lungs as it ripped through his decaying throat. Being undead did not look easy. Watching Josef was proving to be both unimaginably painful emotionally and physically. Holes riddled his body, but the way he spoke seemed as if every movement and word took a huge amount of effort.

"I see. The hellhounds I noticed on my way in are targeting the village, after all." Cedric hummed a moment before continuing. "Was there a chimera leading them?"

"No sire, no chimera, but a pack of the same kind far as we could see. Do you think the sorceress Morrighan sent them, or perhaps one of her sisters?" Josef signaled to the other zombie to watch the gate as they walked into the main section of the village. "I did not see any branding or collars on the beasts. Does the custom remain the same as in my day? Magic users tend to bind them with collars, whereas demons brand the hellhounds?"

"For the most part, yes, but Morrighan would have sent a more loyal creation to at least lead them. Her sister Nemaine has meticulous taste and is known for using snakes and spiders. As for Badbh, she would have just done it herself."

They stopped by a door and continued the conversation.

"No brandings or collars?" he mused. "That is odd. With the over-powering smell of all this rotting flesh and magic, a wild pack would have moved on to the orm carcass upon sensing its death. I saw signs of them staying close, as close as their noses would let them come. Without a demon involved, there is nothing here of value."

"This, this is my house," Angeline whimpered, on the verge of crying again as she stood staring at the door. "Why are we at my house? Oh no, Father..."

"Not this again." Scoffing, Cedric crossed his arms, staring at her with disgust. "I will have to take you back to my home at this rate. You cannot possibly cry like this about everything for much longer, pet. Your annoyance is outweighing your worth."

"He is fine and well; alive, if that is what you fear." His intentions to comfort her failed. Looking at Josef's cloudy blind eye, along with the dangling eye making a poor effort to peer at her, added to the nausea churning in her gut. "Lord Cedric, will you come with me so I may show you our findings? Let Angeline catch up and get some rest. Perhaps she is feebl—"

She shoved past them both, flying through the door that slammed behind her with a great bang. Cedric spit at the ground and sucked on the side of his cheek, agitated. Regrets of dragging her along this far were already plaguing his mind.

I should have left her to the orm and its scavengers. I have no patience for such ignorance...

Nodding to Josef, he followed the broken form further into the village, where a larger group of undead farmers and herdsmen surrounded an object of great interest. Much to Cedric's surprise, he found they had managed to catch a hellhound, despite how fragile the zombies appeared. The hound's hellfire was barely evident; bound tightly to the ground by ropes, it wheezed.

It was nothing like a wolf or dog, with its pig-like snout and wide nostrils. They were known to push up dust and scents from the dirt in order to track their victims. The fur was thick, unkempt, and wiry, curling outward in random places, with the overall color a deep gray with black splotches. Its overall physique was boney in structure. Muscles stretching across the delicate frame lacked any fat, giving the creature a mangy appearance. Even its stomach sucked inward, toward its ribs, something you would expect to see in a wormy dog. It was odd seeing a hellhound in the daylight. These demon dogs tended to track and remain invisible during the daytime, while at sundown, they would burst into their true physical form. In doing so, they shrouded themselves with the flames of hell, which provided them with immense power. The tomes spoke of how the rangers would snare hellhounds long enough for the sun to come up in order to weaken and kill them. With each passing hour of the sun's touch on a hellhound, the closer to death it came.

He turned to Josef with a confounded look on his face.

"I see you managed to capture one, but I am a little confused as to why I am needed for this. The beast is dying; unable to become a spirit again during the day is costly for hellhounds." Kneeling down close to its gnarled snout, its smell engulfed Cedric's nose. The scent held a salty musk fragrance that caught his attention. "This is not any hound. It is a Coinn Iotair! He's a long way from home if he is."

"Precisely," Josef creaked and popped as he kneeled next to Cedric. "The witch woman said there was a chance if you fed on the beast, that maybe you could te—"

"What did you just say to me?" Cedric's eyes shot a furious glare as he stared at the undead man next to him. His voice came through his clenched teeth in a growl. "The witch woman said for me to what?"

"Lord Cedric, there are no living souls near the beast. We undead can see souls and knew immediately what you are. The witch woman has summoned you here for many reasons that we do not understand. Her magic is older than the land itself." With a nod of his crusting head, the other undead made a covering wall around them and the Coinn Iotair. "She said you increase in power when you feed on other magical beings or demons. Her hope is in this feeding, you might be able to reveal some information as to who has sent these beasts here to find her magic."

"When I am done, I want to meet this witch of yours." Cedric snarled as his fangs extended to their proper length. "No one is to disturb me until I am done. If any living man sees me, I will kill them."

"Father? It's me, Angel." Angeline was struggling to slow her breath. She held her back against the door, waiting for her eyes to adjust to the low light in the room.

"By the gods!" Embraced in her father's warm arms, her tears fell as relief washed over her. "She said you were coming! I cannot believe such magic was possible!"

"Oh, Father! I have been given away as a prize at a tournament by your brother!" Clinging to her dad as her knees started to give way, she cried on. "I have been married to a demon! A nightmare is all I have been rewarded in life!"

"What on earth are you sobbing about?" Sliding her to the floor as she choked and sobbed, he did what he could to calm her. "Angeline, my girl, it cannot be as bad as you make this out to be. Come now, you made it back home, did you not?"

"But he's a monster!" Wailing, she threw herself into her father's arms again. "Please! Please do not let him take me away!"

"What manner of behavior is this?" An icy voice sliced through the room. "Stop that right this instant. I will not have the heiress to my power behaving in such a manner!"

"Angel, honey." Her father pushed her back, his heavy hands on her shaking shoulders. "Your fate has taken its place in your life. You must be brave."

"But, I don't understand." She let her father lead her to a chair where she sat down. "I don't understand at all. What have I done to anger the spirits to earn such a horrible fate?"

"You will soon understand, girl. Your fate is far from horrible, yet." Angeline winced, acknowledging the sharp presence that demanded her attention. "There is a reason why that monster was attracted to you and a reason why you were drawn from your bed that night. The magic beating in your veins seeks protection where it can, and it chose Lord Cedric."

"How do you know about that night?" The warmth drained from Angeline's face. Across from her was a skeleton dressed like a gypsy fortuneteller, its fleshless frame well concealed. With each gesture, its bony hands creaked. "I—I haven't told a soul. I wasn't sure. It was like a nightmare, but then I saw him..."

"Your magic is far from coming into full bloom. It is a long ways off before you'll have access to it, that is, if you ever do." The witch scattered tomes across the table before her. The skeletal fingers picked through the pile as the witch continued, "I have information for Lord Cedric that he will need to know. In order to climb ranks, all manner of demons make pacts with one another—"

"Why is the information for him?" Feeling thrown to the side and discarded, Angeline's anger started to seep forward. "What is so important about helping a demon? Why am I to be the messenger for him? Can't you tell him yourself?"

"That's more like it!" Dry cackling echoed from the skeleton. "Perhaps I am mistaken about you. You have not come into yourself just yet! Now listen closely child, it will fall to you to make the decision to accept what needs to be done. For both of you to gain something, and for him in terms of power, you play a very important role. The most powerful creatures that walk this land are bound to another demon or being. The sorceress Morrighan is bonded to her incubine lover, Boto. Having bonded himself to that sorceress, instead of a demon or the succubus queen Lillith, the king of the incubi was granted a larger leap in power than anyone has ever seen. Both he and Morrighan's powers were exchanged, shared, and increased beyond what they started with. This can be the same for the two of you, but you must willingly accept Lord Cedric."

"Why do I need to accept him?" Shifting in her chair, the hair on the nape of her neck started to stand on end. "What does this have to do with me willingly accepting Cedric and the binding of an incubus and sorceress?"

"Are you daft?" Cold bones gripped her hand from across the table, dragging her closer to the shambling figure. "Listen here, and remember well! If you are to do your bloodline justice, and me, your ancestor, you will bind yourself to Cedric, girl! You will be called upon to consummate this marriage of yours. In order to do so, your lord will have to succumb to his incubine flesh and feed on his lover as his moroi roots demand. He must satisfy his bloodlust and his lust for the flesh—the binding rights for both his bloodlines need to receive the proper offerings! You must willingly let the magic accept him as it has already chosen him! Failing to do so will cost you both your lives later. Horrible things are still to come; this present is nothing to what it will become! Be warned!"

"Witch!" Cedric jerked open the door with a great thud. "I have business with you!" The rage in his eyes and fanged mouth was harrowing.

The bones at Angeline's aching wrist fell to the table. Fragments of the skeleton scattered across the floor as cackling filled the small house. An icy wind blew by Angeline whispering, "Remember..." in her ears before flying through and past Cedric. Her eyes locked with his enraged emerald ones. Marching across the room, he jerked her out of the chair by her arm. Burning pain from his twisting grip brought tears to her eyes as she staggered to gain balance.

"What have you dragged me into?" The smell of blood was on his breath, and his fangs were still visible as he glowered at her. "Speak swiftly, pet, before I make you pay for holding your untamed tongue! Tell me now!"

CHAPTER 6

HELLHOUNDS

"I don't know! You're the one dragging me into this!" Angeline struggled to free herself from Cedric's grip, but it only caused him to tighten his hold. "You're hurting me! Stop!"

"Where did the witch go?" he barked at her. Angeline could sense that something had seriously gone wrong on his part as well. "She will pay for this stunt she has pulled as soon as I find her!"

"She is gone." Her father approached Cedric, but he made no move to help his daughter. "Angeline knows nothing. The witch has left."

"Worthless." Snarling, Cedric released her with a shove, knocking her to the ground and against the chair. "I have no patience for riddles and games. Someone better tell me something, or it won't be the hellhounds that destroy everyone here."

"She's the witch's heiress." Disbelief took hold of Angeline as she stared at her father, feeling betrayed. He continued to explain, "Angeline is the current carrier of the old woman's powers, but she may never be able to use them. The hellhounds were sent to seek her magic."

"Those hellhounds are Coinn Iotair! They crossed the English Channel and traveled miles to get here! Their powers have been magically enhanced beyond their normal means! Whoever is seeking this witch out is a very powerful magic wielder." A look of repugnance came across Cedric's face as he looked down at Angeline. "And I am cursed to have this wench for my bride if what you tell me is true. Why do the spirits taunt me so?"

"You? I'm the one who's cursed!" Pulling herself to her feet, she attempted to shove him. "I hate you! You have made my life a living nightmare! You're the one who chose me as a prize! How dare you point the finger at me! You're the monster!"

"GO ON! CRY SOME MORE ABOUT IT!" Yelping at his shout, she shrank back from him, noticing his tanned skin growing paler. "That's all you've done since I took you from your precious court! You should have stayed in your bed, whore! I had no desire to pick you over the others except you were there the night before. I should have killed you with the other piece of shit human instead of lulling you to sleep. You have been nothing but misfortune and worse, you are of magical blood. You disgust me."

"You asshole!" Angeline gathered enough bravery to look him in the eye; she could see he wasn't focusing on her like normal as his eyes lacked their sharp stare. Despite wanting to continue their argument, her nerves were pulling at her joints. As her stomach tightened, she held her tongue a moment, looking him over before she spoke in a far softer tone. "Wait, what's wrong with you? What happened?"

"I'm fine." Jerking his face from her, she saw a flush of color hit his cheeks as sweat dripped down his forehead. "It's only recoil. What did the witch want with you? She clearly had several motives luring us here. Why is she so enthralled by me instead of her own flesh and blood? Did she not tell her own kin of her intentions?"

"Nothing..." Her arm was throbbing from where Cedric's hand had released it. "She—I was told I am to go with you, despite what I wanted."

"How insulting..." Brushing past her, Cedric took a seat in the chair, his breathing growing more restricted with each movement. At times, it sounded as if he was panting like an animal. "I think this is the longest I have seen you go without tears or wailing like a banshee. Did she cure you of that? If so, perhaps I can look past this nuisance she has placed on me."

"Is he alright?" Her father was staying far out of their dispute as he continued to watch. "He isn't well, is he? Lord Cedric, are you well?"

"I, I don't know if he's feeling normal. We haven't been together long, but maybe." Keeping her distance, she looked Cedric over as he struggled to breathe, failing to respond to their questions. "Cedric, are you...? Are you dying?"

"No!" He shot her an irritated glare, but his body was having a hard time with the power he'd taken in. Between the orm and an enhanced Coinn Iotair in such a short space of time, he was overloaded and his body was drunk on the rapid increase in power he had gained. His lust was raging, greedy, demanding more. "And don't talk like I can't hear you. Now, tell me what else she told you. Surely, you had some exchange of words with the old hag. I have no patience left for stalling, pet."

"I... she didn't say much else before you barged in." For once, she was starting to feel sorry for the demonic knight. The sweat now soaked his clothes and heat from his sudden fever radiated from him. "C-can I get you something? Do something? Perhaps some cool water?"

"Don't touch me." He shot a cautionary glance at her, making her heart skip a beat. "No one touch me. Stay far from me. I don't know how long this is going to last. I am in no mood to isolate myself until this wave subsides."

"How long this will last?" Angeline dreaded what answer would follow. Her stance became unsteady as she felt her knees shake. "What do you mean by that?"

A panicked knocking came from the door, startling everyone. It was followed by a desperate cry through the wood. Her father opened it, finding a hysterical old woman. Tears soaked her face and her jumbled words led to more confusion. Through her pointing and screaming, it became clear that the witch had left them vulnerable. All the undead residents were crawling back into the ground. Josef, the guardsman from before, shot a sorrowful look toward them before he, too, returned to the earth. Deep in the woods, the sounds of howls filled the air. There was no mistaking the thudding of the paws as the hellhounds ran back and forth outside the outer fences. Unnerved, the remaining villagers gathered their things. The sun was sinking behind the trees, signaling the day's end. As soon as night fell, they would be open to attack.

"That bitch!" Angeline jerked at the sound of Cedric's outburst, followed by the screeching of the chair as he stood. Huffing and panting as sweat dripped from his chin, he gritted his fanged teeth. "She purposely set me up! She knew! The old hag will be dead if I ever find her. I will not let her mock me like this, that manipulating magic-wielding whore!"

"Knew what?" Angeline's heart quickened as Cedric approached the doorway, still raging. "Cedric, what's going on?"

"Tell everyone to stay in their homes. No one is to come out until daybreak. I have no choice but to deal with the Coinn Iotair and finish the work the witch has put me to do." Looking back at her, he gave her a warning glare. "Lock your doors tight and pray I do not return tonight, either."

"But, can you fight?" Angeline asked, baffled by his orders, trailing behind him as Cedric walked out into the street. Seeing his failing health, no one understood his intentions and watched him with a mix of confusion and panic. "You look like you are about to pass out. You can't fight like this! Are you mad?"

"I mean it! Stay in your homes! I will kill any man or woman who dares come out before daybreak!" The dwindling sunlight reflected in his eyes, glowing as if she were looking into the face of an animal. Sweat glistened across his face and shoulders. He winced suddenly, as if in pain, before he continued, "You have no idea what you are looking at. Heaven help you if you realize what's wrong with me. If you ever do, I will kill you one way or another. That, I can promise you, pet."

Stopping at the inner fence, she watched him walk away into the woods toward the howling that urged the night to come. "You're a monster. Why should I care what is wrong with you?"

Cedric could hear the village clamoring behind him as shouts echoed over the trees. His skin crawled with lustful excitement and his fangs itched to be set loose. What they mistook for pain was much of the opposite. Each flinch was a wave of arousal, almost pleasure, hitting his core and sending his blood boiling. After a normal feeding, this drunken sensation was manageable, but the enchanted dog sent him over his limit. His body was in a state of ecstasy from the recent power absorption. Sensations that would normally be nothing but whispers were snaking in the background, screaming at him. There was no doubt his incubine blood desired power gain. There was a new and more obvious lust for Angeline in the mix of his exhilaration. The rage he felt with each wave and pull toward the girl did nothing to tame the incubus within him.

His only relief came from increasing the distance between himself and Angeline with each step. The incubus bloodline was exerting its influence on him, instincts attempting to override logic. Everything quickened while he was in this state. His heart and lungs doubled their pace as he stomped away from the village and ever closer to the hounds. Anger fueled his thoughts with every step; he could not stand losing his will in the face of his incubine desires. Sounds of panting and the pattering of invisible paws followed him along the path through the trees. The heat from the hellhounds' breath caressed his skin and made him quiver in delight. Once the sun set, there would be a burst of hellfire as the Coinn Iotair manifested themselves on the physical plane. They were ready for battle, minutes away from nightfall.

How did the witch know that power consumption made it difficult for me to hold back my incubine bloodline?

He spat at the ground as he came to a stop, satisfied he'd attracted all of the Coinn Iotair. Horns extended from his head, spiraling into a sharp point like a ram's antlers. Letting some of his self-restraint ease back, he could feel his claws and fangs grow more ferocious, like those of a lion.

It has been a long time since I last struggled against my incubine instincts. The old witch had to have known devouring too much power would trigger it. However, I am eager to gain more power. I have much to gather before I can take my vengeance upon my creator. Perhaps this was more of a blessing than a mockery of my weakness.

Anticipation slithered across his skin as he inhaled, smelling the power that the enchanted hellhounds held for him, adding to his arousal. He felt drunk with desire; no feat seemed too big when he was in this state.

I have to keep away from the village long enough to ride this wave out. If I get too close to the girl, my instincts will shatter what willpower I have held onto. At least the hounds will provide a distraction. If I am quick, I can devour their power and have more than enough time to ride out the lust until daybreak. Why would a witch toy with me, then give me enough to feed on to triple my current power? Is the girl so important that I am the best escort she could have? What manner of magic does she hold? Why does the old hag require me to jump in power so quickly?

More sweat poured from his arms and face as a throbbing sensation pulsed through him.

Damn it, thinking of the whore triggers my incubine instincts! Curse this bloodline of mine! This relentless desire for the flesh will be the death of me!

Roaring filled his ears as a flash of hellfire brightened the night air. The Coinn Iotair, fully formed, stood nearly as tall as Cedric. Three of them stood before him, growling as light smoked from their eyes. They were starving, which provided Cedric with the advantage. All at once, they leaped at him. Catching the first attacking dog in both hands caused it to snap and snarl inches from his face.

Cedric threw his weight into the large canine, falling on top of the hellhound, still gripping its neck. The other two were short-tempered and snarled at one another as their starvation fueled a fight between them. Taking the opening, Cedric quickly made his first kill. He dug his fangs deep into the beast's neck, the warm blood dancing on his tongue. Eagerly, he gulped down the bitter, metallic taste of magic mixed with blood that invaded his mouth. With his incubine blood taking hold of his senses, he was draining the power with ease. His instincts greedily urged him to take in every drop and left him hungry for more.

Sensing the death of their pack member outraged the remaining hounds, and they immediately turned their focus back to Cedric. One darted forward and was met with a hound carcass to the face, knocking it back. Before he could shift his attention, the other took action, landing a bite on one of Cedric's arms. Hellfire boiled out of its mouth, burning the flesh as it spilled across his skin. The smell was ungodly. The heat seared Cedric's skin while the hound's teeth tore the flesh. Blood bubbled in the flames as it oozed from where fangs penetrated the melted skin. Despite the savage damage being inflicted on his arm, Cedric grinned. An animalistic persona crept forward, adding to the chill on the breeze.

"You'll pay for that!" Snatching the hound's nostrils with a thumb and finger, he twisted. Yelping, the hellhound released its hold on his arm.

The hellfire was still smoldering and flaming on his arm as he jerked the canine's head to the side, slamming it into the ground head first. Breathless, his chest heaving, Cedric glared down at the heap at his feet. A gurgling sound came from the beast as it struggled to stand up. The other hound circled back. In an effort to defend its pack mate, it leaped onto Cedric's back. Fighting to chew at his head, the hound found the horns to be stronger than it expected. Reaching back, Cedric grabbed a fist full of fur, flinging the great beast onto its injured partner on the ground. The hellhound's short trip ended with a sharp crack, pop, and muffled yelps. One of them was not returning to the fight.

Rolling up on its feet, the other hellhound snapped and barked at him, flecks of foam flying from its mouth as it growled. Hellfire was building as purple and blue flames poured out from under its teeth, giving the foam an eerie glow. An uncanny howl rolled forth with hellfire riding it, aimed for Cedric. In defense, he raised his burned arm. As his flesh smoldered more, he did not flinch from what should have been a painful impact. Green eyes caught the glowing hellfire ones, mocking the large hellhound's efforts. It was useless trying to harm him at this point. The feedings had already let loose his incubine desires; pain was pleasure in this drunken state. The hellfire plume died as the Coinn Iotair faltered in its focus.

With lightning speed, Cedric pushed back the beast, his fangs locking onto the hellhound's neck. A hair-splitting yelp escaped the canine in its panic. Eagerly, he pulled power out of the beast, suckling and slurping. Growling came from the injured hound on the ground, still struggling to move with its broken legs and back; it was unclear if it aimed to flee or wanted to fight. Steam and smoke wafted off Cedric's blackened arm as he continued drinking, feeling engorged. Each gulp brought immense pleasure and his eyes rolled back in response. Excitement crept through his body, overriding his sense of self. The blood in his veins burned through him with a new level of power, and he wanted more.

Pain in this form comes to me like pleasure, dogs. Incubi crave such harsh battles, and after I have drained you both, no marks from this battle will remain. You have only granted me a moment of pure bliss, like whores to the depraved. I know nothing but desire in this form, and with no way to stop or distract me, you were dead before sunset. Nothing is more satisfying than the sensation of my claws ripping through flesh or the ecstasy of the teeth and claws that rip through my own skin.

Angeline opened the door, watching the sunlight fall across the dusty cottage floor. She poked her head out to have a look. The presence of the hellhounds from the day before was gone. Despite the battle she knew had taken place the night before, the village looked to be intact. However, there was no sign of Cedric. Daybreak had passed hours ago, but still, no one dared to venture beyond the safety of their doors. Yesterday had been so eerily quiet that it was a relief when she heard the songs of the birds. It no longer felt like anything was wrong in Raven's Den. Turning to her father, she finally saw him for the broken man he was. Mustering a smile, she hoped to add a sense of forgiveness between them. He truly was a coward, and at least her mother didn't have to see what little of the man was left in him.

"There is a chance he is hurt." Her father's words were low, nothing but a whisper. "Do you not worry for Lord Cedric?"

"Why would I?" Her smile failed, appalled at being asked such a ridiculous question. "Why would I care for a demon like that? He mistreats me! You saw how he shoved me to the ground like a rag doll! I am not his—"

"Pet." Her nerves rattled from her feet to the top of her head at the sound of his voice, sharp to her ears. She could feel his breath, warm and steady, grace the back of her head. There was no denying he was alive and well. Taking in a deep breath, he continued to speak, "Hate me all you want, but you're mine. I can do whatever I wish with you. Don't you ever forget that, precious."

"No." Tears slipped their way down her cheeks as she whispered to herself, "I won't cry."

"What was that?" Cedric stood close behind her. She could feel the warmth of his body radiating into her own. Huffing onto the nape of her neck, he continued his stinging words, "Are you crying again? What a waste."

"I won't cry for you anymore!" she yelled, fortifying her nerves. With a deep breath, she turned on her heels, glaring at his sharp dagger eyes. "I will not entertain your insults by crying for you! No more, demon!"

"What a relief." A smirk vined across his mouth, and she bit her bottom lip. He seemed different to her somehow, and far more powerful than when he left last night. "Now get your things. I need a more dependable horse, and I'll need you for bait."

"We have horses here!" She fought the startling sensation that pulled at her. Every time she got close to him, it heightened, and she struggled to find a safe distance to prevent this new feeling. "I am not your bait to lure your—"

"Still your tongue!" His fingers dug into her jaw and cheeks, forcing her to stand up on her tippy toes. Tears welled up in her eyes as the pain shot through her and all she could stare at was his sour face. Cedric had lost all patience for her. "You can spit your venom at me when we are on the road! Get your things now!" Echoes of his angry words bounced around her eardrums. Cedric released his grip on her and she lost her balance, landing hard on the ground.

He strode outside to wait for her at the far fence. There were no signs of his horns; his injuries from the grueling fight filled with hellfire had vanished. No clues were left for anyone to gauge what the battle had been like. It took longer than expected to get his blood to sit still, but he knew his incubine half was pushing its way to the surface, filled with desire. He'd gained so much power in the last two days that he could feel it down to his fingertips. His enhanced senses were gathering more information and his muscles even twitched and seemed larger just from last night's feeding frenzy. It was clear that there was a faint smell of magic in Angeline's blood.

Did I smell it before and not realize it? It's such a distinct smell of magic. I have a hard time believing I missed it before. Perhaps my incubine blood desired her more than I originally feared. If so, I will have to find a way to get rid of her before I lose myself to that side again.

The sound of Angeline's dragging feet interrupted his thoughts. She was several minutes later than she should have been. A bow strapped across her chest, she looked less fragile in her woodland outfit. Proper boots, long sleeves and pants, and a turtle-necked shirt covered her chin, resting just below her bottom lip. The skin on her cheeks and jaw was purplish red, possibly bruised from his grip. Catching his glare on the bruise, she tucked her face further into the shirt. Her rosy lips frowned at him, and he scoffed in response. Spitting at her feet, he made her back up several steps.

In all her eighteen years, she had never felt so much like an object. Not even after her uncle revealed that he took her in for his own benefit, she still had not felt like a piece of property. To a nobleman, marrying your daughter off to a high lord, like Cedric, came with rare prestige and even money, and higher positions within the castle hierarchy. Her father had been shamed, banished to the family holdings on the outskirts of the kingdom where his position defaulted to that of a farmer. Allowed among the ladies of the court, she was grateful to have been living in the castle, even if it was only to make her cousin look more attractive. Cassandra was the rose among thorns. She was even more beautiful than the rest of the ladies. To her uncle's thinking, his daughter needed someone by her side to remind the kingdom that not even her own family could do better. Her farm girl appearance was like a mahogany backdrop to a gold and sapphire trinket.

It hurt that her father said nothing but a weak goodbye as he hugged her. What she once took as warm and comforting now felt cold and false. He had no way of protecting her or helping her. Cursed, she found herself traveling down a path to her death. It was only a matter of when she would be meet her assured death.

"Let's go," Cedric ordered, snapping her out of her thoughts. "Don't fall behind. I won't come back for you if a scavenger takes advantage."

"Why are we walking? They had horses." The resentment in her voice made him smile.

"We are getting a better horse, the best kind in the world! I can smell one not far from here. Perhaps my luck is changing after all, pet."

CHAPTER 7

SHADE FOR A HORSE

Sweat rolled down Angeline's flushed cheeks as she tried to maintain a half-speed run to keep up with Cedric. They had taken a turn down an animal trail and were walking through heavy underbrush. She stumbled over yet another stump as they made it to a small clearing, sporting a few boulders and a small cave on the opposite side from her. The sun hit her face and she moaned at the heat that welcomed her out of the trees. She couldn't help but wonder why she bothered to even follow Cedric. The image of hellhounds out searching for her crept back into her mind and she picked up her pace again. That was why.

"Fine." Cedric stopped, glaring at her in loathing. "You sweat like a pig. Set camp here, while I go look around for any signs of what I am looking for. We are close enough that it shouldn't be far from here. Try not to get yourself killed while I am away, pet."

Twisting her mouth, Angeline found nothing to say to him. She was far too exhausted to go any more rounds with him today, and the sun was setting fast. Pulling her pack off her back, she went to work setting the camp up for herself. At this point, she was no longer worried about catering to what his needs were. Cedric disappeared into the woods next to the cave. Sighing, Angeline could feel her muscles relax as she cleared a spot and managed a fire. All she had with her were some supplies she scavenged from her dad's things. Dreading the heat of the fire for the moment, she crawled onto a nearby boulder and took a few swigs of cool water from her canteen. At least she was better equipped, with no need to ask his lordship for anything.

The sound of neighing came from the woods behind her. Stunned, she turned in the direction of the cave and saw a solid black horse. It stood there, staring at her, shaking its head and neighing again. As far as she could tell, it was the largest horse she had ever encountered. There were no signs of tackle, harness, or saddle; this must be a feral horse. Much stockier than a Shire or Clydesdale, its thick legs were embellished with long hairs from its knees down. A thick and wild mane crested its neck as it flicked a massive tail twice before stepping closer to her, curling its lips up. Perplexed, Angeline started shushing it as if she were talking to a baby.

"It's okay, I am just here to sleep for the night." Its lips closed and the black horse snorted, pawing at the ground. "I have no intentions of staying any longer, I swear. I respect this as your territory. You can keep it."

Huffing at her once more, it came closer to the camp. Angeline pulled herself farther onto the boulder, praying she was out of reach in case the horse decided to attack her. It was not unheard of for a horse of smaller stature to kill a stableman; she would have no chance against this horse. It nuzzled at her belongings and snorted at the smoking fire, pacing around the camp. The massive stallion inspected everything, flipping its ears at her as he went from item to item. He came closer to where she sat on the boulder, staring up at her. It neighed at her, pawing the ground once more, as if it were trying to tell her to come down.

The woods were growing darker by the second and Cedric still had not returned. Looking back at the large black horse, Angeline watched as it snorted at her, shaking its head again. She could see its large round eyes; a red glow seemed to crawl out of them as the sun started to fade ever faster over the horizon. Angeline whimpered. There wasn't much else she could do but hope for either Cedric's arrival or the horse's departure. Hugging her knees did not comfort her as she exchanged glares with the thick-muscled brute.

"Go away," she whispered. It was a weak attempt and her voice was not very convincing. "I don't have anything for you. I just want to sleep here. And just so you know, you're rather hairy for a horse."

Its massive head turned to watch the last of the sunlight fade. Rearing up, it let out a bone-chilling scream. Flames erupted from its hind hooves, swarming their way across its entire body. What once was long hair now blazed with patches of blue and orange flames. It snorted smoke and steam from its nostrils as it turned back to face Angeline. Shocked, her eyes opened wide. They reflected the image of the horrifying creature. Before her stood what she remembered in children's stories being called a night mare or shag foal. The stories told of the shaggy-haired horses with fiery eyes that would chase travelers who were alone to their doom in the middle of the night.

"Cedric!" she screamed his name, so loud that it hurt her throat. "Cedric! Where are you?"

The fiery horse pawed the ground and snorted at her again. Tears tried to fight their way forward, but her stubbornness took hold and kept them at bay. Watching closely, she noticed that it was behaving the same as earlier. Stretching its muscled neck out, it attempted to nibble at her feet. She couldn't back up any further without the risk of falling. Once more, she cried out for Cedric, but the woods were deserted. Looking down at the shag foal, she watched as he pranced around the field and returned to try to nuzzle her boots with his nose. A game of sorts was starting to take root as the fiery horse repeated this for a while. Her eyes took turns between watching the horse and seeing if there was any movement in the woods around them. *Where is he? Didn't he hear me?*

This went on for what felt like hours and still no Cedric. Angeline was becoming warier as she took another sip from her canteen, watching the horse poke around her pack and sleeping bag. Amazingly, despite the fire rolling off the horse, none of the things he touched caught on fire. She found herself entertained as she watched the creature. It was curious about everything that was hers, snorting and nibbling at all her belongings. Despite its demonic looks, it acted no differently than most of the horses she had come across in the stables. The more skilled riders seemed to have horses with larger personalities, much like this shag foal. Now her campfire was smoldering and smoking as the last remnants of wood became ash and the flame dissipated. She found herself in darkness with only the light of the shag foal.

"Oh, no." Capping off her canteen, she took the chance to stretch her legs out. The horse had stopped his attempts to get her, as he had grown tired of that game hours ago. "There goes the fire."

The horse pulled his nose from her bag and snorted steam in her direction.

"It needs some wood. I doubt his majesty, Lord Cedric, was out gathering any wood." Pulling her knees close again, she rested her chin on them. "Maybe I can sleep like this."

After a few minutes, she heard the hooves pacing back and forth. Neighing and stomping sounds began, but she ignored the horse's antics. After several moments, curiosity got the better of her, and she finally gave the demon horse a reluctant glance. Nodding its head, neighing, the stallion looked silly as its flaming mane reminded her of a candle flickering in the wind. It walked over to the fire, pawing at it. After all this time watching him, she thought that maybe the shag foal enjoyed communicating with her. Perhaps he was just as lonely as she felt.

"No, please don't do that," she whined, standing on the boulder, frustrated. "Why don't you go spook some other lonely traveler off? I am stuck on a boulder and not coming off!"

Shaking its head, it nuzzled the ashes, breathing fire onto some newly placed sticks of wood. Awe took hold of Angeline.

"Who put the wood there?" The horse exchanged a look with her as it flicked its ears. A new campfire had started in a poorly shaped pile of sticks; it was a weak attempt to rebuild what had been there. "You're trying to get me to come down. It's not going to work demon horse. Making a new fire isn't going to get me to come any closer."

"What are you doing?" Startled by Cedric's voice, she nearly lost her balance on the rock. "Get down from there. You look ridiculous, pet."

"But, the shag foal!" Her face reddened with anger as he strolled past her boulder from the darkness, toward the fiery stallion. "Wait! Where have you been? I've been screaming for help for hours!"

"He's friendly." Cedric petted the horse's nose and rubbed him down without fear. His hands glided over the fiery mane, completely unscathed. "Shag foals are known for frightening travelers, nothing more. They run off to their own deaths. Nowhere has it been written that they eat people or have ever killed anyone on purpose. I would imagine they get lonely for companionship from the way they frequently approach travelers. Figured it was worth seeing if what I researched was true."

"Ugh!" Angeline sighed as she slid down the side of the boulder, watching as the horse danced excitedly when her feet hit the ground. "He wouldn't let me down."

"Brush him down; he's going to be our ride." Cedric flopped some rabbits down on the ground. "Wait, get some wood for this sorry campfire.

You'll never be able to cook anything on twigs. I thought you were experienced at making camp?"

"That's not my fire! It's his!" Pointing at the horse, she realized too late how ridiculous she just sounded. "Really!"

"I see this is going to be a common occurrence." Cedric removed his leather vest and began tugging his shirt free of his pants. He pulled the shirt over his head as he flopped to the ground next to the dwindling fire. "You may want to hurry. There's not much time left in the night."

"Fine." Marching off, she felt herself blushing at the sight of his scar-filled chest.

Walking off to the nearest patch of undergrowth, she could hear the sound of hooves thudding behind her. Looking back, she saw that the fiery horse was trailing close behind her. Ignoring him the best she could, she started looking for more firewood. A soft nose nuzzled her elbow, startling her. She turned to face the glowing beast. The horse nodded at her, his ears high and forward. Hand shaking, she reached out, and without hesitation, the fiery nose was placed against her palm. Angeline winced, but felt no burn. No abnormal heat came from the encounter, chipping away her weariness about the shag foal. Fears melting off her shoulders, she smiled before turning back to the ground. His flaming mane gave off light, so that she could go about her task more quickly. A sense of security was a welcomed change, giving back some of the hope she'd lost back in Raven's Den.

Returning to the camp, she found Cedric lying on his back beside the fire, asleep for all she could speculate. It was the first time she had seen his masculine face without a snarl or malicious grin across it. Staring, she started to place wood on the fire. The flames grew brighter with each piece, revealing more of Cedric's physique. In the reflection of the campfire's light, his sweat highlighted each muscled curve. He was handsome, with a square jawline and a strong chin under his full-bodied lips. The muscles leading from his neck to his chest were both elegant and succulent, leading her eyes further along. She found herself focusing on the ripples of his abs and thinking of all the men she had seen shirtless. No one else seemed so fit at King Frederick's castle. Her heart was pounding in her throat as she found herself insanely aroused. This was not the same sensation she experienced before meeting Cedric, and she sucked on her cheeks, which reddened in response to the wave of emotions it stirred.

"For a virgin, you stare at me like a hungry whore." His glowing green eyes caught her breath. Startled, she dropped the wood at her feet. "And you're horribly clumsy. You'll have to be more agile than that if you want to keep up with me, precious."

"You're as evil as they come." Embarrassed and angry, she spit at the ground next to his head. "You are nothing but demon scum!"

"Now this is a new side of you, my pet." He turned to look back up at the sky as he grinned. "No offense, but I would never lay with the flesh of a farmhand's daughter. The stench of dirt claims what little you have to offer me. Don't you worry about needing to consummate this marriage of ours. You're not my type."

"If I knew how to curse someone—I hope that you experience the worst heartbreak ever." Throwing wood into the fire, it flared wild and high, a howl whispering from the wood as it whooshed far into the sky. Ignoring it, she set to work to make herself some food, glowering at him as she did so. "I hope that you learn to love and that it's ripped away from you in the most horrendous way so that you can experience one of life's worst feelings. You have torn away any chances of me ever experiencing true love. I will pray the spirits return that favor to you, dear Cedric. I hope it will bring you many years of pain in your miserable existence."

"Watch your words, witch." His grin was wide and Angeline caught a glimpse of his fangs as they crept from under his lips. As his animalistic stare caught her in it, sweat dripped down his temple. "Cursing a demon can be costly, I hear. I have heard there's a hellish recoil for attempting to curse other magical beings. You might regret saying that later, pet."

"What do you know about magic?" Hissing at him as she pushed her items into her pack again, she watched as his smile dropped. "You're an animal that crawls about this earth, devouring other creatures, and lack any grace needed for magic."

"Shut your mouth." The tone of his voice was dark. She'd struck a nerve and his jaw muscles flexed. "You know nothing about magic or what it is capable of doing to a person, regardless if they are demon or human. Do not speak to me about magic, whore. Perhaps I should have left you gawking at me earlier, pet."

Biting her tongue, she decided to end the conversation. Her cheeks flushed with rage as she continued to prep her meal, careful to avoid looking in his direction again.

CHAPTER 8

SHAMAN IN THE WOODS

"How much farther are we going into the woods?" Swiping at a fly, she adjusted her seat on the large steed, trying to keep a gap between her and Cedric's backside. "We've been traveling for over a week now."

"I know how long we've been traveling." He scoffed in response. "Trust me, I dread every day I spend with you at this rate. Wylleam's place is not much farther, no more than two hours from here. Two hours of hell, that is."

"And who is this Wylleam again?" It was so awkward and uncomfortable to sit behind any rider on such a wide horse. The soreness of her legs was going to be a constant battle with the shag foal. "Does he have a saddle that will at least fit the horse?"

"We'll see. He is only a shaman from the Hemicynes tribe from the far north and his people aren't known to ride horses or anything of the sorts." The horse snorted and bobbed its head. He agreed with having a proper saddle over the current bareback riding method. "He may know a skilled leather worker that can make one. Please do not act up while we are here. You've embarrassed me enough in front of your village."

"Act up? Act up!" Crossing her arms, she wished her eyes could burn holes into the back of his head. "Are you kidding me? You picked me to marry..."

"Hold your tongue when we get there." Looking back at her, his eyes cut their message deep. "Save your venom for our most wonderful days of traveling, pet."

"I said to stop calling me that. It's degrading enough I am married to you." The feeling of her hopelessness crept into her chest and she bit her lip to hold the tears. "I have a name."

"I don't care." The words hit her with a coldness that stung her heart. "Now still your tongue before I take it from your mouth permanently."

Sulking behind him, they approached a woodland cottage. Smoke billowed from its stone chimney, and chickens pecked the ground around them. Cedric dismounted and offered her a hand. She shook her head in disapproval. Once more, his jaw tightened, eyes flashing his anger in response to her rebellion. Sliding into a more comfortable position on the horse, she shook her head in refusal again. Her eyes matched the heated intensity of his own, both of them angry. She was voicing silently that she would rather stay on the horse. He reached for her, but missed as the shag foal stepped sideways, neighing and snorting his own disapproval. Exchanging glares with the horse, he spat at the ground before turning his attention to the door.

"Be that way." A sigh of relief left her lips as he walked inside.

"Thank you." Lying on her belly across the horse, she hugged and petted the shag foal. "Thank you. You didn't have to do that. You are very kindhearted and I am sorry for not being nicer on the day we met."

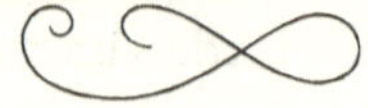

Cedric stood in the dark cottage embellished with dream catchers, talismans, and many other ceremonial items. His nose was invaded by the smells of herbs, spices, and ointments that were housed there. Rubbing his nose as spices tickled his nostrils, he found Wylleam bent over, digging through one of the boxes that cluttered the floor of the room.

Being a Cynocephali, he had the head of a dog with long, tall ears and the body of a man. Wylleam was a powerful shaman and his appearance reflected his position among his tribe. He had feathers wrapped into two long flutes of hair that draped down each side of his face. Across his doglike head and furry chest were symbols and lines that one could only assume helped invoke communications with spirits. The leather chaps he wore had pouches covering them, each with different patterns of beadwork to signify what they held. His canine face turned toward Cedric as he stood, towering over him, flicking both his ears. A long, dark brown mane bordered the short tan fur on his face, like a hairy headpiece. He would have been intimidating, but his tribe was well known as peace-loving people living in harmony with nature, most of them vegetarians.

"Ah, Cedric!" They hugged, patting one another on their backs with great thuds. "It has been a while, my friend. What troubles you today?"

"Where do I begin?" Smiling, he gave a hearty laugh at the shaman and they sat down. "Most of my trouble is outside, sitting on a shag foal."

"Oh! So, our assumption on shag foals was correct, then?" His large, brown eyes seemed to light up. "That is wonderful! How did you manage to get one to approach you, though? I thought they only come up to humans?"

"Bait." Cedric's smile faded as he glanced at the closed door. "And a curse."

"Really?" Wylleam looked at the door, raising his nose to the air and sniffing for a moment. "Well now! What an interesting girl you have with you! I never thought you would travel with a magic wielder, with your past history and all."

"It's not completely by choice." Sneering, he rubbed his hands across his forehead and pulled his hair back, staring at his boots. "I somehow missed the fact she had magic in her blood when I first acquired her. His highness, King Frederick, married me off to a lady of the court after a tournament, and that's what I got. I should have picked the prettier one."

"Married?" The large ears folded back and he shook his lion's mane of fur, ruffling it. "You have been busy with collecting quandaries, I see. Your power has increased immensely, though. That is edging you closer to your goal, is it not?"

"Yes, at the cost of a night of lusting again." Sitting up, he slouched in the chair, almost pouting as he stared off into the chimney's fire. "I have devoured an orm and four heavily enchanted Coinn Iotair within a day's time. An ancient witch, the ancestor of the bitch outside, set me up. She knew how I fed on demons to gain power and had the whole thing planned. It was worse when I got near the girl and had to spend the night out in the woods. This is only the second time I have ever had to battle while lusting, and thinking about it makes my skin crawl with excitement. It... I felt like a whore with a fresh batch of virgin soldiers. Never have I let the incubine blood arouse me like that, and I lust for it to happen again, even now. Its taste is still fresh on my tongue."

"I see. I still do not understand why you deny yourself all of your bloodline's powers, but an ancient witch, you say?" Sniffing the air once more, he hummed, scratching under his canine jaw. "Yes, that is very old magic indeed. That is as old as the magic we use to contact our ancestors, and possibly older than that. No offense, my friend, but that is a very special find you have, both the foal and your bride. I assume you have bedded with her by now."

"No!" His eyes met with Wylleam's, and there the shaman could see a sense of fear in his friend's eyes. "I refuse to touch her. I will not touch any woman that the incubine blood desires. I have made that mistake before, and it still haunts my dreams every night."

"Ah, so there is still fear behind the purpose of your lusting." Sighing, he gave Cedric a thoughtful look. "I do not blame you for being afraid, my friend. What happened the last time would haunt any man or demon. Do you know what the witch's purpose was in increasing your power and sending you into a lusting? Sending her heiress along with someone like you seems rather strange and dangerous."

"I assume as a form of protection for the girl. Her father let me know that she may never discover her powers, but there is some other magic wielder after the powers her blood holds. The Coinn Iotair were sent to hunt that magic down, and as far as I could smell, they came from across the channel in the northwest. They were doubled in power, enchanted beyond anything I have seen here. Morrighan's magic holds no chance against what I sensed within those hellhounds."

"That is clever. May I speak with her? I am curious to meet someone like her."

"I wouldn't advise it. She does not hold her tongue, and she's truly a farmer's daughter."

"Bring her to me and I will be the judge of that. You can go wash up; you stink of sweat and blood and I wish to free my nose of it." Sneezing, Wylleam exchanged grins with Cedric. "Let me meet this bride of yours!"

Cedric pulled himself from his seat and opened the door. Eyes closed, Angeline was still lying across the horse's back, rubbing him down. Whistling jerked her out of her trance. He held the door wide open and flicked his fingers, motioning for her to go in. Biting her lip, she took a moment before deciding to climb down. It was quite the drop. Her foot landed wrong under her weight, making her limp past him into the cottage, too stubborn to make a noise over it. Shaking his head, Cedric closed the door behind her and grabbed the reins of the shag foal, making his way to the water.

"Ah! So you are Cedric's bride!" Freezing in her steps, she looked at the dog-headed man, unsure whether to be afraid. "Not to worry, child. I am a shaman, no more than a priest, in terms of your belief system. I wish to talk to you."

"Are... are you Wylleam?" Swallowing, she sat in the chair across from him. "Cedric's friend?"

"Yes, I see he told you about me." It was awkward seeing a smile on a dog's face. "I want to know what the old witch requested of you. Do not worry, I do not intend to share it with Cedric, but as a shaman, I get whispers from the spirits that follow everyone here. I am being told you were given strict instructions and a task from your ancestor that must be completed."

"A shaman who talks to spirits?" Looking about the room, she could see nothing that made her feel she was in danger. Sighing, she turned back, hoping that relieving the weight of her distress onto a stranger might make her feel at ease. "The skeleton witch told me she wants me to be bound to Cedric."

"Bound?" His ears drooped low beside his head, and a frown crossed his muzzle. "How does she expect you to do this with an unboundable abomination such as Cedric? Unnaturally created, through the means of black magic, he is no more than a toy to his creator, Morrighan. Did she explain to you how this is to be done?"

"Yes." Her stomach twisted as she could still hear the instructions loud and clear. "He is to be in his incubine form when he takes me and then satisfy his moroi bloodline when it calls for it."

"She said moroi?" The ears pricked forward and the hair on the nape of her neck stood on end. "That would be something that Cedric and I had no idea about. We had assumed it was a vampire incubus cross, but this does change things."

"What is a moroi?" Goosebumps crawled across her skin as she could see the concern on his face. "It's not a vampire?"

"It is the offspring of two pure-blood vampires who truly love one another. It is said that the moroi are always female, and every time barren, with red hair and green eyes. They eat and drink as humans do and can walk under the sun amongst us. The only special abilities of the moroi are her stamina and strength. It is said she outlives her husband, if she does not overwork him in the bed."

"Always female?" Cedric's red hair and green eyes flashed across her thoughts. "But Cedric isn't female."

"You can thank the incubus bloodline mixed with Morrighan's black magic for what he became. Incubus are known for strong stamina and strength as well, with an insatiable thirst for the arts of the flesh. It is through these means that an incubus gains his power. Unlike vampires, who increase with feedings and age, the more women he beds with, the more an incubus's power increases. Strangely enough, Cedric has discovered by instinct that he gains power by feeding like a vampire on demons. As for how he obtains any power through the incubine standards is still in the dark to him, or he has never revealed that much to me. Other means of gaining power would be terms for binding him to another demon or a magic wielder, but it was thought impossible. Cedric's only purpose in life is to gain enough power to destroy the sorceress Morrighan, his creator. He will gain it in any manner necessary."

"According to her, it is very possible." This time she lost her fight to the tears as they slid down her cheeks. "I want nothing to do with magic or Cedric. I don't want to bed with a demon. I'd rather be sent to hell, if I am not already there."

"And he is too afraid to bed with you. This is interesting."

"Afraid?"

"Please understand that over one hundred years ago, he made a horrible mistake. It is not my place to tell you that story. I will keep your secret as I keep this secret, but he will have to make a decision just as you will. Morrighan was a virgin sorceress when she called the incubine king Boto to her bed. She willingly bound herself to him and him to her. We can only assume she knew what kind of pact she was making with him, since the ending result was the strongest power gain of all time. Your ancestor has no concerns with Morrighan, but something we all know nothing about. The power gain from your binding will easily surpass theirs."

Wind rushed through the room, rattling the hanging charms and sending the fire in an uproar. Angeline hugged herself as she watched his flicking ear as he eyed the fire. The room went silent and the wind fell, leaving objects swinging about them. The same cold breeze had shot through her before from the skeleton witch. In silence, she continued crying, having nothing else she could do in response. As she saw it, her life had no purpose worth treasuring.

"Dear child, you have a strong ancestor that watches over you." A gentle smile came across his face, and he got up to dig through a large chest. "I have something for you. I hear you are an excellent archer, yes?"

"Yes. I am good with the bow. Did Cedric tell you that?" Rubbing her tears away, she welcomed the change of conversation. "I haven't had a chance to use it in front of him."

"I do not rely on Cedric for information." Chuckling, he pulled out a gorgeous bow; its wood golden and gnarled. "Here, this is yours. I haven't used it in a very long time. At least you can carry it to protect the both of you. You may not care for Cedric, but he has been a good friend to me. He needs someone to look after him, and since you are stuck with the task of being his companion, you can do this for me."

CHAPTER 9

VENOMS, POISONS, & TOXINS

Shifting the large bow across her chest, Angeline pulled her collar over her mouth and nose. It was the second time that month they had no choice but to travel across a field laden with decaying bodies from a battle. There was nothing out of the normal seeing a sight like this with so many lords and kings in this region. Looking across the land, the corpses were stacked in piles with crows and vultures covering their peaks. Feeling sick, her stomach twisted as a wolf dragged entrails away from his pack members. The scavengers were fighting one another for any piece of it. She buried her face in Cedric's back. He grunted in response, spitting at the ground as the shag foal delicately stepped its way through the rotting filth.

They had both given up on arguing with one another at this point. The only words that were spoken were out of necessity. Cedric's routine was to tell her where to camp and he would leave her there with the horse he now called Barushka. She would stay there next to the fire, he would come back, drop off rabbits, and leave again. He never stayed any longer than that. Sleeping elsewhere in the woods was her guess. Every morning started with him nudging her with his boot and nodding for her to pack up. It was hard to say who was avoiding whom in terms of eye contact. There was a sensation of dread that was ever-growing each time they mounted Barushka and were forced to be close to one another for yet another day.

The rank smell hit her nose despite using the collar and Cedric's back as a shield, her stomach lurched. Gripping his shoulder, she jerked the turtleneck down; leaning as far as she could manage without falling off, she began to vomit. Barushka neighed and stifled to the side, shaking his head. Stopping to let her finish, the horse watched with great concern as his friend fell ill. Cedric had found it annoying that his rare steed had grown attached to Angeline to the point that he would cater to her and not what he needed him to do.

"Is that necessary?" Spooked to hear Cedric's voice, she winced as she spit out the last of the foul taste. "Could you hold it for when we get past here? I don't find it appealing myself."

"Sorry, it hit my nose and—" Lunging forward, another round started as it fell across the ground with a splatter. "I tried to hold it, but it was either you or the ground."

"Oh m." A female voice came from the top of a nearby body pile. "She looks rather green. I must admit, it's a pretty shade."

"Nemaine," Cedric growled up at the woman. Her Greek goddess attire was revealing; gold accessories were loud and decorated with skulls. Thick green hair fell behind her, as long as she was tall. The white cloth only made the green snakelike markings across her face, arms, and legs stand out. "I have no business with you, Sorceress."

"Oh! But are you not my sister's lost puppy?" Sitting there on the decaying bodies, Nemaine was holding a half-rotten head in her hand, picking off the remaining flesh. "If I were a good little sister, I would be eager to return you to her, but we all know that's not me. I am more of the type of sibling that sneaks off with everyone's favorite toy. Unfortunately, I carry the reputation of breaking them."

"I am not your sister's toy." Cedric's hand gripped the hilt of his sword as he snarled at Nemaine. "Let us pass. I have no quarrel with you, only Morrighan."

"I have no intentions of stopping you. I am up here, collecting new skulls for my collection." Pausing from her grotesque activity, she leaned to get a better view of Angeline who buried her face into Cedric's back, feeling a mixed wave of security and the need to be as close as possible to him. "Wait a moment. What is she doing there behind you anyhow, dear Cedric? It's been a while since you have carried a female with you."

"A curse." Spitting at the ground, he made some clicking sounds with his mouth. "Move Barushka, we have no time for this."

"A curse? You lie! Since when does our abomination carry a girl with him?" He could feel Angeline's fist grip his shirt in response, and he shifted in the saddle as Nemaine laughed. "You are like a long-lost little brother to me! Which brothel did you find this one in? Oh, please do tell! She must make love like a starving animal for you to keep her! Let me have a look at your new toy! Or what was the other name you gave them? Oh yes, pet."

"I've heard enough of your taunting." They cantered down their path, but Nemaine leaped off her mountain of rotting flesh, walking close behind them. "Nemaine, I am in no mood for talking. Perhaps you should call upon your sister, Badbh. She should still be close, I imagine, by the looks of this battle."

"Badbh?" Nemaine's face twisted in disgust, making her stop in her steps. "We never see eye to eye. She tells me how inferior my methods are and I point out how she has destroyed her body in her barbaric methods of battling in wars. I have nothing to talk to her about."

"I am too busy to hear your complaints. I have much to do before I go pay Morrighan a visit." Angeline could feel his back muscles tightening, and once more, another wave washed over her, making her feel aroused. "There are other things I rather be doing, besides riding my horse."

"Of course! I would expect the offspring of Boto to have better things to ride." Cedric pulled Barushka to a stop, looking back at her, his jaw tight. "Oops, did I let that slip? How forgetful of me. It never crossed my mind you would want to know that. It's amazing, the older I get, the more forgetful I am of such important information. Dear Cedric, please forgive me for not remembering who your daddy was. I hope I helped you and made your day so much more delicious!"

"I am the spawn of the king of incubi himself?" Another wave went through Angeline, making her exhale to attempt to relieve this new sensation of excitement. Shuddering, she refused to move, afraid to be caught in the crossfire of his eyes or worse, subject of Nemaine's taunting again. "It explains a lot. Perhaps your tongue has more information for me, perhaps my mother's hierarchy?"

"Nope, doesn't ring any bells. He must have humped her good to get something like you out of her. I hear he's infamous for killing a majority of the females he beds with." Shrugging, a coy smile crossed her red lips, wicked in nature. "Not a thing more for you, little brother. I am so sorry. Are you going to cry about it?"

"Feh, then I will be on my way." Barushka tried his best not to start in a gallop, feeling the urge Cedric was implying to stay calm.

"See you again! Soon, I hope!" She waved as her impish laugh began to take hold.

Barushka was traveling faster across the field, his concentration focused on gaining as much distance as possible and, more importantly, into the woods. He no longer was concerned about whether or not his hooves were stepping on bodily contents. Angeline was almost panting, sweat crawling across her body as she clutched onto Cedric's back. Cedric's muscles were still taut under his shirt and the rhythm of the horse was not helping relieve her of her troubling feeling. It was a sensation flowing from him that had her worked up. Never had she felt the yearning that haunted her entire body like the one she was feeling now. It was embarrassing and atrocious, yet in a strange way enjoyable.

They were in the shade of the trees, but she dared not move a muscle. It was hard to say how long they rode through the woods before he brought Barushka to a stop. Aching in her chest did nothing to still the throbbing sensation that was taking hold elsewhere. Cedric reached back, gripping her thigh. She moaned with excitement at the touch, but it ended as a quick jerk pulled her off the horse. Landing on the ground, she yelped as a stick cut across her arm. Tears welled up in her eyes as she looked up at him, confused by the sudden toss. Cedric was enraged as he sat on Barushka, who neighed and stifled in protest.

"Is it necessary to pant and moan like a whore on the whole ride?" His eyes were wild, degrading her in every way they could. "What was so arousing about a battlefield of rotting flesh? If my nose wasn't so insulted, I'd give you a royal fucking in hopes this virgin nonsense quits."

Holding her arm, she sat there crying, confused, and relieved that she felt normal again. Climbing off the fidgeting horse, he stood over her with his arms crossed. Staring at the ground, she had given up on the idea of fighting him as warm blood trickled between her fingers where she held the cut. It was still unclear to her what she was doing. Though the sensation was exciting, it was misplaced. All she could tell was that it was something that had leaked out of him and she was merely reacting to it. Kneeling beside her, he tried to grab her hurt arm, and she jerked away. Grabbing it up, she cried out in pain as he jerked her sleeve up. Eyeing it for a moment, he simply covered it back up, releasing his hold.

I don't think she realizes what was happening. Good.

"Just leave me alone." Wailing as the horse nuzzled her, she held her arm close to her.

"You'll live." Standing, he walked toward the woods. "Set camp. I have no desire to ride with you anymore today."

Cedric had a lot to think about. Wylleam had been clever at letting it slip that the girl's ancestors revealed his mother was a moroi, and not a vampire as they had originally thought. Now it was confirmed that Boto was the one used for his creation, like many of Morrighan's other favorite creations.

Nemaine started in on me, and Angeline's magic mingled with the untamed incubine senses. I could feel it tug at me. Hell, I had a hard-on for the whole ride with how worked up she was getting. Shocked she didn't start humping me like a dog in heat. There is no doubt I have an incubine touch that would rival the king of incubi, but I am going to have to keep it under control. I wonder if this is why Boto takes so many virgins? My instincts crave it. My skin crawls with excitement at the idea of taking a virgin and being close to her makes it worse. Dammit, why did it have to be Boto?

All of his offspring are chimera these days, loyal to Morrighan. He's killed all of his bastards, that is, if the creature he mounts lives from his desire to inflict pain on them. Morrighan had bound herself to him so she could take advantage of a black magic technique that would allow any seed to take. Somehow, she managed to get a moroi to be fertile on top of it all. I wonder how something like me managed to escape her fortress. Did my mother find a way to escape?

The muscles in his abdomen tightened, and he stopped. There was something wrong. Turning around, he ran in Angeline's direction. *She said see you again... soon.* Flying out of the woods into the clearing where Barushka and Angeline were, he halted. Startled, the two of them stared at Cedric with looks of bewilderment. After a moment, Angeline resorted back to dismay, and she finished wrapping the cut. Barushka shook his head and went back to nibbling at the patches of grass at his feet. Cedric sucked on his cheek, trying to place the sensation of danger that was boiling his instincts into a frenzy. Nemaine was up to no good, but there were no signs of anything happening. *I hate magic. I can't always tell what it's doing and where.* With a sigh, he began breaking branches off a dying tree for the fire.

"What are you doing?" Pausing, he looked over his shoulder at the sound of her broken voice. "What's wrong?"

"Gathering wood for the fire," Scoffing, he went back to popping a few more large pieces off. "Something wrong with that, pet?"

"It's just a cut. I can handle this on my own." Biting her lip, she was hoping he would go away. "Plus, it's not like you to be kind to me. We weren't going to run off without you, if that's what you thought."

"It doesn't have anything to do with being kind to you or fear of being left in the woods." Dropping the wood next to her, he flopped down on a grassy patch. "Do you even realize who that was back there?"

"Nemaine, the Venomous Sorceress." Angeline piled the wood in a way so she could get a strong fire. "Sister of the dark sorceress Morrighan and Battle Goddess Badbh. It has been said she travels on the back of a monstrous spider and keeps the company of snakes who can swallow a man whole."

"At least you're not completely daft." Watching the last of the sun fall behind the forest trees, he groaned. "It's hard to say if she is going to try anything tonight."

"I'll pray that she gives me a quick death, then." Bitterness was in her voice as she motioned for Barushka to come over, and with a snort, he started the campfire for her. "Don't worry about any food. I'm not hungry."

"I wouldn't recommend eating anything near here. She's notorious for poisoning local animals and water sources." He watched her unroll her bedpack and go through her routine. She took off her boots, pulling her feet free of the woolen socks, and began rubbing ointment on the blisters that covered them. "How long have you gone with your feet like that?"

"What does it matter?" Exasperated, she looked his way as he lay on his side, watching her from the other side of the fire. "I haven't traveled like this in a very long time. You get soft living the life of a lady of the court and wearing silk-lined slippers. You're a lord. You should know this."

"Yes, I am a lord. That much about me is true." A smirk met his face as he observed her growing frustration when she looked at her torn sleeve. "I am from the House of Romulus."

"But you are a demon and they are far from that." Digging through her pack, she managed to find a small field-dressing knife. "The House of

Romulus is the oldest house in the land. How on earth would a demon find a way to not just claim he is from their house, but prove it?"

"I was the previous lord's adoptive son. His wife fell ill and passed before his son could be properly born. On one of his many travels, he came across me and took me under his wing." She wasted no time cutting the torn sleeve off the main part of the shirt and doing the same with the remaining sleeve. "I like your new look."

"It's only temporary. I'll need these scraps to make more bandages. So, the last lord of Romulus adopted you. How long ago was that?" She shredded the good sleeve into two pieces. "How long ago did that house die off, then?"

"I think it's been over a hundred years ago now." Pausing from her task, she caught a glazed look in his eyes as he glared into the fire's flames. "I wish he had died in battle."

"How did he die then?" His tone was downhearted, and it had her full attention.

"I rather not bring up the past." His eyes came back to the present and caught her curious brown ones in their green glow. "That is none of your business."

"Well, excuse me for holding a less hostile conversation." Scoffing, she threw her blanket over her shoulder and laid with her back to him. "It was a welcomed change, but I won't push my luck any further."

Barushka screamed, sending both of them to their feet. His flames exploded from his mane and hooves as he reared up, stomping at something in the grass not far from them. Cedric glared at the ground about them, hoping to catch a glimpse of what was coming. Shuffling backward, Angeline's feet bumped into something hard, sending her falling on her back, hard. Hissing erupted and, as she looked up, a large cobra stood tall. The snake was large enough to eat a man, just like all the stories she had ever heard whispered over the tables in the castle.

CHAPTER 10

A Cure

Mesmerized by the size of the cobra, Angeline lay there, shocked and unmoving. Once more, the snake hissed at her and she caught sight of the fangs wet with venom. Another head stood up out of the grass and she was facing two identical beasts, their eyes aimed for her. One lunged forward. She flinched, and they withdrew, as if enjoying teasing her. They coiled themselves in their spots, showing that they were long and lean, with scales bigger than her hand. The second snake raised himself taller, flared his cobra crown, and went for a strike. Closing her eyes tight, she waited for the pain that was coming.

A thud and vibration from the ground met her hands. Jerked to her feet before she could register what had landed so close, she struggled with remembering to breathe. Cedric had managed to get between her and the snakes, freeing the striking snake of its head. Stepping back, her feet bumped something hard again, making her hair stand on end. Forcing herself to eye her feet, she was relieved. It was the bow that Wylleam had given her. She wasted no time to snatch it up and frantically searched the ground for her quiver of arrows. A clash of metal and fang jumped her heart to her throat as Cedric put his full focus on matching speed with the strikes. Everything was going fast and her movements felt slow. A strap under her thrown blanket called her attention to it. Her swift dive for it was matched with another bang as the snake attempted to strike in her direction, and Cedric blocked once more.

"Stop moving!" He was furious sounding, and she was glad that his back was to her. "She sent them after you! I can't focus on killing it if you keep changing where it's striking!"

"I've got my bow!" Her shaking hands dropped the first arrow, and she pulled another from the quiver. "I can help!"

"Are you kidding me?" He threw his hands up, making the snake bring its attention back to him again. "An arrow won't do you any good on its scales. I'm going to need a new sword after I kill this one!"

Biting her lip hard, urging her nerves to stay still just long enough, she let the arrow fly. Whizzing past Cedric's left cheek, it landed on target with the snake's eye. It let out a hissing screech, enraged by the attack. Cedric looked impressed as he shot a glance over his shoulder. That was his mistake. The angered cobra lunged forward at that moment and landed a blind strike across Cedric's right arm. The force of it shoved him backward, smashing him into Angeline, taking them both to the ground. Her hand landed square on the arrow she had dropped. Without a second to spare and with all her strength, she rammed the arrow's point into the snake's remaining eye. It released its grip from Cedric's arm and fled from their sight.

"You distracting bitch!" The sound of sizzling flesh caught her attention, and she looked at the venom that had made its home in Cedric's arm. "Damn you! I had this and you—"

His eyes grew wide as he gripped his arm and sweat poured over him, his tanned skin paling with alarming speed. He attempted to stand, but stumbled to the side and fell to his knees. It became very clear that he was not bouncing back from this encounter. Angeline looked around. There were no signs of any more snakes, but Barushka was missing. Jerking the bandages from her pack, she attempted to tie off the poisoned limb. He tried to shove her away, but, engulfed in the pain, he struggled to keep himself sitting. Satisfied that she managed to get it tight enough, and the wounds covered, she whistled several times. Her only hope was that Barushka was still alive and close enough to hear it. The sound of something splattering the ground brought her back to Cedric as he began to puke. The smell was unnatural, and it was a sickening black color.

A light came from the trees and was approaching them fast; Barushka had heard her whistles. The sight of a flaming horse headed across the small break in the woods was a blessing for a change. Bopping his head up and down, he dropped two arrows on the ground at her feet as he snorted steam from his nostrils. It was clear that on his way back he had come across the snake that had taken Cedric down. Barushka nuzzled Cedric, who fought to get himself standing enough to lean on the horse's tall shoulder. Angeline could hear the rattling in his breath and his eyes were dilated like nothing she had ever seen before. Gathering what items were necessary, she snuffed out the fire. Barushka had kneeled himself down to his knees and hocks, and somehow Cedric had managed to pull himself on. There was no time to throw her shoes back on; tossing them in her bag, she leaped up behind Cedric's shivering body. Barushka jumped to a full gallop.

They must have looked like a rider straight out of the fires of hell as the horse's heavy hooves thrust them with great speed through the forest. She had no idea where they were going, but Barushka's flames were high as he took to the unseen path. Cedric was soaked now in his own sweat and losing body heat. If it were not for his constant shivering and gagging, she would have thought he was dead. Green and black lines were steadily growing out from under the bandages where the fangs had punctured his flesh. Nemaine's venoms were magically altered. There was no telling what this version was designed to do. Only one thing was certain: no one lives after an encounter with her toxins.

Neighing woke her from her sleep. At some point, she had passed out, and she found herself laying up against Cedric's back. His beating heart was dull and his chest rattled more so. He was knocked out, unmoving. Looking around, they had reached a very dense and ancient part of the forest. The trees creaked and let little sunlight through. The barren forest floor was speckled with dots of light as Barushka walked over the gnarled roots. Sitting up straight, she wiped his sweat from her cheek and marveled over the massive size of the trunks that surrounded them.

"Where are we?" They stopped and Barushka laid down, looking back at her and curling his lips. "I suppose we get off here."

Slipping off, she took a better look at Cedric. His lips were white and cracked and his eye sockets were dark and sunken. He was near death. They had stopped close to one of the bigger trees, and she looked up at it with great awe. It was as big as a castle tower, if not wider. Roots from the enormous plant snaked and zigzagged in and out of the ground twice the height of Barushka. Ice latched firmly on her injured arm and she yelped. It echoed endlessly as she turned to see Cedric's half-opened eyes.

"Help me off." The pupils of his eyes were so wide that she could see just a green outline about them. "Help me to the tree."

"Ok." It made her sick to her stomach to feel how cold and weak he was as she struggled to help him off the horse and over to the tree. "Is this… is this where you intend to die?"

"No." He managed a small fiery glare. "She owes me a favor."

"Yes, I do." A voice made of wind, water, and the rattling of leaves came from the tree, sending Angeline's heart sprinting. "Lord Cedric, I see you have fallen victim to Nemaine's sorcery."

"He was bitten by one of her giant cobras." Angeline's shaken voice did not help the unnerving sensation in her joints, and Cedric had faded back to his coma. "We rode as fast as we could."

"Let me see the bite." The bark in front of them shifted and a wooden figure of a woman leaned out of the tree for a closer look. Angeline stared with amazement as she observed the exposed bust that used its vine-like hair and arms to keep her attached to the trunk. Her face was like that of a wooden figure from a throne room, but lacked any signs of a mouth. Cedric was now wheezing in his unconscious state. "I must see it to know what enchantments to add to the ointment or elixir."

"Ok." Angeline uncovered the puncture wounds, wincing as flesh pulled away with the last part of the bandages and her nose met a smell more foul than the corpses from the field. "Oh no, it's infected already!"

"Worry not, child of Eve." Roots snaked from under Cedric and dug into the wounds. He did not react, though she had to look away and cover her mouth. "This is most foul. The sorceress has outdone herself this time. Fortunately, I have something I can make for this."

"Will he live?" Barushka nuzzled her, and she hugged his giant head in response.

"Yes, if you take him to Wylleam from here." Looking back, she watched as a bottle of glowing blue pulled free of the ground and poured over the wounds. "This will stop the poison and relieve him of some of the symptoms. As for the healing process, the shaman will know what would best suit Cedric's needs."

"Barushka can take us there. He got us this far somehow." Cedric was tossing in a fitful sleep as the elixir boiled and mixed with the streaks that had worked their way as far as his chest and neck. "I did promise him if anything happened to Cedric, I would come back to his place. I suppose this would be what he was talking about when he said Cedric was reckless with his life."

"He should be stable now." Her roots held Cedric up and placed him back on Barushka's back with great care. "My favor is now paid in full. Let him know he is not allowed back into the Black Forest unless otherwise summoned. The same goes for you, child. This is not a place for mortals."

"I understand." The nearby trees shook and howled; the warning was not to be taken lightly. "I will pass the message on."

Pulling herself onto Barushka, she watched the woman's figure fade back into the trunk of the tree. Cedric lay in the same position as before, belly flat on the horse's back. At least he was starting to get some of his warmth back. With a swift turn, they wasted no time to return to a full gallop. It was comforting not having to panic over where to go and where to lead the horse. Somehow, Barushka knew. After everything that he had done, she couldn't imagine ever having a normal steed again.

It was dark when they made it to Wylleam's cottage. Angeline had stopped acknowledging the passing of time after the Black Forest. Wylleam was already standing outside, grabbing hold of Cedric before they even came to a complete stop. Watching the door close behind them, she and Barushka could take a moment to release the tension that they were still holding. Hugging his neck, she let the tears free that had been there, demanding that she fall apart. After a moment, she unstrapped the saddle, shocked that Barushka hadn't been rubbed raw from the whole ordeal. Brushing him had been a good way to get her tears to slow, as they both enjoyed a moment of calm.

Angeline wasn't sure how she felt about everything that had gone down. Part of her wished he had simply died off so she could be free, yet another part knew that she needed him. Every time the word "need" crossed her thoughts, she would pause and mull it over. The question was, what kind of need did she want from him? Protection? Attention? Or did she really like him, after all? *After all the spiteful comments, shoving, and abuse, was there something else there?*

"Angeline." Wylleam's softhearted voice cut her thoughts short. "I need to ask something of you."

"What do you need me to do?" She gave Barushka a good pat on the back and he walked off. "I am more than happy to help you, Wylleam."

"I wouldn't say that so soon. It's for Cedric." His ears were flat, and the sadness across his muzzled face made her stomach knot. "What I am about to ask may not be received well. I know how you feel about things."

"At least you are kind enough to be honest and gentle on delivering me with bad news." Her chest ached from the depression that was seeping forward. "What kind of horrible task do I need to do now?"

"There was another way, but we will choose the less daunting choice. Neither would sound pleasant to you. I know you do not like Cedric, and he's not exactly the best company for a lady, but he will not be able to heal properly otherwise." With a great huff, he held her hands in his massive ones and looked her in the eye. "He is a moroi crossed with an incubus with the use of black magic binding him together as one creature. The venom is no longer in his body, but the damage has been done. I simply need to take some blood from you, since you are a human magic wielder. Your magic will restore order in his body and blood. I should be able to make a healing elixir to get his bloodlines healing right again. I would give him mine if I thought it would work, but despite being a creature of magic, my blood contains none. We Cynocephali depend on our ability to listen to the spirits and use the land's gifts for the medicines and healing we do."

"Then what was the other choice?" Swallowing, she wasn't sure if her ears wanted to hear it. "If giving you blood was the more feasible option, what was the other way?"

"You should already know that answer." Wylleam broke eye contact, pulling a small knife and jar from the pouch at his hip. "The only reason that wouldn't be an option isn't because you would not lay with him. It's because he would refuse to do so. I did not tell him that you knew how to bind yourself to him, but even then, I think he would refuse."

"Am I that repulsive to him?" She unwrapped her cut arm. Anger was replacing her despair as her thoughts scattered over the matter. "It's one thing to hear it from his vulgar mouth, but coming from you makes it true to heart. The very idea hurts."

"You don't understand, Angeline. He has a very good reason for that decision." Despite how gentle he was trying to be, she hissed as he reopened the cut with the knife and encouraged it to bleed. "So sorry for hurting you, but I have some ointment for this. It'll be healed by morning, promise. As for the other, it is not my place to share that story with you."

"Thank you, but it still hurts that even a demon like him has no interest in me." He handed her the ointment and more bandages from another pouch. "He's lucky to have a friend like you. I don't understand how, though."

"He has a bigger heart than you think." Swirling her blood in the jar, he started chanting low to it. She watched as a bright yellow glow developed and peaked to the point it hurt to stare at it for very long. "My, you do hold some very strong magic indeed. I may have taken too much at this strength."

"Is that what the glow is from?" The ointment relieved the pain instantly as she watched Wylleam nod and head back into the cottage. "So I do have magic in my blood..."

Her arm felt good, so she braved half dragging the oversized saddle to the small stable by the cottage. By the time she managed to get it to a good enough spot, Barushka was returning from his walk to the watering hole. Nuzzling her once more, he then set out to lie down in the fresh hay. Wylleam had gotten word about them coming from the looks of everything. He was far better than any priest she had known. At least she had crossed paths with someone caring, besides the shag foal. Sitting on the soft hay, she hugged her knees, leaning against the stall panels. She was far too tired to do much else as she drifted off to sleep.

"WHAT THE HELL DID YOU DO!" Yelling came from within the cottage and shook her from her dreams. "How dare you do this to me!"

"Oh no," Sitting up, she frantically pulled hay from her hair. "This can't be good."

"Calm down, Cedric." Wylleam's look of panic did nothing to ease the anger that steamed from Cedric. "It was either this or the other. I already knew that was out of the question."

"You fed me an elixir full of her blood! Do you know what that does?" He was breathing hard as he paced the floor; no signs were left of his wounds from the venomous bite. "I should leave her here with you for this! I am in enough trouble with the wench, and now you've ruined me! Ruined me!"

"You were barely alive. It was the quickest way to heal you. Moroi do not thirst for human blood but still can take advantage of receiving vampire healing properties from consuming it." Cedric's green eyes held pupils like a cat as he gritted his fanged mouth; common sign of a vampire who recently fed. "My research—"

"I don't care!" Cedric's jaw twitched as the rest of his muscles bulged from his seething temper. "I have a hard enough time with the incubine traits! I do not need you to encourage the other half to savor the flavor of her blood on my tongue!"

"I don't understand." Wylleam sighed and sat down in his chair. "What are you afraid of? It's not like I let you bite into her."

"My senses are running rampant. She becomes more and more distracting. I wouldn't be here if she hadn't attempted to use that bow you've given her!" He jerked up his shirt from the floor, and then, disgusted by its dampness, tossed it across the room, continuing his tantrum. "Her flavor will haunt me, as does her touch and the way she looks at me. I am going mad! I feel like a dog in heat!"

"Did she land the shot?" Watching Cedric pace and kick objects did nothing to discourage his curiosity. "Did she hit her mark?"

"Yes." Stopping a moment, he looked over at Wylleam. "She's a damn good archer for sure. Landed the first shot in the snake's eye, just past my cheek. Amazing for a girl shaking like she was."

"Then why did that distract you? You should have continued to be her shield, not look like a peasant watching a tournament." Cedric's face flashed red, and the red in his hair was waning to its black tips, making it look half-black and half-red. "You know I am right. Why would the archer you are defending be a distraction? You are too well versed in battle tactics to be making a rookie move like that."

"It doesn't matter! You should have just let me heal on my own." Punching into the wood, he disregarded the splinters that bit into his knuckles. "Boto was the one. My incubine blood is far richer than we thought Wylleam. Boto was the one used for my conception. I wasn't a conjured being; I was born into this curse."

"Boto?" Wylleam matched Cedric's sensation of concern. "The king of the incubi demons was the male half. Now I understand why you're not so keen on what I did."

"She's a virgin, Wyll." The red in his hair took its place again as his green eyes met his friend's in pure fear. "I don't know if I can handle this. Not with her taste in my mouth. It's not looking good at all. Boto is ruthless, and I am starting to understand it is instinctual. His want for being over-aggressive, his taste for virgins, and the excitement of her blood on my lips. It's haunting me."

"Morrighan out did herself when she made you. She only uses Boto for her favorite or rarest mixes. It is amazing to think she managed to find a moroi old enough to conceive. Most of them are killed at birth or hunted down at an early age. Perhaps your mother's bloodline can keep Boto's at bay?" Wylleam started pulling books from a nearby stack and flipping through the pages. "Not many of his mixed bloodlines are allowed to live. I wonder how you were able to slip under Boto and Morrighan's aim all this time."

"I couldn't care less. My only concern is getting these wild incubus cravings to sit still. I can hear her heart, her breathing, even smell her from here. No doors, walls, or dung-covered stable can interrupt what I want from her." Cedric sat, holding his head in his hands as he stared at the ground. "It's this overwhelming excitement and want. My skin feels as if it's crawling, and pain is replaced with pleasure. Nemaine's venom was the first real pain I have felt in centuries! It's getting stronger. It was getting like this before I came across Angeline, but now it's building up too fast for me to keep a good hold on it. Shit, she's walking this way."

"Stay there, I will take care of this." Stumbling to his feet, Wylleam grabbed a pack by the door and closed it behind him. "I see you woke up. I packed some fresh clothes and things for you. You should go down to the water hole and wash up while you still can, Angeline."

"Is everything ok?" She took the pack as she stared at the closed door. "He didn't sound too happy when he woke up. Is he that pissed with me?"

"He's not upset with you." One of his ears dropped as he stared at his closed door. "But he's quite angry with me. Perhaps one of these days I can explain it, but for now, it would be best to leave him to ride his temper out."

CHAPTER 11

DESIRE

Wylleam pointed her in the right direction and almost shoved her off. After she vanished around the bend, he opened his door to a grotesque smell. Cedric was squatted in front of the fire, one arm dug deep into the logs gripping the iron below. The look on his face made him look intoxicated. Covering his sensitive dog nose, Wylleam was oblivious about what to do or say. He watched as Cedric's red hair faded to a solid black as he began to pant. His eyes were far off, and the look of pleasure on his face was beyond disturbing. Sweat dripped across his skin and the horns snaked from his head. They were larger than the time he had battled the Coinn Iotair hellhounds. Wylleam stared at him with wide, doggish eyes. He had never seen this version of his friend in person. All he had prior was Cedric's description of the demon form that he fought against every second of his existence.

"Cedric?" The dream catchers and charms rattled in the room, spirits whispered amongst themselves in response to the power being leaked into the room. "Cedric, what do you need me to do?"

"Nothing." His breathing was quick as he glanced up at Wylleam. "She was too close to the door. It was the only thing I could think to do. I—I'm losing control."

"But your arm. You can't possibly hold it there forever?" Curling his lips, he looked more like a dog for a change. "What will you do when you are on the road?"

"I'll need a small knife or two." Closing his eyes, a wicked smirk crossed his face as his shoulders shuddered. "It's like self-inflicted pleasure rather than pain. She's at the spring. I can smell her even from here. Her bare skin is touching the water... I never imagined my senses to become this far advanced."

"How can you smell anything over your own flesh burning?" Scoffing, Wylleam pulled a rope that would open the chimney chute wider, praying to relieve his home of the smell. "I will get you the knives and a new sword. Will you be ok alone in here?"

"Yes." He opened his eyes, still drunk with pleasure. "I am more than good with this."

"Here." Wylleam tossed a dagger at Cedric's feet as he started out the door. "Perhaps you can switch out and free my home of your burned flesh? I will be a few hours as I visit a friend to obtain a sword for you. Are you sure you're ok being alone with her?"

"I think this will work." Pulling his arm free of the fire, he frowned as it quickly healed over. "That's working far faster than before. I'll switch to stabbing my thigh."

"You didn't answer me." His ears dropped flat, and they exchanged glares. "Will you be ok alone with her?"

"I don't know." Cedric's eyes flashed back with the same fear his friend's question held. "I will not let myself take her, if that's the concern."

Wylleam shut the door without another word or glance. His focus was on making this a quick visit. Praying to the spirits, he hoped that Cedric could continue to hold his demons back as he had done before. Barushka neighed at him as he walked past the stall. After a moment of pause, Wylleam sighed and decided perhaps riding a horse would be the best way to limit the risk. Pulling himself onto the horse, he whispered where he wished to go, and Barushka was more than happy to canter that way.

"How is the water?" Cedric's voice frightened Angeline, and she shoved herself chin deep into the spring. "Oh, come now! Stand back up, pet."

"Where are you?" The heat her cheeks produced was frustrating as she looked about for him. "I see you are feeling better!"

"Yes, and no." Her eyes caught his green glare from atop a rock behind her. "I figured I would see what my wife actually looked like without dirt-covered clothes."

"Why is your hair black?" There were no signs of his horns, but his intoxicated manner was still taking place. "Shouldn't you be resting? You're not quite acting right. Anyhow, I would like to finish bathing. Alone."

"What does it matter, pet? You are mine and if I wish to look at you, then you cannot deny me that." Cedric dug the knife deeper into the side of his thigh, just out of her field of vision. "Now continue. Just go on as if I am not here, as you were doing a moment ago. You didn't seem to mind me here until I spoke."

"This is wrong!" Tears were rolling up, and she swallowed the panic in her throat. "I will not do anything for you!"

"Don't worry, dear. I have no plans to mount you here on this rock." His eyes were untamed as his fanged mouth took its cold tone. He was twisting the knife, testing his limits of control. "I only want to see what I have ended up with. If I am to talk about your chest to a fellow soldier, I wish to be accurate to the last detail. If you'd like, I could do you the pleasure of seeing what you'll never get?"

"They're all the same, aren't they? That's what the drunks bark about in the whorehouse!" She turned her back to him, hoping he hadn't seen the tear that was starting to fall. "You have nothing I want."

"Fine." Ripping the knife from his thigh, he had managed to ease his fears. Confident that he would be able to keep himself in check, he was done using her. "I'll be in the cabin. Get some rest. We leave in the morning."

After several minutes, she was confident that he was gone. Her moment of peace was ruined, but at least she had clean clothes. The attire Wylleam had given her fit firmer than the ones she had gotten back in Raven's Den. It was high-quality leather, and the workmanship made her movements flawless. She would not have put it past Wylleam to have had them made for her. After putting on her new boots that laced as high as her knees, she began her walk back.

Something flashed sunlight at her from the top of the rock where Cedric had been sitting. Coming closer, she gasped. A bloodied dagger and a large pool of blood flowed down the back of the rock. There was so much of it that one would have thought someone butchered a cow on top of the boulder. Her hand shook as she picked up the knife and watched a trail of blood leading up the path. As she followed it, it had stopped before the bend in the trail. *What on earth is going on?* Barushka neighed hello as he returned with Wylleam on his back. There was no mistake. The blood she saw came from Cedric.

Weeks had gone by since they left Wylleam's cottage. Cedric had returned to being silent and distant again. Angeline had made it a new habit to keep her bow and quiver within reach at all times. She wanted to be ready for anything. After asking Wylleam about the dagger and blood, they decided it best not to acknowledge she noticed it to Cedric. Wylleam insisted that she keep the dagger for herself, just in case something should happen. It did nothing to ease her concerns about whether the venom had changed something in him. His hair had gone back to being red with black tips, but he had moments where she swore the black was trying to creep back in place.

"Where are we going?" Angeline was tired of not knowing. "How long are we traveling this time?"

"Williamsburg." He shifted in the saddle. "It's not much further. We can reach it in a few hours if we ride hard enough."

"Williamsburg?" She rubbed the scar on her arm. After hesitating, she asked the question that came to mind. "The town that was massacred by demons a long time ago, is that the Williamsburg we are going to?"

"Yes." His tone had a cold bite. "That would be the correct Williamsburg."

"Why?" It was strange to not receive any angry glares this far into her questioning. "That place has been desolate and abandoned for a very long time. What are we going there for? The stories say not even the foulest creatures come near that place. The travelers stay there for a quick rest because it is safe, but they still say they can hear the cries of the people. It may even be another old highwayman's rumor. The villagers were slaughtered, and the village was wiped out. No one knows what happened to the creatures that consumed the people there. It's a great mystery. Why would you want to go to a barren place like that?"

"It's my home." They sat on Barushka in silence as they continued down the path. "I need to do some research and the books I need are in my study."

"Your home?" She did her best to hold her composure, biting her bottom lip.

"Yes." Looking over his shoulder, he shot her a look that made it clear that she was not to ask the question that was rolling across her mind. *Did you wipe out Williamsburg?*

The silence that they held was tenser than what it had started as that morning. They both sat rigidly on Barushka, with the occasional shift in the saddle. Angeline would push herself back away from Cedric as far as the saddle would allow. The more time she spent with him, the more she started to see him as a monster. It was amazing to think that the gossip that was whispered about him was concerning only that he had no wife. Luckily, she was the quick fix for this small rumor. He had everyone fooled about what he truly was. No questions about the fact that he was the only knight capable of the demon jobs he took. Perhaps society had chosen to accept him despite the obvious signs. A groan came from Cedric, and she stopped, staring out into the woods. He was hunched over in the seat, sweating once more.

"What's wrong? Is the venom still..." The heat radiating off his back was alarming. "What's going on?"

"I don't know." He pulled Barushka to a stop, slid off the horse, and fell to his knees on the ground. "It's not the venom."

"What do you need me to do?" She slid off the horse, pausing in her steps when she watched the red in his hair fade to black. "What's happening to you?"

"Stay back! Don't touch me!" He was panting as sweat dripped from his face. "Don't come any closer to me. Not a step closer."

Angeline backed away. If her taking a step closer was the borderline for him, then a few steps back would be safer. Her hand gripped the hilt of the dagger she had been given, stained with Cedric's blood still. Neither she nor the shaman could wash the stains out of it, but it looked as if she may have to use it on Cedric himself. He pulled something from his boot; she stepped back further. With an angry shout, he stabbed a knife into the center of his hand, pinning it to the ground. Jerking from the action, Angeline looked away, grimacing. After a moment, she looked back, but what she saw did not help the knots forming in her stomach.

Cedric squatted there with a vacant stare, sweat and heat pouring from him as he smiled to himself.

It was hard to say how long the two of them stood there, both unmoving. She had a tight grip on the dagger's hilt while he grinned, like an intoxicated fool in a brothel. The huge flapping sound interrupted the awkwardness and called their attention elsewhere. Landing in the path in front of them was a creature like nothing Angeline had ever seen. It stood as tall as Cedric, bat wings spread wide, a tail like that of a snake swished side to side and she was humanistic from the knees up. A set of horns crowned her head, like a ram. One had been broken, and it complimented the massive amount of scars that covered her gray-colored body. Her clawed fingers and gargoyle's feet made her menacing as the dark red lips smiled at them. Closing her massive wings, the single clawed fingers that topped the top joint hooked around her neck like a clasp for a cape.

"Dammit." Cedric cursed as his panting increased and he pulled the knife from his hand. "Who are you?"

"I was going to ask you the same thing. I thought I sensed Boto, but instead, I find something far more desirable." Her grin exposed the double set of fangs that sent chills across Angeline's skin. "You must be one of his mixed offspring. Interesting. So pretty and fresh. I like this option."

"Who are you, and what does it have to do with me?" His green eyes flashed up into the red-colored eyes of the demon. "I am in no mood to play games, demoness."

"So angry and aroused, I see. That incubine blood is a pain, isn't it?" She placed a hand on her hip and looked over at Angeline for a moment before continuing her conversation with a giggle. "And traveling with a virgin must be difficult with your blood boiling like that. Ha! You are an interesting find. Not many halflings would be able to fight off that level of want."

"Who are you?" Clinching his teeth, fangs were seeping out and the excitement he was feeling was gaining leverage over him. "What do you know of incubine blood?".

"I know a lot. Don't you realize what's going on, boy?" Baffled, her smile faded for a moment, but crawled back across her face. "I am the queen succubus, Lillith. I was looking for Boto, and between the heat you're giving off and the smell of your blood, I thought you were him. Amazing that I would mix the two of you up like this!"

"Lillith." Paling, he struggled to keep his fears in check as a wave of arousal came across his skin, one of the many he was feeling coming from where she stood. "What would you want from a mixed-blood like me?"

"I have a problem, you see. It was annoying to think that tomorrow night was my heat's peak, where I am obligated to conceive more incubi and succubi to spread across this world. That buffoon bonded himself to that bitch-of-a-sorceress and there is no pleasure in having a half-dedicated mate for this. I choose the strongest to mate with so that my clutch can benefit the most from our powers, but here you are, Boto's offspring. Unbound and just as strong, and the heat coming from you is turning me on as well." She leaned forward in a provocative manner; she allowed her breast free of her insanely lose chainmail top as she leaned to meet his eye level. "I want you to willingly bind yourself to me, my future mate."

"And if I refuse?" Cedric forced himself to look away, feeling the tug of Lillith's powers encouraging the incubine blood to continue to push forward. "If I choose not to bind or mate with you?"

"Well, it may not be fun for you." Standing up right again, she sighed. "In that case, I will be coming for you tomorrow night. At my peak heat, there is no incubus alive that would be able to refuse to lay with me. You will be more than willing then. Especially for a half-blood. You'll be bonded to me whether you intended to or not."

Flapping her massive wings, she took to the air again. Angeline had fallen to her knees, shocked by the visit and relieved for the fight that hadn't come. Her hands shook as she leaned forward and puked the contents from her stomach. There wasn't a nerve left in her body that hadn't unraveled in the encounter. Cedric was still breathing fast as he continued to remain frozen. Lillith had made it clear that the waves of pleasure and excitement had been her this whole time. The struggle he was having had nothing to do with Angeline these past weeks, but the succubus queen's heat coming near. For a moment, he stared at the blood dried across the dirt under his healed hand. He would have to make a decision, and he had no time to decide.

"Angeline." His voice was soft, and it caught her attention to hear him say her name. "Do you understand what a binding is?"

"Ye-yes." The pounding of her blood hit her ears, and she shivered. "Why do you ask?"

"I will have to lay with you tonight and pray to the gods I know how to bind us." He balled his hand in a fist, grabbing up the bloodstained dirt with it, staring at it with a long mournful look. "But you have to willingly accept me. Can you do that?"

"I-I don't know." Shuddering, tears started to fall down her cheeks. "I don't want to."

"I don't know if I know how to." Standing, he let the dark grains fall at his feet. "But I do know that being Lillith's bonded mate is a fate worse than hell itself. She's tortured all of them. There is a reason Boto never allowed her to bind with him, and that tells me all that I would ever need to know."

"I know." Her voice cracked as she hugged her knees. "I know how."

"What do you mean by, 'I know how?'" Looking back at her, his green eyes against his black hair gave him a frightening appearance. "How to do what?"

"The witch, she told me." Angeline buried her face into her knees as her throat tried to close off her next words. "The witch wanted me to bind myself to you. She said I had to do it. I was to tell you, tell you that you needed to be in the full form. And then ... then you would need to satisfy your moroi bloodline at the moment it starts. You would have to do that in order to complete it."

"That was the purpose, then." He spit and marched over to her, jerking her to her feet and shoving her on Barushka. "You should have told me. Damn you and your stubborn tongue."

The horse neighed in protest of how rough he was being with her. Cedric shot him a boiling stare, and the rebellion ended. He mounted and they took off full speed down the trail. Angeline sounded like a banshee behind him as she wailed and sobbed. He could feel her shaking from how hard she was crying. She would find herself too close and would wiggle away, a desperate plea to stay away from him. The sun was fading fast at their backs as they approached the fork in the road. There sat an old cottage, broken in the dim light as they slowed.

Cedric dismounted Barushka, digging through his pack. Pulling out a key, he unlocked the dusty shelter and went in to inspect it. Angeline was rocking and shuddering as she let her torment come out in shrieks. He pulled her off, carrying her into the musty room, slamming the door with a swift kick. Dropping her on the bed, he worked on getting a fire going. She scrambled to sit up straight and make some distance between them and started hugging her knees once more. Warmth started filling the room as the light of the fire danced shadows across the dusty house. Cedric sat at the edge of the bed, staring off with a glazed look in his eyes. She was being swallowed by fears while Cedric stared out to the unseen as if mourning.

"I need to tell you something." His voice was tender and low, and she took a moment to catch her breath as she stared at his back. "I know this idea is devastating to you, but you need to understand how I feel about this. You need to know why this was never supposed to happen."

"What is it then?" She watched as the muscles in his back tensed and he drew an unsteady breath. Angeline sniffled as she tried to slow her breathing.

CHAPTER 12

HAUNTING DREAMS

"I wasn't raised as a monster or an abomination. The old knight told me he had found me, just a babe crying in the rotting filth that I had been left in. He was on his way home, to Williamsburg, when he crossed that battlefield and discovered a red-haired, green-eyed baby boy. The knight's heart was touched, and had mistaken me as a blessing. Losing a wife and unborn son the year before, he had thrown himself recklessly into one battle after another to drown his sorrows. His pride kept him from giving up life entirely, but it did not stop him from gambling it away in countless wars and insane hunting missions.

"Growing up as a lord's son was an easy life. One free of realizing what I was or who had made me. Lord Cedric de Romulus will be a man I will cherish for the rest of my wretched life. The name which was passed on to me and one that I am trying not to stain. He was the one who taught me the skills to fight. Preaching to me how agile a fighter must be against the darkest creatures this world contains. I was taught in many arts: sword, archery, spear, and more. Spending countless days training, I dedicated myself to mastering riding and war tactics fit for a king. I was just as swift on horseback as I was on my own two feet by the age of twelve. Sparring with the other squires, I rose in the top ranks with alarming speed. I should have known something was wrong. It was far too easy to outdo the rest of the men in any challenge.

"My skills brought the old man joy, and he then turned my focus to educating me in reading and writing. He wanted his son to have the best books and teachers. My thirst for knowledge was enormous, as I would not sleep until I had finished the tome I was introduced to. The teachers he brought from all ends of the land marveled at the speed I learned. Once more, it brought great pride and joy to Lord Cedric to see his adoptive son do the house good. The Romulus House would survive through me, in essence. That's the least I could have done for such a great man. A man that not only gave the world hope, but even made a monster like me love him.

"Then there was her. Her skin was soft like the petal of a rose, with eyes the color of the sky. Her name was Yvette, a nobleman's daughter and a family friend at best. We had grown up together and as I became of age, my heart and desire were to be with her. I could tell that she was feeling the same. We were no longer the children that chased one another down the hallways, but two fools in love. Looks and comments exchanged were undoubtedly flirting and lust growing. It all seemed good-hearted and nothing in the world could break us apart.

"What I didn't know was the cost. My foolish, selfish wants would take everything from me. I would soon reveal how much of a monster I could be. The lord and I had returned from the nearby castle. You wouldn't recognize its name. It was dying out in that time, but that is where I found it. A ring with a bluestone that matched her eyes and just the right size to place on her finger is what I came back to Williamsburg with. That would be the last time anyone came back home. It was the last day the village would exist after what would happen that night.

"We had snuck off to the stables, and we were all over one another. The excitement was intoxicating, and if I had recognized the sensation for what it truly was, maybe... I had slid the ring on her finger, proposed to her to be my lady. The kiss she gave me was far better than the words anyone could have used. Hiking her skirts up, we gave way to our desires. That excitement took hold, and her moaning let me know she could feel it, too. As she gave herself to me, I felt hungry for more. There was no mistake that the more she enjoyed it, the more powerful I was feeling. I started to be more aggressive, making her scream in pleasure and pain. Startled, she tried to pull away, but I had lost myself to the craving that had taken over.

"I was met with the spray of her blood across my face. At some point, I had become animalistic, and with a monstrous motion, I had bitten her neck and shoulder with an ungodly thirst. I realized at that moment what she was afraid of. The man she knew was no longer to be seen, but the horned figure of an incubus lay on top of her. In my panic, I pulled away from her to watch the blue in her eyes fade into death. They reflected her killer, and all I saw was myself. I ran as far and as fast as I could. That was the other mistake. I should have stayed, and more importantly, given my father the chance to slay the monster I had become.

"The sun came up in a red color that morning, and something in my gut told me I needed to go back. The closer I came, the richer the smell of blood was in the air. Screaming soon came to my ears, and I started running. What I found was harrowing. My love, Yvette, had become something dead and hungry. Everyone she had attacked turned, and there in the center of town was Lord Cedric, the last standing man. He was far too old to be fighting such monsters, and it was clear to me as I approached that he did not know I was to blame. A mob of mauled undead were swamping him. In that moment of distraction, the old man saw me, rejoiced that I was okay, and I watched as Yvette crawled unnaturally across the earth, across the other monsters, and latched on to the front of his face. I will never forget the crunching sound, his scream of pain and sheer horror. I stood there frozen and watched as my desire, my true love, devoured and turned the man who gave me everything.

"What made it worse was they were loyal to me. After destroying the man who I held as my own father, they came crawling to me, groveling at my feet in their bloodied and broken forms. They were like the imps you would expect to see crawling about in hell. I kicked one in anger, and it whimpered and asked for more. The begging and pleading for what they could do to please me was disgusting. Some fought amongst each other at times to be the first to hear my commands, while others were still seeking out any remaining villagers who may have lived through the first wave.

"I don't remember how many days it took. With the old man's sword, I had slain them all, every last villager, friend, family. I killed them all. The only command I gave them was for them to line up, kneeling before their grave as I took their heads and buried the rest. The infectious bite that I had left Yvette with had spread its filth in one night. Every child had been struck, and it took even longer to find all of the little ones. There was a baby. Ginger's third child was ravaged across its stomach and turned into one of these things. This was when I knew that I was an abomination from the depths of hell.

"I buried him last. My adoptive father; the man had given me the world and I had sent him to his death. Leaning over his grave, I took my own life over and over again. The pain that I felt every time I woke up alive and had to try yet again was cruel. I was even confident I had managed to decapitate myself, but the screaming always brought me back. It was as if Williamsburg would not let me die. Death was a privilege and I would never have it. This was my prison, and I would not let myself leave it.

"The ground there had been stained black from all the blood spilled. It was foul, and no scavenger would come close. Those who dared to attempt to dig up what I had buried were slaughtered, and those who did come across the defiled village in the beginning were not human. It was a long while before the fears in men's hearts and memories faded enough to step foot near there. Before that, I had my share of battles against demonic scavengers that even I had never heard of in my studies. A shaman was hired by a neighboring village to come and calm the spirits of the people who died in Williamsburg. It was a mystery to them what had happened here, and no priest would come to do such a daunting task. The people would seek out a safer alternative and a Cynocephali was more than welcomed to risk it. That's when I met Wylleam. I had managed for the last 20 years to be unseen by those who traveled through there, but for some reason the spirits let him know. He still will not tell me what the ghosts and souls of the town have told him about me. The old dog just tells me I already know the story. Neither of us knew what I was or what to do with me at that point.

"The fight we had over me leaving here was ugly. I had no desire to leave this place. It was my ball and chain, and a reminder of what I did wrong. All I know, is he said something just right. It was a phrase that my father had used, and I knew that he had forgiven me. With that, Wylleam was able to make it clear that they all knew, but wanted something more for me. Over the last one hundred years, I have aged very little. I have made several mistakes, but never allowed that excitement have what it wanted. Every night I repeat every gruesome detail of Williamsburg, from Yvette to my torment of wanting death. Not one night has been free of these images, this pain.

"And that now leads me to what I am forced to do tonight. I will have to face a side of me I have spent every day hiding and fighting against. This will require me to give in to what destroyed the life I could have had."

Cedric's eyes were still looking into the past as the muscles in his jaws twitched. "Angeline, I can't promise you anything."

She sat there staring at him. He had told her his deepest secret without a second thought. This monster had experienced the worst kind of pain. Her heart sank as she remembered her words to him. *If I knew how to curse someone, I hope that you experience the worst heartbreak ever.* There was no way for her to know, to understand that he had suffered through that already. Her heart skipped a beat when his green eyes looked at her, meeting her own. No words came to her as she looked at him for the first time as a broken man. He had wanted her from the beginning, but had been too afraid of what may happen to her in allowing that feeling to be set free. This was the type of sincere love that most spent a lifetime never finding, but was this the person she really wanted it from?

"Do you understand what I am telling you?" Her brown eyes couldn't break away from the sharpness of his stare. "I have attempted this process once before. It destroyed me. I have been struggling to deny myself the pleasure of being with you because I can feel that same excitement that took me to hell and beyond. This isn't the type of pleasure I indulge in at the brothels, but something deeper. Do you understand I may kill you tonight?"

"I—I understand." Her voice was low and barely audible as she took in the pain that he wore on his face as a tear ran down her cheek. "But I don't know what I am doing. I don't want it to be like this. I've never done this. Do you even love me? How can anyone want to do this without love? I don't think I can..."

Frustrated, he stood up. Jerking his shirt and boots off, huffing. "You're too young; you don't get it at all."

"I'm sorry." Hugging her knees tighter, she watched nervously as he started to unbuckle his belt. "I didn't mean what I said that night. If I knew, I would have never said it."

"What night?" He paused, looking back at her, baffled. "What on earth are you talking about?"

"When I said, *I hope that you experience the worst heartbreak ever. I had no idea.* If I knew that..." Burying her face into her knees, she began to sob. "What happened to you is horrible. I am so sorry, but I can't help but feel scared! Worse of all, I can't stop this sensation of being alone and abandoned. I am nothing and I have nothing. If this kills me, at least I could stop feeling, but I'll never know what love will ever be like."

"Heh." His lips brushed up against her ear. His breath tingled across her neck as he spoke. "No matter what happens, just keep your eyes closed. No matter what you feel, I promise that you'll at least be in a state of bliss when you die. Perhaps you'll even know what love is when I am finished with you, pet."

Gasping for air, she sat up in the bed. Sweat poured over her body, and she felt as if she had been holding her breath far too long underwater. Grabbing her head, images and waves of pleasure recapped what she had experienced the night before. Moments of blindly reaching down, the gripping of the horns that he had on his head had increased her excitement. Every touch had sent her senses reeling. Her skin crawled with excitement as she tried to hold on to the sensations that poured from her memory. Her last thoughts were those hungry for more of the pleasure he was bestowing. It was clear that there had been four hands, all working her over one-way or another. Two had been those on his wings. She had failed to keep her eyes shut!

Then the flash of the moment in which she felt their souls pull away from one another and when they returned, they were complete for the first time in their lives. His wings had been large, and his eyes flashed when he caught sight of hers staring up at his demonic form. She should have been frightened, but she just wanted him to have her. Her heart was racing as she recalled the rhythm of his motions and the overwhelming thrill of his lips and tongue that he ran across her body from her breast to—

She gripped her neck but found no bandage. A lasting image of his fangs came to her mind, but her injured arm sent her a sharp ache. It was bandaged and the smell of ointment was overwhelming. Blood splotched it heavily and her stomach turned. It was scarred before, but there was no telling how bad the new wounds would look when she healed. Shivers crawled across her skin and she pulled the covers over her, still naked under them. He had chosen her arm over repeating the bite on the neck with his past lover, Yvette. Despite this, she couldn't shake the sensation of how much she wanted him to have her. She wanted to be his, and when he first took her, it was the most amazing feeling she had ever felt. She was his lady and wife, he her lord and husband, and what happened last night was something they could have every night for the rest of, at least, her life.

"Don't worry. I dressed the wound as soon as we were done." Cedric's voice caused her to jerk and waves of bliss washed over her, begging she remember more. "There is no doubt we are bonded to one another. Your body has been trying to beg me to it all morning with waves of pleasure."

"I, I am having a hard time remembering it all." He was sitting on the edge of the bed, both hands and chin leaning on the hilt of his unsheathed sword. "Have you been there all night?"

"Yes." Sighing, he sat up straight and looked back at her. "I didn't want to take any chances. If you turned, I was going to make sure that you did not make it out of here alive."

The thumping of her heart and the rush of her blood all were new sensations as they exchanged glares. There was this sense of connection, a thrilling fulfillment of power even. She was feeling a wide variety of things that were never there before and there was no denying these were the things given to her from the binding. Despite these new experiences, she was still wary of Cedric. He had sat at the edge of the bed, expecting to kill her at any moment. "I'm okay, right?"

"Yes." Sheathing his sword, he threw her clothes at her. "Hurry up and get dressed. I want to get to Williamsburg before Lillith finds us."

"Do you think she'll come for you still?" Hugging the blanket to her chest, she pulled the clothes to her, still lost in his green eyes. "Even after you bonded yourself to me?"

"Lillith will want to kill me and you over this. I need to get to the manor before she arrives tonight." Her face was turning red as he glared at her, waiting. "What's the matter now?"

"Can you at least turn around?" Biting her lip, she looked down at her fidgeting fingers. "Or go outside?"

"Why?" Now his temper held something new. She could literally feel her own blood boil with his and it resulted in feeling aroused. "Are we really going to keep doing this even after last night?"

"Sorry." The door slammed and her heart jolted as she mumbled to herself. "It's too much all at once for me."

CHAPTER 13

LILLITH'S RAGE

The closer they rode to Williamsburg, the thicker the air was with the smell of death. The plants were getting more aggressive in growth and looks. She watched as the green faded into the black bark, the ground burdened with vines and limbs. Barushka snorted and Cedric fought him, urging him down the path. There were no distinguishable remnants left in what used to be the center of town besides the thorn-covered well. On occasion, Angeline could make out a random rafter stretching out from the undergrowth. The dirt was a rust color with blotches of black and shivers ran across Angeline's back as she recalled Cedric letting the blood-stained dirt drop to the ground. She realized he was remembering the way he had left the sand in Williamsburg. Blood had spilled in unspeakable amounts over a hundred years ago, and she was leaning on the back of the beast to blame for it.

Cedric was growing tenser by the moment. With their new connection, she was having an easier time seeing his reactions for what they truly stood for. He was recollecting every detail that had happened as they slowly made their way down the road. Luckily, she could not see the images that flew through his mind. That was something she could live without ever seeing. Barushka made his way to the large manor that sat at the far end of the ruins of the old town square. It was just as large as King Frederick's castle. It could have been mistaken for a pile of black wooded trees with the way the vines covered it.

Heat was starting to pour from Cedric and sweat ran down his back. He was feeling aroused, and it wasn't from her. Lillith was close, still having her fun, calling to his incubine blood as she took her time waiting for the sun to set. For the first time, she wrapped her hands around his waist, her hands sliding across his abs. He grabbed her and shoved her arms back behind him, making it clear that this was not the time for that. Cheeks red, she still felt feverish from last night and didn't know if she should act on the sensations that filled her from top to bottom. It was frustrating for Cedric as they stopped in front of the manor. *The more aroused Lillith tries to make me, the more aroused I am making Angeline. I don't think the girl realizes she's taking half of the load of Lillith's power off me. This is going to get very difficult the closer Lillith gets.*

"Well, are you going to come with me?" His tone was starting to sound softer, but Angeline was unsure if she was fooling herself. "You might find something you like in there, and the beds are far better than the ones you slept on as a lady of the court. The House of Romulus only had the very best of everything."

"If Lillith is coming, I suppose I should see if there is anything else I can do to defend myself." She waited for him to finish digging through the pack and followed obediently behind him. "How does one defeat a succubus?"

"That's why we are here." The door creaked open and revealed nothing but darkness. "I was coming to read more about Boto, the Incubus King, but now I am going to have to research his other half's lore."

"It's so dark." Cedric disappeared into the pool of blackness, but her eyes met with a torch as its flame grew larger. "Is it always this dark?"

"Yes, ever since." A wave of sorrow astounded her and she gasped, letting him know she felt it. "Stay close. I'll light more as we walk to the library."

As one torch after another danced into life, the massive great hall came to its own again. The large tapestries of epic battles against men and demons hung down behind the head of the table. Huge and stunning, Angeline's assumptions on how noble life should be were smashed. King Frederick's court was nothing but a sheepherder's dinner table by comparison. This is what it meant to be the best house in the land. No king of today that she knew of could come close to the extravagant appeal that Cedric's manor held. This is what a castle should be like. The hallway was tall and massive with so many doors it made her head spin. Armor, tables, and more tapestries decorated the hallways. She kept pace with Cedric, struggling to take it all in.

The hallway dead-ended into two massive doors. The carvings across their wood were amazing. Woodland creatures ran rampant with embellishments of gold, silver, and the occasional glint of a precious gem for their eyes. Unlocking the doors, Cedric pushed them open and the air greeted them with a musty, stale scent. He tossed the torch into a brazier that was the central focus of the room, and its light revealed walls and shelves that held more books than she had seen in her entire lifetime. One shelf in Cedric's library held more books than the alchemist studies back at the castle. If she had been like the other ladies, she would feel like she had scored high in advancing in the noble caste, but this added to her unease, not realizing who Cedric was. With no new information on the House of Romulus, no one knew if the family had money, since the last heir was throwing his life to the werewolves at every turn.

"Here we go." She watched as he shoved a ladder across the room and climbed it. "Come grab these and set them on the table there."

"Ok." Much to her surprise, the room was not covered in thick dust and cobwebs like the hall had been. "Do you come back here often?"

"When I find a reason to." The tomes he handed her were heavy, and she was making several trips back and forth. "I can't remember everything I've read."

"You've read all of these?" Finishing, he climbed off the ladder and sat at the table, flipping through the scriptures. "There are so many books here."

"Remember, I am well over a hundred years old. I have had more than enough time to find, read, and collect resources." It was hard to say how much time had passed as she watched the apprehensive look on his face as he dug through the books. "Dammit, there's nothing here saying anything about how to kill an incubus. The only weaknesses listed for both are their insatiable thirst for the arts of the flesh. Mixed offspring can be killed in several ways and are smaller in size, but nothing about full bloods."

"No stories on ever defeating one?" Her skin felt like it was crawling for a moment and she shook the sensation off. "Are you sure?"

"There are no records of ever defeating one. There are a few lores on how Lillith and Boto fought their own kind to earn their seats of power, but that means only another succubus or incubus of full blood could kill her. And even then, it doesn't clarify how they go about that task." His eyes had their catlike pupils as they stood there in the poorly lit library. She could clearly see he was at a loss for what they would need to do. "Let's hope she gets bored with me and leaves."

He motioned for her to follow him and they walked from one end of the manor to the opposite side. The manor was as if it lay frozen in time as they reached another set of carved doors depicting battles. Inside this great room were enough weapons for three of King Frederick's army. The brazier here was much larger, and in one corner, there was a blacksmith's forge, which sat cold. This was the place where weapons were made to fit any man. Javelins and spears of several types lined a section of the wall, all made at various lengths to best match the height of any warrior. Cedric whistled, spooking her from her admiration of the handiwork before her. Coming closer to where he stood, she saw that he was going to show her what he had found. There were bows of several types and arrows made in ways she had never seen before.

"Do you know much about arrowheads and what each is designed for?" She looked lost as her eyes jumped from one stack to the other. "I suspect that no one would have bothered to teach you that. For now, I will cover some of the ones that will matter the most when Lillith comes."

"I have never seen arrows like these." She picked up one that had a star-shaped jagged point to it and the head of it seemed loose. "What is this designed to do? It feels as if the head will fall off at any moment."

"That's exactly it. It's designed to make a nasty hole in the beast's flesh." He pulled the head of the arrow off so she could roll it in her hand and get a better visual. "When they attempt to pull the arrow out, they only pull the shaft out. This sits in place, encouraging the wound to bleed out and the more they move, the more the ridges dig into the flesh. Very handy to use on vampires and other blood-sucking creatures, too, since losing blood slows their powers down drastically."

"Ok, good to know." He handed her a quiver full of these and a few more quivers of other kinds, explaining the purpose of each to her. "Wow, I don't think any of the rangers I have met ever carried more than one kind of arrow."

"For some reason, this has become a lost art. I believe Williamsburg was the training hub for demon-hunting rangers." Again, a wave rattled her nerves, and sorrow mixed with excitement sent her blood rushing. "But since you are skilled enough, I should take advantage of you. I didn't expect you to be confident enough to shoot across my shoulder and hit your target when we faced Nemaine's cobras. I suppose the old dog got his whispers in the ear and that's why he gave you the Black Forest's enchanted bow."

"Enchanted bow?" She pulled the bow off, looking over its gnarled wood in curiosity. "The Black Forest where we took you to the tree spirit?"

"Yes. She gave that to Wylleam as payment for sending me to help them." Cedric was digging through armor, putting on some greaves and arm guards. "And then made it clear to me she would return a favor when I saw fit. She kept her word. But now I can't take my shortcut through there to travel anymore. The other tree spirits will not hesitate to kill me, despite the fact I saved them from being torn apart by one of Romasanta's wild packs."

"Romasanta?" She was trying to decide which arrows she wanted to use, or whether to mix a lot of them into one quiver. "That name sounds familiar."

"He's the father of werewolves, and he attempted to defile this place at one point." He spat at the ground. Her blood boiled in unison with his. "But he can wait. Lillith is getting very close now. The sun has finally set."

"How can you tell?" It was baffling that anyone could tell where the sun was in a place so closed off to the outside world. "How can you—"

Pausing in her words, they both watched as the other broke out in a sweat. The potent wave of arousal hit them both, and their glares told each other they were glad they weren't any closer to one another. Grabbing a sword as he walked out, she followed with two of the heavy quivers. He shoved the front doors open, walking ever faster toward the town's center. She couldn't keep pace with him, and her boiling blood only added to her nervousness. There was an ever-growing concern building in her stomach for what other sensations they may share. She would know as soon as this battle got underway. There, standing by the well, was Lillith. Her eyes glowed red and with her wings spread wide, making her menacing in nature and frightening to behold.

"What is this I sense?" Her tone was not as cool leveled as it had been the day before as her tail swatted back and forth like an angry stable cat. "Who on earth did you find to bind yourself at such short notice?"

"You should have known I wasn't going to let you do that to me, Lillith. If Boto refused you, then I surely wouldn't settle for it." Rage seeped out of her, and as waves of it hit him, his excitement was growing. "But I will not lay with you to create any offspring. Go back to Boto."

"I will have to, but not until I kill you first." With a quick flap of her wings, she came at Cedric. Her claws were met with his sword, and with a fanged grin she hissed her next words. "Then I will send your pet to Boto and let him have his way with her."

An arrow hit Lillith in the shoulder. She grinned wider as she leaped back from Cedric and shot a glance at Angeline. Angeline had kept as much distance as she could from the battle. Sitting on top of Barushka, her hope was she could ride away if things got too dangerous. Lillith twisted the shaft, pulling it from her arm. With an annoyed sigh, she saw the head of the arrow had stayed behind, leaving a gaping wound that was continuing to bleed. Cedric took advantage of her distraction and caught her off guard, landing a slash across her abdomen. She had moved enough that it produced nothing but a scratch.

Rubbing her hand across her belly, Lillith licked her own blood off her palm as her eyes became wilder. They came at each other, her claws meeting his sword's strength without fault. Sweat poured from Cedric as he fought the waves of thrill flying out from her every time they came close. Lillith was pulling his incubine blood into a state of excitement. His hair was turning blacker with every strike they exchanged, and Angeline managed to land another arrow in Lillith's back. This time the succubus laughed as she pulled another arrow shaft from her, lacking its arrowhead. Cedric came in for another chance to strike, but he missed and she landed a strike across his cheek. The overwhelming sensation of arousal took him off-guard and he lost his balance, crashing to the ground from his momentum.

Trying to regain his focus, he barely made it back on his feet when Lillith struck. Her claws gripped deep into the flesh of his arm and her smile became wider. The wave of pleasure had him panting and his heartbeat throbbed in his ears. Hissing at him, she bit into his shoulder, putting her weight on top of him. He fell to his knees, losing some of his hold on himself as his horns pulled forth. In desperation, he managed to tighten his grip on the hilt of his sword and rammed the blade through her stomach with enough force to knock her off him. Her bite released, and she moaned, grabbing his wrist, pushing him and the blade further into her.

"Oh! More!" As she began panting, Cedric realized his mistake and withdrew away from her, leaving his weapon behind. "It's been a while since I've felt this aroused in battle! Give me more!"

The back of his neck tingled and instead of throbbing pain from his arm, he was receiving waves of pleasure. With a reluctant sigh, he allowed himself the use of his own claws, and they came at each other. Lillith managed to land a scratch across his shoulder and he failed to hit his mark. Before he could back away, she managed to grab him by the throat and his feet searched for the ground below. Desperate, he kicked the hilt of his sword into her stomach. A sickening gush came from the motion, but all that escaped Lillith was another moan of pleasure. It was enough of a sensation for her to lose her grip on his neck and he gained some distance to try again. Another charge at her managed to strike the side of her neck.

A thud landed on his head as they locked horns, and the red glow of her eyes met his furious green ones. Before he could pull back, Lillith's hand dove deep into his stomach. This time, he moaned from the motion and his body begged for more. She gripped the flesh within him and twisted, sending another wave of arousal. Part of him wanted more, but he was losing himself far too fast in this fight. Her lips brushed against his lips as he struggled to keep his eyes from rolling back. The glance of flesh was electrical in sensation and it was overwhelming all his other senses.

"Does this not bring you great pleasure? You know what makes it more exciting for me, don't you love?" The lick that crawled across his neck and ear sent shivers of desire and waves of unimaginable wants through his mind. "Watching your bound pet fall off that horse when I rammed my hand into your gut. Oh, and the way you indulge in this pain as she screams from every twist."

Pulling his intestines, Lillith's laugh did nothing to overturn the sound of Angeline's shrieking. Coughing blood, his pleasure from the crude gutting wavered and there was a pull at his soul. Instinctually, he brought the pain to himself, wanting nothing more than to feel pain instead of pleasure. Holding his guts into himself, the pain poured forth; it brought his incubine blood to his control. All pleasure dissipated and the unspeakable weight of crude agony took its rightful place. Angeline's screaming had ceased, and she was on the ground, not moving as Barushka nudged her. Anger fueled him as he struggled to stand and face Lillith.

The red in his hair was returning, but the horns on his head curled tighter as he seemed to increase in size overall. Sweat poured across his paling flesh ,and he now panted from the ache in his stomach as the sound of his own blood spilling on the ground made its way to his ears.

"I see you didn't know about that small disadvantage." Lillith was rubbing her breast and thighs as her excitement grew. "Didn't you know that's why I bonded myself several times? I have tortured and killed many of my mates for the sole purpose of pleasuring myself. It's a very rare form of arousal for even a succubus as high as me in ranks."

"You whore." It was unclear where he was pulling power to heal himself from, but he had managed to heal enough to keep his guts inside once more. "You'll be screaming from pain when I finish with you."

"Oh, really?" Her laugh was taunting as she stretched her wings for a moment. "That's what Boto promises every time. Amazing how much alike you are to him."

Cedric's speed caught her off guard as his hand buried itself into her open abdomen, gripping the hilt of his sword that still lay within it. Ignoring all the pain that haunted his body, he pulled it out the way it had come in. Blood spilled in ridiculous amounts, and Lillith was feeling the effects. Her strength was starting to waiver, despite her continued arousal from the violent move. Backing away, she started panting and sweat crawled across her gray body. Cedric stood before her, her blood dripping from his hand and sword as he watched her stumble away. She spread her wings wide as she moaned, shrouded by the pleasure. He came running forward again, intending to take a limb if possible, but sliced through air. Blood rained down on top of him as he looked up, Lillith humming in the excitement as she floated there.

"I would continue, but if I play any longer, I am afraid I would not live through Boto's mounting." The pleasure was too much for her, and it was clear the fight had ended. "We'll play another time, boy. It was most delicious."

It was hard to breathe with all the pain that enveloped him, but watching Lillith fly away was a godsend. He turned his focus to Barushka and was relieved to see Angeline was at least sitting up. By the time he made it to her, he could see that she was sweating perversely, panting there on the ground. Bewildered, he touched her and the wave of arousal took its hold on him again. It was like breaking the tension on a lake flat as glass. Overwhelmed, he leaned forward, kissing her as he put his weight on top of her. She moaned, grasping onto him, both feeling desperate to be close again, both eager to feel alive. Pulling away, he made distance between the two of them, and tears fell from her cheeks. Neither of them could decide if the yearnings they felt were of their own anymore. Baffled as they stared into each other's eyes, the same thought came to them, *Why does this feel so natural? Do I really love...*

Shivers ran across Angeline, and he shook off his own wave. The pain she felt of her own guts mangled was still gnawing at her stomach. The moment it switched into pleasure, it had taken her breath away, and the throbbing excitement had astounded her. It was clear to her why he was able to fight in such a reckless manner. Every scratch, hit, and wound was like making love. Closing her eyes, she could see the shadow of Cedric from the night before, his wings spread wider than that of Lillith's.

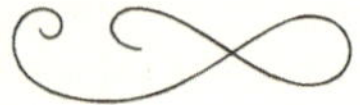

Cedric's wounds had healed quickly, but the unnerving of the encounter with Lillith had taken away his want to continue his journey right away. His revenge against Morrighan would have to wait until he understood what was going on with himself. They spent months at the manor in Williamsburg, researching and, more importantly, training. Angeline's archery had found room to improve with access to different types of bows and arrows as well as one of the most amazing training setups she had ever witnessed. She no longer waited for Cedric to hunt for her food. Her focus was to practice the techniques in a tome he had given her about hunting, stealth, and archery. The ancient arts of the rangers had been recorded in great detail, including images. Her muscles were growing ever taut, and she was picking up speed when running or climbing the trees for better shooting range.

It had been awkward at the beginning when she had revealed to him she could not read. He had failed to consider that even after becoming a lady of the court that no one wasted any efforts to educate the girl from the farms. The days in the study learning to read, sitting so close to him, had fueled moments of excitement. There were countless flashes where lust took hold, but one of them would manage to break away before going any further than the wild groping and kissing that would spill forth. It was hard to say who had the best heartbroken expression when the other pulled away, but neither of them felt they could trust their own feelings. It was an animalistic sensation, but with each instance, the both of them became fonder of the other's company.

Despite the harrowing outlooks, the manor was cozy and very accommodating to them as they rode out the peak of winter. They slept on opposite ends of the house, and met in the study or in training sessions. It was strange shooting arrows at Cedric, but he had toned his focus, reflexes, and speed thanks to the idea as well as increased her ability to follow a moving target. After a while, this became redundant, and he moved on to training her with the dagger, the rangers' secondary weapon. Thanks to her ability to feel what he felt, they kept themselves from constantly fighting. Then again, she felt the most aroused by him when he was angry, which led to the overwhelming confusion they had about one another. There were times when he had similar reactions to her feelings. Moments of extreme frustration on her part led to him being angry suddenly, and in turn, they both broke away as the sense of lust started creeping in. It was exhausting, feeling what the other felt, and the waves of excitement that followed those torrents of passion made the ordeal more daunting.

"I need to find Badbh." Cedric's voice was soft and low as he straightened her arm, showing her the correct motion of the swing for the dagger. "I can't find anything and if anyone would know, it would be the Battle Goddess herself."

"Badbh? Nemaine's sister?" She practiced the corrected swing a few rounds. "How are we going to find her, and how is this going to go? I hear she loves to battle and appears as a raven on a battlefield before picking a side to fight against. One can only pray she sides with you, or death is assured."

"We'll have to travel around in the more populated areas. There are more wars going on and she is bound to be at one of them. Luckily, she's nothing like her sisters. I have come across her before with no issues. I have even spotted her in a few taverns and brothels that I frequent." He leaned over her from behind and moved her arms in a different angle, showing her how to lead into a second move after the initial swing. "We'll be headed back past King Frederick's court. Did you want to drop by Raven's Den?"

"No." A heavy sensation hit his chest, and he paused as her tone of voice became sharp. "I don't ever want to go back there again."

"If that's what you want, I won't mention it again." He cupped her within his body as he used her arms like a puppet with the swings of the dagger. "Here, let me show you some more ways to keep a line of strikes going without stopping. You never want to pause in a fight unless you have made enough distance between you and your enemy."

Feeling the warmth of his chest against her back, she bit her lip as his hand gripped on top of hers on the dagger. They made a wide swing which led into a quick jab, then his knee pushed into hers, causing them both to kneel on it, low to the ground. The hair on the nape of her neck stood on end as his weight made her lean forward, leading her into two more strikes. His breath against her ear and neck made her skin crawl with excitement. Tightening in her chest let her know he was feeling the lust as well, and he released her hand, but stayed in that overpowering position. His lips gently kissed her neck and shoulder as his hand slid around her abdomen, keeping her from breaking away.

Dropping the dagger to the ground, she leaned back into him, and they both gave way to the passion. Both had exhausted themselves in fighting the inevitable, there was no denying it. Their feelings hungered for this chance to be with one another again. They both wanted to have something more compassionate, a better memory to replace the dread that had painted over the one desperate night of fears when they had first lain with each other. No demon came forth, but that overwhelming want and need to be complete, to be with one another, for time to stop and sigh. Pure bliss with each touch encouraged them to give way to their desires, their bonding tying their moments of climax so one another could share it was nothing like either of them had felt before.

Breathless, he held her tight as they lay on the floor, drunk in the moment of lust. Both feeling a great burden lifted from them. Skin to skin, it was easier to feel one another's emotions, and it was simply relief that they felt between them. Angeline shivered as the cold air caressed her exposed skin, and he pulled her tighter to him, giving her more warmth. For the first time, she could say that her feeling of loneliness had finally broken away from her. She was his lady, and he her lord, and together they were bonded to one another's souls. This was beyond what it meant to be married to one another. They had truly touched one another on a more spiritual plain, and it had lasting effects. He nuzzled her neck and kissed her once more.

"I'm glad we got that distraction out before we left." He could feel a tension of hurt coming from her. "Stop getting upset. You felt how I was feeling. I wanted it and passionately gave it to you. It was not for my advantage, completely."

Distraction, the word echoed in her mind, leaving the moment shattered. Breaking away, she quickly dressed again, avoiding looking his way in fear that the anger she felt coming for him might encourage another moment between them. A tear managed to work its way across her cheek, and in panic, she turned away, hoping he had not seen it. She was now struggling to get her boots on as she failed to see past the tears that blurred her vision. Her chest ached more now, as anxiety was building, but broke into a startle when a firm grip grabbed her jaw. Forced to look up, her lips crushed against his, and she let the tears fall. After a moment, he pulled away, taking her breath with the glow of his green eyes. "I think I do love you after all."

CHAPTER 14

MORRIGHAN'S CHIMERAS

The steam puffs from the rabbit's nose were soft, and nearly invisible to see so close to the snow-covered ground. Angeline did her best not to snuffle her nose and slowed her breath. She crouched low to the icy ground from her hideout in the far-off shrub. Her fingers were numb and ached, as she had held herself in her ready stance for several minutes. She refused to let the arrow fly until she was sure which lump of white she was staring at was the rabbit and which was a snow-covered rock. The rabbit perked his ears up, the steam shifting and revealing a better definition of where his head was. The arrow flew with a keen sound, cutting the air as it hit its mark with a thud. Waiting a moment before moving, she made sure there was nothing else interested in her prey. Cedric had made it very clear that in the wintertime, you are most likely hunting the same prey as a local beast or demon.

The snow crunched and popped beneath her steps as she came up on the carcass. He was rather plump for this far into the winter, but that made her meal heartier. She went about her normal routine, skinning, gutting, and prepping the rabbit. Very little went to waste, and she had found it quite satisfying to be self-sufficient. The thrill of hunting and practicing her new skills gave her an improved sense of purpose. There was much she still did not know about this world of Cedric's, where every shadow held a new nightmare or truth. Returning to camp, she propped the meat over the fire and started working the skin over more. Cedric and Barushka watched her with curiosity. Angeline was unsure if Cedric had changed his thoughts about camping with her since their last travels, or if it was just that cold.

"What are you planning to make with that skin?" Cedric had paused from his sword sharpening as he continued observing her task. "There's not much there. It's a small skin, barely enough cloth to patch the crotch of my pants."

"I will make gloves or something for my fingers to keep them from going numb when aiming in cold weather." Ignoring him, she continued focusing on her work. "So what has been keeping you in camp so much?"

"In camp?" A smirk crawled across his face, and her cheeks flushed at the sight of it. "Do you really want me to answer that?"

"No." She rubbed snow in her hands to wash off the blood that clung to them, and then took a cloth to wipe the last of it. "I can only imagine what you want."

"It's not like that." Grunting, he sheathed his sword and stretched. "No signs of anything big still?"

"None that I saw. The rabbit was rather plump." She rotated the meat over the fire. "Considering we are on the back side of winter, it seems there is a lack of predators in this area."

"No, that just means there's something big enough to be eating the rabbit's predators." He gave her a stern glare before watching the last of the light fade away to its wintry purple. "Just be on alert at all times. I haven't seen any evidence of deer since we started into this area a few days ago. No signs of any large animals."

"Understood." She huddled closer to the fire's warmth, throwing her hood over her head so she did not have to risk meeting his eyes. "I'll keep an eye out."

"How long are you going to stay this bitter?" His voice cut her thoughts, and all she could manage was to bite her cheeks. "You're as stubborn as they come."

His footsteps were heavy as they crunched away into the frozen darkness of the woods. They were both still struggling with their emotions. It seemed when one would submit to the idea of love, the other would become abrasive, and it was a volatile reaction. She was still hurt from the night prior to them leaving a month ago. It was impossible to shake the word distraction from her mind and the disconnected sensation it brought. They had managed to get better at keeping one another from feeling the other's emotional peaks, but this led to the fighting again. Both could not help but ask themselves whether it was best to give way to the instincts or keep a distance.

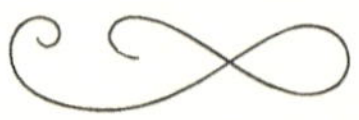

They were a day shy of clearing the dense patch of forest. Camping out in the thick brush, Angeline had come across a large buck. A 10-12 pointer with shoulders as wide as a large stallion scrapped its antlers against the tree in the distance. Her heart thudded in her ears; this was going to be the largest kill she had ever taken down. Thinking over her studies, she took her time, identifying the different kill spots, choosing which would leave her the best chance to hit her mark. It was unclear how she was going to manage to drag the deer back to camp, but she was not going to let this one go. The fur was worth the effort alone, not including the amount of meat and use of the horns for new handles on her daggers. Drawing her arrow back, she paced herself. Deer were fickle, and utter silence was of the utmost importance. She was blessed to have started her life as a farmer's daughter, learning the art of skinning, preserving, and, more importantly, knowing the many ways to stitch the leathers to common goods.

The snapping of a frozen branch caught the buck's attention, and he drew his head high, eyes wide as his ears flicked about nervously. Squinting, holding back the cursing, she looked down at her feet expecting to see the branch she had leaned into, but found nothing. A crunching of the snow to her left sent her hair on end as a large paw rested there next to her. She could smell blood and dirt coming from the creature as it crouched in the shrubs close to her, clearly unaware of her presence. Her eyes grew wide as she took in the sight of the chimera. The heat of its breath melted the snow in front of it, its massive lion's head and mane crowned with four curving horns of a goat; its back half flowed out from its feline front into a split-hooved creature. The tail whipped side to side as its scales glittered in the sunlight. The sight of the eyeless serpent's head at its end made her bite her bottom lip until she tasted the iron of her blood across her tongue. Repeating lessons of stealth, she hoped to keep calm as her thoughts flew. Her lip remained in her mouth, fearing the smell of her blood would reveal her to the massive creature.

The sound of something metallic caught her attention, and she saw that it wore a crude collar buried in its mane. This was a sign that this creature belonged to the sorceress Morrighan, and as she looked back at the large buck, it was obvious he was part of a pack. Two smaller chimeras were stalking on the other side of the deer, which stood stone still unaware of the glowing eyes approaching. Another pop of a branch from a smaller chimera sent the buck jolting toward her and the larger monster. With effortless grace, the beast pounced, shattering the antlers of the deer with one large, aggressive bite. The three creatures fought over the deer, ravaging it across the snow, painting it a gruesome red in the sunlight. Slowly, she backed herself out of the shrubs, hoping that their prey and hunger kept them blind to any movement in the area. Panic was causing her to shake; she struggled to switch her focus from the chimeras to her feet. They were consuming the deer so fast. There was no way she could make enough distance to get away. Her shoulder bumped against a tree, and looking up, it became clear this was her only chance to remove herself from the immediate danger. Climbing as swiftly and silently as she could, she was thankful for her new rabbit's fur gloves. Managing to get a good height up, she pulled her bow off her shoulders and readied herself, just in case.

A sensation of anger hit her and instinctually she looked back toward the way of camp. She could see glimpses of Cedric's red hair through the far-off trees approaching. He had sensed her fear but could not possibly know the cause for it. Panicking, she whistled the bird song he had taught her in case of danger in order to warn each other. In the process, she neglected to prevent the spraying of blood from her lips. The chimeras froze and started sniffing the air in her direction, and Cedric broke into a run. Sucking her lip back into her mouth, she turned her focus on the chimeras smelling their way closer to the tree. Pulling the arrow back, she waited for the right moment to release it. She could feel Cedric getting closer, his anger adding to her anxiety. He broke through some shrubs, catching the attention of all three creatures, and she let her arrow free. It landed its mark in the largest chimera's paw, bringing his attention back to her. This would give Cedric a chance to kill the others if she could keep the larger, stronger one's attention.

The tree shook, and snow-covered branches rained down around her to the ground, threatening to knock her off her perch. Another thud of its massive lion's paws made her hug the trunk of the tree. Looking down did nothing to soothe her fears, as the flames rolled between its teeth. Chimeras were infamous for breathing fire and with nowhere to go, she had to think fast. She sat on the branch and wrapped her legs firmly around the limb. Locking her feet and ankles to one another, she readied her bow. Swinging upside down confused the chimera, who mistook the motion as falling, canceling his fire breath, thinking to catch her in its jaws, opening his enormous mouth. This was just long enough for her to take aim and make her shot count. Roaring, it pawed at its mouth, knocking into the tree, desperate to free its tongue from the arrow she had placed in it. According to the *Book of Rangers*, an injury to the mouth would keep a fire-breather from using this tactic. Now she struggled to right herself as the beast bashed itself against the trunk, still occupied with the arrow lodged in its tongue. A branch fell across her left hand, causing her to shriek. She flailed wildly, her legs losing their hold, her fingers possibly broken. The mixture of pain and pleasure was adding to her hysteria.

Cedric's jaw twitched as he dropped his sword from the unexpected pain in his left hand. There was no time to waste. It was clear Angeline was not going to be able to recover her position on top of the branch after smashing her fingers. Running head-on against one of the smaller chimeras, he picked it up with amazing strength and flung it into the larger beast. The two slid and rolled across the snow, and without missing a beat, Cedric launched himself up the tree. Angeline's wild, tear-filled eyes met his enraged green ones. There was a large jolt against the tree, and a large crackling like thunder roared from the bottom as it started to tilt and roll. Her legs slipped from the jerking and she braced herself. Catching her in time, Cedric gripped her waist, hugging her close, and together they abandoned the falling tree. The pack of chimeras had regrouped quickly and rammed the tree in unison, breaking it at its base. They were fast and worked in union, unlike the hellhounds he had faced.

The popping and snapping were deafening as they stood close to the falling behemoth. They landed nearby and she let her feet touch the snow. The ground shook violently before the tree settled in its final resting place, and there in the snowy ruckus was the approaching pack of chimeras. The eyes of the larger one were glowing red as they drew closer, blood dripping from its mouth, now free of her arrow. Cedric shoved her behind him, and she winced as she tried to get her fingers to grip the bow, but failed. It was clear he was taking her pain from her, and each movement was causing her to feel aroused. The chimeras stopped just a few feet from them, and the jaws of the larger one opened. Purple mist flowed from its eyes and mouth as it began to speak.

"You have been busy, Cedric." The voice was female and the tone was smooth and articulate in manner. "I was astonished how much you were able to work Lillith over. The latest information I have received on your activities as of late has certainly caught my attention. Is this what you wanted?"

"What do you want, Morrighan?" The heat from his anger astounded Angeline, and she leaned against his back in response as a wave of pleasure and anger pulsed through her. "It won't be long before I come for you."

"Clearly; but I was curious to see this witch you had bound yourself with. It seems the magic in her blood has been catching a lot of attention as well." The chimera shook snow from its shoulders and mane as Morrighan continued her conversation through it. "First, I was told my sister Nemaine had killed you, and then Lillith nearly outdid herself fighting you. Here you are with my chimeras, so I could not sit back without at least engaging in some small talk. It is clear my little sister failed to dispose of you for me, and there is no doubt that you have grown in power at a rather alarming rate. It saddens me to think I did not see your full potential before. Here I thought you were a failure, but now I see that I was more successful than I had originally expected when I created you."

"I am not one of your handmade puppets." Sweat poured over her as Cedric's anger continued to grow with every word. "I will stop your madness. Even if I die, I will make sure your days of creating abominations like me end. You're a plague upon every living creature here."

"Such a big promise. I am curious to see if you can keep it." A wicked laugh came from the chimera's gaping jaws. "That's if you can even make it past Boto? Moreover, before that, how do you propose getting past my army? You cannot possibly think you would gain enough power from binding with a witch to get on the same playing field as your own creator? I am your God and you can only dream of being blessed by my presence, if I allow it. You forget, I made you, and I can undo the magic that stitches you together."

"Like I said, I will knock you off that pedestal if it kills me." The purple mist faded, and the chimera shook its head at Cedric. "I will kill you, Morrighan."

"Cedric." Angeline slid to her knees. The hatred she felt coming from him was breathtaking. "I am so sorry. I had no idea how much…"

"I need you on your feet, Angeline." His glare cut the air between them as she stumbled to her feet again. "I don't care if your fingers are broken; I need you to keep them off my back long enough for me to get two of them down."

"Ye-yes." Her fingers gave her a pleasing sensation, despite the purplish and black colors that stained the skin under her ripped glove. "I'm ready."

Cedric charged headlong at the largest chimera. His rage for Morrighan fueling the attack, he gripped the massive horns and buried his knee between its eyes. Angeline managed to land an arrow into the cheek of one of the smaller beasts, interrupting its attack on Cedric. She ran across the snow for a better shot and sent another arrow into the back hock of the other, slowing its movements drastically. She was recalling everything she could on ways to delay an attacking beast. Watching as Cedric leaped backward to dodge the swiping of a large paw, he ran forward, making his way behind the beast. Desperate, she grabbed up an arrow, paying no heed to the chimeras limping her way. The arrow glanced Cedric's ear, pausing his attack as it made its mark on the other side of him. Looking up, Cedric saw she had risked cutting him to take out the serpent's head on the end of its tail. He had failed to take note of it. Frantic, she shuffled back, trying to gain distance between her and the other two chimeras.

Cedric gripped the tail of the massive chimera, and with all his might, pulled and swung the beast into the fallen tree. Blood oozed from the ears, forehead, and mouth as it struggled to keep a focused attack. It curved back, swiping at him from where he still pulled at its tail. Yanking, Cedric pulled its balance off, and its jaw slammed to the ground with a loud clamp of its teeth. Kicking his heel into its hip, he positioned himself on top of its shoulders. Fangs long, he bit into the back of the monster's neck to deplete it of its life. The beast released an ear-shattering roar as it attempted to stand and claw at Cedric. Ignoring the slash across his shoulder, Cedric indulged in draining the last of its life force as it slumped to the ground, the light in its eyes fading.

The other two chimeras had shifted their attention back to the commotion of their dead leader. Angeline sighed as she pulled another arrow, taking out one serpent tail and quickly the other. She was determined not to face a repeat of Cedric being poisoned again. Once more, she had called their attention back to her, and she just kept the onslaught of arrows coming, hitting one, then the other. By the time Cedric caught up to them, she had managed to blind them both in one eye. He gripped one by the back legs, knocking it off its feet, and jumped on top to continue his feeding.

Angeline couldn't help but compare him to a hungry wolf as he took it down. It was clear that the chimeras were never the predator here, but it was Cedric. A demon that devours demons and the darkness that all creatures fear is what she was staring into the eyes of. In her moment of distraction, she had failed to keep the other chimera off his back as its claws dug into his back, yet he never released his bite. An arrow in its remaining eye caused it to fall away, but the ravenous stare from the feeding Cedric made her heart race. Breaking the stare, she pelted the remaining chimera with arrows. Deafened by the thudding of her panicked heartbeat, cold tears crawled down her cheeks. All her frustration, anger, and fear went into every shot. The beast stumbled and wavered with each hit as she stood her ground. After a moment, her vision was blurred, and she was just aiming at the heaping blob, only wanting this nightmare to end. Reaching into her quiver, she grasped air. She was out of ammo. Slumping to her knees, she wailed and let herself cry out the remaining dread as it poured out of her.

Arms grasped around her from behind, and she could feel Cedric's breath against her neck and ear. The smell of blood met her nose, and she sobbed more, but leaned into his warmth and security. She had lost touch with the situation a moment too soon, but she had done what was asked of her. There was a long ways before she would be worthy of the ranger title just yet. All she felt was broken, both physically and mentally, there in the cold darkness on the snow.

"It's ok. You killed it, pet." His voice was soft as he nuzzled his lips close to her ear. "You did a good job. It's over, you're safe. You killed it before I even had a chance to finish..."

CHAPTER 15

BADBH THE BATTLE GODDESS

They rode for a day and a half before they came across a bustling town. Cedric's wounds were having trouble healing. He had consumed some of Morrighan's magic from the chimeras and it had backfired. It was undoing the magical binding between his incubus and moroi bloodlines, slowing his healing and draining him of his strength. They had said nothing to each other about the issue. Angeline followed behind him in an obedient fashion as they walked into the town brothel, silent and firm. He looked pale and was starting to sweat like he had done with the cobra's bite. She was in such a daze still, her fingers blackened and sore, but her mind was arguing about which issue to deal with first, Cedric or her hand.

Her ears could not track the conversation he was having with the brothel keep as they stood among the commotion of the downstairs tavern. After a few moments, he turned to her and motioned for her to follow one of the girls up the stairs. The girl wore a long skirt, and her top barely held her breasts in them. Clearly, she was one of the brothel girls that a patron could pay to keep them company at night. She had heard many stories from the drunken merchants and nobles of places like this, but this was her first time in one. The girl unlocked a door and handed her the key. The smell was no better than the drunken tavern scene from the first floor. There was a sour yeast smell, and the bed looked to have been ridden hard for quite some time.

Looking back, she realized that Cedric had not followed them up. No one was in the hallway with her anymore, and she was baffled as to where he could have gone. Closing the door behind her, she took a deep breath, allowing some of her tension to unwind. Despite the rough look of the bed, she flopped herself on it, burying her face in her arms as if to hide herself from everything. After the battle with the chimeras, she had sat in the snow while Cedric tended to his wounds, packed camp, and from there they had traveled nonstop. They were exhausted, but it was no mystery that they both needed to heal. Rolling onto her back, she pulled her left hand free of her glove to have another look at it. It was scattered with dark angry colors, and the left ring finger was crooked. This one had been broken, and would never look right again. She was fortunate enough that she had full movement in that finger, despite the numbing pain that screamed from it.

The bang of the door spooked her from her sleep. Cedric dropped some bags at the foot of the bed and began undressing. Sitting up from where she had passed out on the bed, she caught herself watching him. Blushing, she looked away, afraid that he would notice or that she would find herself losing to her feelings again. He paused for a moment as he dropped his torn shirt to the ground, and with a grunt, he continued inspecting his bandages. Walking over to the washbasin, he began to take off the bandages from his shoulder and back. Looking at him, Angeline could see the deep punctures in his back were still trying to bleed. The gaping holes were painful to look at, as they oozed dark red blood over the muscles of his back. Tearing her eyes away from the gore, he began to wash out the wounds. The sound of the water made her stomach turn, and she tried to distract herself by taking off her boots.

"Make sure you lock the door next time." Stopping for a moment as she worked the first boot off, she looked at him, but met the gruesome view of his back. "We're in a brothel. The type of men who stay here would gladly take advantage of any woman laid out on a bed alone. Next time, lock the door, pet."

"I'm sorry. I thought you were right behind me and then I must have fallen asleep." She jerked her other foot free of its boot, feeling agitated that he was lecturing her. "I've never been in a place like this."

"I know." He threw the blood-stained cloth into the basin, marched over to the bags on the floor, and he jerked something from them. "Never go anywhere without this again, you understand? You should have had it on you when you met the chimeras."

He dropped one of her daggers in her hand. A wave of something she hadn't felt from him before came across and she couldn't stop herself from shivering as goose bumps danced across her skin. Her eyes grew wide as she looked the handle of the dagger over. At some point, it had been replaced with the tip of one of the chimera's horns and the ridged texture made its grip easier in her hand. Pulling the blade from its new snakeskin sheath, she swallowed. The black spatter on its blade kept it from reflecting any light, telling her exactly which of her daggers he had upgraded; this was the blade she had found left on the rock. The dagger that Wylleam and she had decided not to acknowledge to Cedric that she had found and knowingly knew he had stabbed himself with. Her hair stood on end as she looked up at Cedric, lost for words or explanations. Instead of the sharp gaze, she was looking into one that seemed dulled and another wave of the strange sensation hit her again. She could not identify the feeling she was receiving from him.

"It was stupid of me to leave the damn thing on the rock, but perhaps my blood on the blade will give enough scent to discourage an attack." His jaw was tight as he stood there, his eyes demanding she acknowledge he was not oblivious to her secrets. "I knew you had it this whole time, so don't look so perplexed. I broke the handle when I used it last, so I had the local smith fix it as part of my trade. Chimera horns are worth a fortune and it was no trouble to get them to fix it. They paid for the room, supplies we will be getting by morning, and more. Only the best demon hunters have weapons fashioned with chimera horn grips and hilts."

Speechless, she sheathed the blade and sat there, staring down at it. He had acted so strangely on that day she had found the blood-covered rock. She never understood why he felt the need to use it on himself. Perhaps it was all Lillith's doing before they had come across her in their travels, but his behavior had been animalistic in nature. Collapsing onto the bed behind her, Cedric drifted asleep with his back to her. For the life of her, she couldn't recall when he had taken the dagger from her or found it in her pack. Glancing over, she cringed; his wounds looked grisly and were festering. Her thoughts were reeling as she continued to register everything, confused about how she could fix this. Cedric wasn't going to get better at this rate.

It was awkward to think that this would be the first time they would be sleeping next to one another, despite everything they had done together. Laying on the very edge, she hugged the dagger close to her chest, curling herself in a ball. He shifted, and she felt startled for a moment, her nerves still on high from realizing he had known about the dagger. Closing her eyes, she tried her best to slow down the waterfall of emotions and thoughts, whatever it took to not to cry again. It was too much pull on her to continue to fall apart like this with so much danger in her life. Her focus needed to be on resting, on healing, and on preparing for the next battle that was inevitably coming. There could be no more crying. There was no more room for the naïve Angeline in this new world of darkness.

Gasping as she sat up from her sleep, she found herself shivering, the room dark. Cedric wasn't lying next to her on the bed any longer, but the room was too black to tell if he was still there, possibly tending his wounds again. Light splattered across the rutted floor as drunken laughter and slurs echoed on the other side of the door. Music was blasting from downstairs, doors slamming, and a new sound she had not been in the presence of before.

This was the sound of a girl screaming and moaning, the neighboring bedposts knocking on the other side of the far wall. Hugging her knees, she could not help but play through her own lustful moments with Cedric. In her mind, she questioned how she must have sounded in those moments that he had overwhelmed her.

A shiver snaked up her spine, and she stumbled to her feet, looking for the packs at the foot of the bed. As she bent down to pull free her blanket, an icy hand gripped the back of her neck, holding her firm in the awkward position. If it wasn't for the wave of arousal he had given her at that moment, she would have panicked. Her breath was unsteady as she waited to see what Cedric was intending to do with her.

"No crying? No screaming?" His voice was cold as he released her and sat back on the bed. "Were you not afraid?"

"Why would I be?" Pulling the blanket free, she went back to her side of the bed, laying with her back to him. "It was only you. What was the point of spooking me like that?"

"I was curious to see how you would react." The bed shifted and creaked as Cedric moved closer to her. "Did you not just feel aroused? Were you not just thinking about all the times that I have sent you to Heaven?"

"You call that Heaven." The brothel girl's screams became wilder for a moment before turning into laughter, mocking Angeline as she hugged her covers to her chest. "Yes, I was thinking about those times. Aren't you the one who was aroused first?"

"Perhaps." A wave of excitement vibrated through her, and she shut her eyes, attempting to ignore it. "Does that really matter?"

"We need to rest. Don't we have to look for Badbh?" Scooting over more, she realized she was at the very edge of the bed.

A tight grip on her arm rolled her onto her back. Cedric straddled her, his weight crushing as she yelped in surprise. He leaned in but was stopped before he could go any further. In her distress, she had managed to unsheathe the dagger. Hilt against the center of her chest, the tip dug into the center of his chest. They lay frozen, his eyes glowing green with their catlike pupils as she stared up at him with confusion and fear. Something warm trickled across her fingers and began pooling on her chest from where the handle pressed hard into her sternum. Laughter started coming from his chest before it made it out of his mouth. He looked wild and untamed to her. In the dark, he looked like the animal that she had seen on the rock, his fangs glinting.

"You have it in you after all." Letting her go, he flopped on his back. "I was starting to worry you had lost your stubborn side after that fight."

"Don't touch me." It took all her focus to keep calm and to slow her breathing. "Don't ever touch me like that again."

"Just remember to pull that dagger like that and there won't be a next time." Smacking her in the thigh, he rolled over. "I just needed to know you had it in you to protect yourself, pet."

The ride was silent as they rode down the heavily weathered road. They had been given directions to where a recent battle was going on, and they hoped they would see Badbh there. Cedric noted that Angeline was struggling to keep herself from being so close to him on Barushka. A grin crawled across his face; it seemed childish to act that way. Nothing had happened, nor was anything going to happen last night. A chance to pick on her and test that she could protect herself was all that was in it for him. Wylleam gave her the dagger. He knew when they arrived at the cottage, and he caught the scent of it. The glance he shot the old shaman could have killed a man, and the flattened ears told him enough. He had decided it was fine for her to keep it, but had no need to fix its hilt until now. Her fight against the chimeras had exceeded his expectations about her, again. The way she handled the situation was beyond impressive, besides her panicking in the tree when she hurt her hand. The rangers would have had her in their top ranks with that much growth with little training. Angeline was a natural; if only she realized it.

The sound of crows and ravens screeching in the distance was getting louder, and the smell of dirt and iron began to overcome everything else. The battle was close. Barushka shuddered as he fussed at the muddy pathway, broken down from the hordes of horses and soldiers that had traveled down it. His large heavy hooves sank into the mud, making each step troublesome for him. As they rounded the nearby hill, it became clear that the battle had ended, and the victors were long gone. Cedric encouraged Barushka through the bodies and debris. Looking about for signs of anything that could tell him if Badbh had been there, they went deeper into the frightful scene. They passed fallen men who were screaming or moaning as they lay in the filth of the battlegrounds. Their wounds fatal, there was no way of helping them. Angeline had given up on keeping her distance from Cedric and pushed her face into his back, covering her ears from the pleas for help. It sounded like the cries of tortured souls trapped in hell as they worked their way to the heavier section of the battlefield where the fight had peaked.

"Looking for me?" It was a deep-toned woman's voice that broke through the chaos of birds and the dying, sending them all into a moment of complete silence. "I figured I would wait for you before I moved on. I heard you were searching for me."

"Badbh." Barushka halted as Cedric turned him about to a rather large raven on top of a polearm that was stuck in the ground. "You are not the waiting sort, I thought?"

"For this, I am more curious to hear your side of the story. I heard from my sisters of the ruckus you caused them." The bird chuckled before it flew off and to the ground. "I admire the tenacity of your efforts. You're a hell of a fighter and, more importantly, one lucky bastard."

"Not that I had much choice of who I fought against lately. I would have preferred not running into Nemaine like that or Lillith shortly after." The bird grew in size, flapping its wings, feathers flying about as a masked warrior appeared. "I was hoping I could ask you a question about how to kill someone. My research has given me nothing on the matter."

"Ah, I thought that was going to be the case. Let me guess, after Lillith, you realized there was more to killing pureblood succubi and incubi, neh?" Badbh's tanned skin was covered in pink and purple scars of all sorts of shapes and sizes. "To be honest, the only information I have is that it has something dealing with their offspring. My studies have shown that purebloods have been killed by halflings and other purebloods. You may have a shot, especially after handling Lillith so well. Being the offspring of the strongest of that sort of demon may have given you the edge you needed for the task you are setting out to do."

"Lillith was pure luck." Shifting his back and shoulders, he shook Angeline out of the center of his back. "I had to bind myself to a witch at the worst possible time. I had no other chance of dodging becoming her next playmate."

"That's right; your ranger-in-training over there is a witch's descendant. There's much gossiping on that matter as well." Hidden by a bird-like mask of silver and brass, her face was impossible to see and her skirt of raven feathers flickered in the wind as she made small talk with them. Angeline marveled over the rigid look of her muscular arms and abdomen that could rival most men's physique. "Well, she may want to keep that dagger with the black blade close. Not sure how you managed to enchant it, but it is one of a kind. I could not make an enchantment that could match it. As for battling Lillith or Boto, you have a better chance than myself at winning a fight with one of them. There is nothing more I can do for you, Cedric. You know how to be tactful, and you have been around long enough to gain a solid line of experience to call on. Training and building your power to match Boto's should get you closer to Morrighan and defeating them."

"Enchanted?" Angeline felt a wave of emotion from him, and the muscles on his back twitched under her hands. "Did you enchant the dagger, Cedric?"

"I am sure Wylleam had something to do with that. Badbh, do you not want to keep me from killing your sister? Nemaine may not say it, but she would not have attempted to kill me in our last meeting." Cedric spat at the ground as he changed subjects. "Or does the Battle Goddess have other plans?"

"Look, unless you can find some way to pull the demonic possession from Morrighan's body and mind, she is dead to me. She was never right in the head, but after it took hold, her ways went too far into the dark arts. As for my plans, I am following this so-called 'crusade' heading south. King Frederick has received yet another promotion among the human politics and now thinks he can lead these fools to battle in the name of their God. I am intrigued to see what battles develop from this." The wind kicked up, and in the ruffle of raven feathers from her skirt, she had transformed back into the large raven again. "If you figure out a way to set Morrighan free, I would owe you for the rest of my life. Oh, and you, witch?"

"Ye-yes?" Angeline swallowed back her unsteadiness the best she could. "What do you want with me?"

"You are his bounded mate, and you need to start listening to those instincts. They are there to inform you of how you best suit his needs, and he does the same as it calls of him. You are responsible for fixing his wounds. That is your place." A large caw rang out as Badbh flew off to the south.

"My blood." The memory of the glowing bottle in Wylleam's hands shot through her mind and she remembered why it had to be hers. "That's right, I can fix this."

"That's the last thing I want." Cedric jerked at the reins and Barushka started into a light gallop, heading back toward the town. "I don't need your blood. I'm fine."

"But Wylleam had to use my—" A wave of anger shot out of him, knocking the air from her lungs.

"I don't need it." Once more, he shook her off his back.

Nodding at the barkeep, they went back to their room. His body was still growing colder, and the wounds ached with every motion he made. Cedric's focus was to start cleaning the gashes, keeping them from infection. Angeline slammed and locked the door behind him, but he paid her no attention. Running the water across his shoulder stung, but the dried blood that painted his arm needed to be scrubbed clean. Warm hands touched his back, and he paused as he felt the waves of emotion Angeline was giving off. The sensations they shared were hard to control and breathtaking when they were touching. She took the cloth from him and began cleaning his back, and he could feel the mixture of sorrow and guilt she held as she tended to the ravaged scene that lay across it. Sighing, he closed his eyes, enjoying the affectionate gesture. The cloth hit the floor, and she threw her arms around him, gripping him tight as warm tears ran down his back.

"I should have never stopped shooting." She shook as her hands clung to his chest and stomach. "Your back would have been fine, but I screwed up."

"Angeline, it's not the wounds." Looking down, he stared at her discolored hand and its crooked finger. "I let Morrighan rile me up, and my greed got the best of me. I would be healed by now if I hadn't drained the chimeras and consumed her magic. She knew I would, and she made sure I would be punished for taking it in."

"I can fix it." She was pressing her face harder into his back as she shivered. "I think I understand now. Without me, you have no true way to heal..."

"Don't." He turned, pushing her back as he gripped her shoulders, demanding eye contact. "I don't want blood. Not from you."

Jerking away from him, she worked her sleeve up, exposing the arm with the scars, holding it up to him. Wide-eyed, he stared at the slash and the ravaged bite mark that made its home across her soft skin. She was biting her bottom lip, tears rolling in her eyes as her face blotched. Compassion was flowing out of her, but it did not change how he felt on the matter. It was hard for him to decipher which side wanted her blood more, the incubus or the moroi. Before, it had been clear that it was the incubine blood that cried out for the virgin's blood, but now, it was replaced with a hunger that he hadn't known before. This new want had started shortly after Morrighan's magic began wreaking havoc on his system. She shoved her arm closer to him and he pushed it away, the thirst choking him. Her emotions made it harder for him to bury and push the new urge down; it was exhausting. There was no way for him to know what his new need was intending to do.

"Stop it." His eyes were sharp as he snarled at her. "I definitely have no desire to ravage your arm again, and especially with you making that sort of face, pet."

"Wylleam explained it to me. You don't understand." Desperately, she wiped the tears from her face while he pushed past her. "Magic in my blood can undo hers. That's how we got your bloodlines to go back last time. My magic can replace the broken parts."

"Do you not get that I know that?" He jerked up a shirt and started for the door.

"Stop!" Again, her hands wrapped around his waist. "You can't."

"Let go." Growling he sent a wave of anger through her, but all he got in return was the immediate pulse of arousal. "This is not the time for this."

"Does it matter?" Another wave. Now she was doing it on purpose. "Does it matter who starts first?"

"Angeline, you are treading in the unknown." His incubine blood was stirring as she continued using their new ability to share emotions. "You know I can't promise."

"I know." Her voice was meek as she nuzzled his back and lightly kissed it.

His skin was crawling, his breath had quickened against his will, and the blood in his veins was rushing with excitement. Gripping her arm, he pulled her out from behind him and locked lips with her as they fell to the bed. She shuddered as he started kissing her neck and his fangs graced the skin. His hand slid across her back, working its way under her shirt. The exchange of excitement between them was washing away the fear and contempt that was keeping them apart.

Her scent filled his nose, and the sound of her heartbeat as her blood rushed from his every touch pulled at the hunger that had been haunting him. It was something foreign to him, but if she wanted this so badly, he would give it to her. Giving way to his instincts, he latched onto her neck, his fangs popping through her skin. The moan of pleasure that escaped her quivering lips fueled his longing. Sweet and thick, her blood ran across his tongue and sent a shiver of desire across his entire body.

Her fingers clawed into his skin as he continued drinking with all his weight on top of her, keeping her still. The magic in her blood weaved its way through him, and it was intoxicating. Morrighan's magic lost its hold as hers touched it, replacing the broken ties that allowed him to maintain his existence. His wounds were no longer aching, but healing as they continued groping at one another. Releasing his hold on her neck, he licked at the bite mark as his hands crept across her body, making her release wave after wave of arousal. Panting, sweating, she opened her eyes, staring into the narrow slit pupils of his green ones. She ran a hand across his wounded shoulder, and relief flowed from her as she could see the skin growing back in its rightful place. Hugging her close, he pushed her farther onto the bed, kissing her neck again. It was a sentimental thank you for him as he let his incubine blood drive him further as she panted and moaned in response. All he wanted was to make her scream in bliss. Cedric grinned as he stared down at her, knowing she had earned a night of unfathomable ecstasy for being so courageous for a change, despite her tears. *Does she know how fortunate she is to be the lady of an incubus? Will she ever understand that the love she receives from her lord is the ultimate desire of those around her, to lay with someone who can bring them such great rapture that it spoils their soul?*

CHAPTER 16

LEGEND OF THE MOROI

Rubbing her neck, she could feel the two scars where Cedric's fangs had dug so deeply into her skin. It was a constant reminder that she was a living elixir and needed for his survival as much as she needed him for protection. Winter was starting to give way to spring, with a few places showing the ground and patches of green. They had continued traveling from one village to the next, still looking for information on Morrighan and the king incubus, Boto. Instead, they had come across a story about a moroi that had lived in a small town north of where they were. No one could say if she was alive, but her tale was well-known to travelers before the packs of werewolves started to overrun the surrounding woods.

They had taken out three werewolves on their way down the path leaving the town. The woods here held an abnormal infestation of the turned. Cedric showed Angeline the signs of werewolf activity, from the clawing of trees to how to identify their tracks from other beasts. He told her of how all werewolves came from the same one, Romasanta. The books referred to him as the Father of Werewolves and it was unclear how old he was. There had been a conflict between Cedric and him back in Williamsburg. Romasanta neglected to show respect for those who had died when he looted several of the homes and graves. Since then, Cedric has had a hard time tracking him down. The werewolves he creates are banished, never allowed to be near him or his immediate territory. This causes nearby woods to become infested and they tend to gather in packs instinctually. Angeline noticed that Cedric did not feed on these as they dispatched a few more. Then again, the last thing he had fed on was her, weeks ago. *Is my blood that strong that it gives him no reason to feed?*

Passing a broken signpost, they worked their way closer to a clearing where a shattered village lay. Cedric slid off Barushka and took a closer look at the calamity that decorated the place. Houses were barely standing with large gaping holes in the side of them. A few had signs of a fire erupting and a large pillar near Barushka's hooves bore claw marks across it. Smelling a handful of soil, Cedric sighed as he looked about in the dimming daylight. This was the right place, but they were years late. In fact, it was impressive that the place was in such good condition considering the time that had passed. His best guess was over a hundred years ago when it was ravaged.

"Did werewolves do this?" Angeline petted the side of Barushka's neck as they both watched Cedric. "This is horrible."

"No." Standing, he pointed to a charred mark on the well. "Werewolves don't breathe fire. This is a sign of Morrighan's chimeras, which means that the moroi that lived here could be the one she used to mother me."

"Mother?" Pausing, she looked about. "Was this done by the same chimeras we killed?"

"Possibly, but she has several. We are talking about over a hundred years." Walking around, he kicked a few things, looking for clues. "I wish there was something here that had some more information. No one knows much about moroi. They are killed the moment they are discovered. I wonder why this village chose to keep her. If there were any survivors, I am sure the werewolves plucked them from here. In fact, most of the mutts we see were likely from this village before the curse took them."

"What is a moroi?" Cedric started digging in one of the packs, ignoring the mumbling manner she used to ask her unsteady question. "I haven't heard of them before."

"Not many have. The Romanians are some of the few that have records of them. Moroi are the offspring of two strigoi, pureblood vampires, who were able to conceive a child. You can recognize one because they are always female, red-haired, and have green eyes. It is noted they are infertile and incapable of nurturing life in their cursed wombs. They say they can walk in sunlight, eat no different from a human, but have abnormal stamina and strength. Being of great beauty, they woo many men, causing trouble in any village they come to. One lore said they will outlast their lovers in bed and life. No one has ever recorded how long they can live, due to the fact they are hunted down. I assume they can feed on other creatures for blood and may become stronger by doing so from my own experiences. Other than that, not much else is known." He flipped out a book and started writing in it. "We'll camp here tonight so I can look for more clues tomorrow."

"What's that?" It was the first time she had noticed him writing. "What are you writing about?"

"I am making note of this place. I'd be an old fool to think I could remember everything." He shot a sharp look at her as he placed it back in the pack as if to say do not touch. "We can use what's left of the house over there to camp in. It's at least sturdy enough to use the fireplace."

Shivering, Angeline watched with chattering teeth as Barushka started the fire. It seemed awkward to be sitting in the abandoned cottage with a huge hole in the sidewall. The air was cold and wet, and she could not wait until spring took full swing. Cedric returned with more firewood before sitting next to her, pulling her close. This was another strange sensation they were starting.

Cedric had given into the idea he was stuck with her and indulged in being close to someone for a change. He couldn't help but smirk with each move. Her waves would result in her sensations of being alarmed, physically stiff for the first few moments. It was clear she was more at ease when he treated her this way. She fell asleep faster when he took a moment to show her some tenderness, but he was starting to enjoy it. Part of him resented the idea, but out here, away from prying eyes, he felt there were no risks. Barushka would eye him suspiciously from time to time, as a silent form of jealousy and protest as he snorted. Much to his own surprise, Cedric found himself smirking as she shuddered and pushed herself harder into his arms for warmth. *When was the last time I enjoyed something so simplistic? I have strived so hard to distance myself from my past that I forgot about the humanistic things that I cherished most. Too bad my time with her will not be a long one. Her life will end well before my own, if I even live through killing Morrighan and Boto.* A sigh escaped his lips as he closed his eyes, his thoughts trailing over his times in Williamsburg and the things he missed so much.

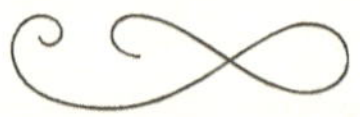

At some point, he had dozed off. The fire was low as its coals popped and crackled. Placing more wood on the fire, sounds started coming from outside. Barushka flipped his ears at Cedric; both of them had heard it. Grabbing up his sword, he took one more glance at Angeline, sleeping on the ground, as he backed against the wall to conceal himself. The noises of several animals pacing out of view, followed by an occasional growl, met his ears. Another pack had tracked them down, but this one was much larger. Nodding at Barushka, the shag foal started nibbling and nudging Angeline awake. As she came to, her eyes locked onto Cedric's and she grabbed up her bow and the quiver from Barushka's back.

Looking out the opening in the far wall, glowing eyes stared back at Angeline and she pushed back her fear. She drew an arrow and waited as she tried to decipher how many were out there. Drool dripping across the ground resonated in her ears like rain, causing her hair to stand on end and she bit her cheeks. The werewolves they had come across were all starving and these were no exception to the fact as she observed their ribs protruding out of their skin. There were eight sets of glowing eyes, but more were undoubtedly waiting from the movements she could see from the hole in the wall. She lipped the number to Cedric, whose jaw twitched in response as he tightened his grip on his sword.

Looking back, she gasped. A large, mangy head of a werewolf was poking into the opening. Focused on her, it had failed to notice Cedric against the wall as it slowly crept over the wall. With one hard swing, his head dropped and his body followed, leaving it hanging halfway into the room. Howling erupted all around, deafening in manner, as it thudded through Angeline and Cedric's chests. Two more werewolves charged at the opening, managing to bottleneck each other. Growling and snapping at one another, they were larger than the first one that had entered. Letting an arrow fly, she landed a hit in the smaller beast's temple, killing him instantly. Reading the tome of the rangers, half-human monsters had easier kill-spots if the archer was skilled enough to hit the key areas. The other one was now biting and tearing into its fellow pack members in order to free itself from the blockage. Once more, Cedric decapitated the werewolf, making a stack of corpses as their wall of protection from the snarling pack waiting on the other side.

Barking and growling erupted as they started to chew and pull their dead comrades out of the hole. Barushka, engulfed in his flames, stood tall and ready to do his part in this fight as he stomped and snorted. A wolf's head squeezed between the corpses, but was met with the back hoof of Barushka and sent out again. Cedric stood back from the wall as the werewolves started to bang themselves against the cobblestones. Rocks were falling, and their faux shelter was not going to handle much more abuse. Nodding at Angeline, Cedric was about to clear the doorway. She hopped on Barushka, ready.

They could feel the waves of emotions from one another; Cedric's waves of extreme calm managed to relieve her bursts of panic. What was meeting them on the other side was unknown, but the sudden pulse of anger from Cedric was enough to snuff out her fears. She hugged herself low on his back, afraid of catching the top of the wall. Cedric gave the top corpse a hard kick, sending it flying into two unsuspecting werewolves. Before the others could register what was happening, he managed to take two more out with a toss of the last two bodies.

Barushka cleared the cottage and Angeline wasted no time to right herself, taking down werewolves with each arrow. Cedric guarded against one attack in time to receive a slash across his back, and once again, Angeline experienced extreme arousal from his injury. Barushka bucked, launching the offender off Cedric, but sent Angeline face-first into his mane, causing her shooting to come to a stop. Catching her balance, she focused on the closer werewolves in hopes of not forcing Barushka to make that mistake again.

The pack was pouring out of everywhere like roaches in a dungeon. It was hard shooting from Barushka as he did his part to fight. He had managed to save Cedric and her several times already. For some reason, the werewolves had no interest in the shag foal, but it was a blessing for them. If it were not for his flames, it would have been harder for her to see the incoming hordes. Cedric pushed back a werewolf, gaining enough of a break to dispatch another coming from the side. Shoved up against Barushka's shoulder, he had never seen a pack this large in all his travels. The villagers were turned here after facing Morrighan's chimeras, which had been nothing more than food for the werewolves in the area. Usually, if the cursed ones were from the same area, they tended to group together.

He ran forward, slashing two more down before head-butting a third without his horns to absorb the crashing force of his forehead on the massive wolf's head. It sent him flying, and he knocked Angeline off Barushka. Landing on top of her, his green eyes stared down at her in bewilderment and for the first time, she caught a flicker of panic from him. A werewolf pounced onto his back and he knocked him off as he stood over her. His horns and claws came forward; there was no choice in the matter after losing his sword. Angeline coughed and wheezed as she gripped her ribs, astonished by the overwhelming sensation of excitement that flowed from him. Managing to get her hands on her bow, her skin crawled with the feelings that he was receiving by giving way to his incubine blood. This is what he hated the most as lustful sensations pulsed from him, but without her quiver, she was useless and unable to help.

Barushka was caught behind the torrent of fur as they pushed him farther away from them. The fiery stallion was unable to break past the attacking mammoth of werewolves. Cedric clawed at the attacking horde, which became more hesitant in confronting him as they continued to lose more pack members. Angeline pulled her daggers, ready to slash any that came too close. Both of them were carrying the same thought on their minds, if she were to receive a single scratch or bite, there was a risk for her turning as well. There were plenty of accounts of witches and sorcerers being victims of vampirism, were-syndromes, and more.

They were back to back, but somehow he seemed agile enough to dispatch them before she had no choice but to attempt to strike. Barushka cried out, his flames bright as he broke through. Cedric gripped her by the arm and threw her into the saddle. Immediately she began making way with her arrows, trying to make a path through the chaos of drool and blood. A howl erupted and the werewolves scattered. Panting, the three of them stood alone, baffled. Nothing but the dead left on the ground and the flurries of winter's last snow falling.

Sliding down to his knees, Cedric tried to slow the boiling of his blood and bring his incubine excitement back to normal, suppressing his horns and claws. It was unclear as to why a pack of that size would retreat despite their hunger and tenacity. Barushka snorted and nudged at Cedric, insisting he stand. Something else was coming; Cedric could smell it over the scent of dog and blood that was engulfing the area. It had a smell of power and decay, which meant whatever was approaching, was an undead type of demon. Walking over the bodies, he found his sword and turned to face the direction he sensed it coming from. Shuddering from the ambiance of its power, Cedric tensed further knowing that this demon was either the master of the werewolves or something they feared. It was not long before a cloaked figure showed itself, pausing at a comfortable distance for both sides. Looking at the remnants of the battle for a moment, it lowered its hood revealing the yellow eyes, pale skin, and pointed ears. This was a vampire and a pureblood type. Tainted bloods tended to be disfigured, unable to keep consistent human facial features when near blood.

"What do you want?" Cedric stood between Angeline and the vampire, unsure of his intentions of interrupting their fight for survival. "Are you the master of these werewolves?"

"Yes, I am." It sheathed a sword that had been held out of view. "I apologize for the trouble, but I must ask you what is it that you want? Why have you come here?"

"I came here looking for information." Out of mutual respect, Cedric sheathed his own blade and motioned for Angeline to lower her bow. "I had no intentions of defiling this place, but the pack gave me no choice. I apologize for disturbing your territory; I didn't see any of the customary markers."

"Ah, understood. There were no markers indeed." Rubbing his chin, his long black hair ruffled in the snowy breeze. "I am Count Vladimir. Normally, I would not interfere with their eating, but I smelled something familiar. Was one of you hurt?"

"Just me." Cedric tensed up. "Why?"

"Who was your mother?" It was a deeply grave look he shot Cedric, his eyes sharp. "And who are you?"

"All I know is my mother was a moroi possibly from here. I am Cedric, the Demonic Knight." He huffed himself onto Barushka, keeping close to Angeline. "I was looking for information on the moroi and was told this had been the home of one."

"Then you have found it. Come, follow me if you wish to learn more about the moroi." He put his hood back on and motioned for them to follow.

Barushka had to stay at a solid gallop to keep up with Vladimir as he ran through the woods. There were no more signs of werewolves as they came to another clearing where a mansion sat in silence. Stopping at the gates, they waited for their host to unlock them and wave them in. The courtyard was large and overgrown as they approached the front doors. Cedric hesitated before going another step, his mind filled with the dangers of entering the home of a pureblood, where their powers held greater influence.

"Do not worry. We have no interest in the girl." Angeline bit her bottom lip in response to this notion. "She is your bound mate and we hold such bonds sacred. Purebloods often do the same with one another. Feeding from someone's bonded mate is a sin in our culture."

"I hear you can always take a vampire's word." Cedric's eyes flashed a warning, reassuring that the statement held weight. "I have never had the chance to test this. Don't make me regret it."

"My word is true. Come, I will tell you about this moroi you seek." Cedric gripped Angeline's hand as they followed him inside. She was sending wavering waves of panic as she struggled to keep herself calm. "It is your blood that has caught my interest; its scent was overwhelming. It holds my greatest concerns and not in terms of feeding, but in regards to the information you are seeking."

They came to a tall room that was much like the library at Cedric's manor, and there in the center sat a woman in a crimson dress. Her skin was white as milk, her brown wavy hair reached the floor, and her yellow eyes widened at the sight of Cedric. Vladimir removed his cloak and offered the seats that faced her before taking his place next to the woman in red. One bloody tear fell from the girl's eyes as she stared surprisingly at Cedric. Chills crawled across Cedric's skin as the scent from her tear, her blood, hit his nose. There was something uncanny and familiar about it. He had never come across a pureblood vampire before and here he sat in the home of two as their guests. There was something going on and centering on him.

"You said you suspected that the moroi from here was your mother, no?" Vladimir shot a look at his silent companion before looking back at Cedric. "I assume this relates to Sorceress Morrighan."

"Yes, since it's the only recent account in the last several hundred years of one being old enough to be forced to conceive a child through the use of dark magics." He looked from one to the other, seeing a look of concern that they held on those solemn faces. "What do you know about her?"

"She was ours." The woman's voice was like that of a songbird's and she looked off into the distance. "Was ours. She has left this world."

"Yes, that moroi was our daughter and there is no mistake that you are her son. I can smell our bloodlines within that magical concoction you call your blood." His yellow eyes faded for a moment before continuing his lecture. "The village here was kind to us. We provided protection to them on numerous occasions, and they were more than happy to raise and care for her. Our hope was to give her a normal, human life. We envy how fragile and simple their lives are and it was our hope that she get to experience that. Morrighan's chimeras came for her, destroying that dream, as we all failed to track them down in time. By this point, Morrighan and her bounded mate Boto had conducted their experiment, and she held the fruit of their efforts within her belly. There were no hopes for a pureblood to face Morrighan's magic and the army of the King Incubus. We had no choice but to give up after word had traveled of her and the newborn's deaths. The relief was that their creation had failed and she would not be suffering from a second attempt. They had shattered the village here, and those we had held dear. Seeing you here, and free of her magical leashes, gives me some hope after all. At least she bore a son capable of being a free-willed spirit."

"I'm an abomination." Cedric broke away from their hopeful stares, failing to keep the wave of anger that he sent up Angeline's hand before releasing his grip. "I have lived a wretched life and destroyed what I held close. I live to destroy Morrighan and to put an end to this torment she has created for everyone. My hope is to see her last breath before giving my own."

"I see." The woman's voice was soft as she reached over to touch his hand, her flesh cold. "You're so warm. She was warm like that."

"Excuse Charlotte." He pulled her hand away, wiping the tear off her cheek as she sat still as a statue. "She has been broken from this. There isn't much life left in her since she stopped feeding. In her eyes, she lived to see her daughter have a life of happiness, free of torment, and that was shattered."

"It's ok." Cedric's voice softened as he looked into faded, yellow eyes of pain. Charlotte's eyes held a look that he knew all too well from his own experiences. "It's not easy. It doesn't matter if you aren't human. We all hurt from loss."

"Precisely." A hint of a smile hit Vladimir's face, the first signs of his fangs they had seen all night. "And don't forget that. You and your lady may rest here. Please find sanctuary in our home whenever you find a need in the future. You are, by blood right, family and entitled to anything that is ours. Tomorrow, I will see what we can discover about inherited abilities. It seems there are some there, but that can wait until you've recovered from your wounds. I assume you were also looking to see what abilities a moroi held, being that you've fully mastered your incubine traits thus far."

"Thank you. That is one of my greatest concerns, in fact. With no books or knowledge out there of moroi traits other than how to identify them, I fear I have a harder time knowing when that bloodline comes forward and how to even use it. It's a great honor to be accepted in a pureblood's home like this." Cedric stood and bowed as he stared deep into Vladimir's eyes, having a newfound respect for him and his kind. "I look forward to learning more about my heritage from my very own grandfather."

Motioning Angeline to follow, Vladimir led the two of them to a room down the hall. The decorations in the room were extravagant in nature. Everything was covered in gold, silk, and ivory, far more outlandish than House de Romulus had been. The bed was huge and softer than any other she had sat on in the past. Cedric flopped face down onto the bed, exhausted from the fight still. Looking over, she was astonished to see that the wounds had already healed on his back, but her side was still throbbing. This was far faster than she had recalled he could heal. She reached over to rub her hand over it and in response received a wave of curiosity from him. His green eyes caught her brown ones, freezing her in the act.

"What are you doing?" He seemed irritated as he frowned at her. "Do you have to constantly touch me now?"

"I was just surprised." Jerking her hand away, her face reddened. "Your wounds are gone. Did you always heal this quickly?"

"Yes." He looked away. "I told you before; it wasn't the wounds that were the problem."

"I see." Relieving herself of her bow and pack, she curled up in the bed. "Sorry, I should listen to you more."

"How should you ever understand it?" It was a sour note that struck her hard. "You're too young and naïve."

Sliding out of the bed, Cedric left her sleeping there, knowing if anything should happen he would feel it from her directly. Pacing down the hall, he found Vladimir and Charlotte sitting in the library still. Nodding to one another, he followed his newfound grandfather to an empty ballroom where they both could speak freely. After smelling Charlotte's blood, Cedric understood the sensation which they had felt when they sensed his. It was the sensation of being part of one another and it resonated throughout the body. It was neither pain nor pleasure, like his experiences with his incubine traits, but something calm and stern. It was the embodiment of power and pride, ancient in touch, taste, and smell. There was no excitement or distraction from it, but a heightened awareness of his surroundings and the slowing of time.

"I take it you can feel it now?" Vladimir started rolling up his sleeves as he gave a coy smile. "That, my grandson, is the stronger of your two bloodlines. That is the same blood and power your mother held and that I even hold still. It is what allows you to push back the vile incubine taint, to be able to take in the energy of other demons and increase your healing by dining on humans. This is what adds to your strength, speed, and stamina. It is why the moroi are feared and hunted so severely. The moroi instincts fuel the tenacity in which you push yourself to your limits in order to survive, but also refine who you are. Do you feel how it vibrates so close to one with the same lineage? Like two crystals of the same pitch?"

"Yes. It is nothing like what I have felt before. It seems I have been using my moroi abilities this whole time, but why is it letting itself be known to me here?" Cedric watched as Vladimir walked over and bowed before a golden statue of a deity he had not seen before. It looked down at its follower surrounded by candles in peaceful calm. "I have never actually felt the blood itself like I have with the incubine blood. I have fought over the excitements, blood boiling over pleasures and pains, yet this one has stayed silent even in times when I now see it was in control. Is this normal?"

"Yes, your moroi lineage would never entice or distract you." Standing again, he walked to the far wall that held an array of strange weaponry from a distant land. "The nature of incubi is an animalistic one. They have been crawling on this earth longer than we vampires have, but nothing has changed through the age of time in concerns to them taming the blood they hold. Their cravings for desires of the flesh rule every movement and thought, yet no signs of them wanting to break free of this behavior. Thus, we consider them lesser beings. You, on the other hand, you have blindly struggled on your own. Using the unknown to drown the known is a courageous feat. It is this aspect that I admire most about how far you have come. Now you have met your rope's end, but fortune smiles down on you. You found me."

"A good friend of mine insisted that I was using my moroi side. I suppose I should have listened to the old dog more." Watching him remove one of the smaller sheathed daggers, he rolled his shoulders and popped his neck. "Are we planning to spar?"

"No, but I will need this if I wish to pass wisdom and awareness to you." Walking back to the statue, he held one arm out and sliced his wrist wide open, letting it spill into the golden cup that the figure held in two of its many hands. "This is not as ceremonious as the ritual would normally be for a pureblood. Under the circumstances, this is the appropriate time for you to take this in. Call this your rite of passage to be here."

"I don't understand." The smell of the blood engulfed him, making the vibration he was feeling increase. "What do you intend for me to do?"

"Drink." Filling the goblet, he allowed the cut to heal and placed the cold, black drink into Cedric's hands. "There will be no masquerade ball, nor the meeting of other pureblood lines and kin in your passage, Cedric. You have passed the traditional one hundred year mark and unlike your brethren, this is essential to your survival. Drinking the blood of one of your elders grants you their knowledge. You will absorb and retain abilities that this line holds, and information about who and what you are. It will be instant; as soon as you drink the last drop. It takes a particular amount for this to trigger and the process hits a point of acceptance shortly after that. In our society, this is handed down, given to the younger ones, but there have been those who take it forcefully for their own lusts for power. These sinners are sentenced to death. Please, take this gift that your mother was never able to give you directly, as I had done for her."

"She lived for a hundred years?" Their eyes locked, but the glare was unchanging from Vladimir. "I see, then I will drink."

Cedric held the cup to his lips, feeling the vibrating intensify his awareness. His own heart and blood had long gone quiet to him. The only sound that thudded in his ears was Angeline's beating heart on the other end of the manor. Other than this melody, the vibration of Vladimir and Charlotte's presence were his pillars of connection to a side he had had no access to until now. Taking one last breath, he engulfed the thick, cold lacquer. It was foul in flavor, almost choking him as he forced it down. As he drew more from the never-ending cup, his eyes began to roll back, fading to white. The last drop hit his tongue and unlike the icy, sour filth that had spilled forth prior, this one morsel was warm and sweet. It cleaned his palette as it slid back and into him, relieving him of the torment that had come before it.

A mixture of ice and heat filled his veins as he fell back in agony. His bloodlines twisted, recreating him in ways he could not grasp as memories from an ocean of individuals spoke to him all at once. Each had something important he needed to know, but there was one in that ocean that shined the brightest. Her red hair was a rose in the sea of black and her green eyes cut through him as it pushed him back out of this sea of chaos. Gasping, he rolled to his side, coughing. His body continued to tremble, his system in shock. His hair had lost its black tips and the way his blood fought to be cold or hot was alarming. It was like dying and coming back to life constantly. There was no pleasure from the pain he was enduring as he began to sweat and shake. He clenched his teeth as his head filled with information, feeling as if his eyes would burst. No longer able to contain it all, he let out a scream as the cold took hold and then exploded into a searing heat once again.

It was slow at first; the relief that the heat brought worked him over and took the pain of his blood battling itself away. Panting, it felt like he had spent several hours without the ability to breathe. After a few more minutes, he could hear the rushing of his own blood in his ears again. His vision blurred. He managed to sit back up as everything he retained started settling in his mind, finding its rightful places. As his eyes focused again, Vladimir drew closer; his yellow eyes seemed to glow. Closing his eyes, Cedric fought to regain his focus of thoughts, but the pain in his neck interrupted him. Vladimir had latched onto his neck, each swallow echoing in Cedric's ears. He could not move, but the pain soon started giving way to a new feeling. It was sentimental and comforting in nature, unlike the pleasure and arousal that he would have experienced before. It made him relax, drowsy even until he felt the release.

"I am sorry to alarm you." Vladimir wiped the blood from his mouth as he walked away. "It is customary that the receiver allow the other to drink from them, in hopes of exchanging any new adaptations or information. It is also how we try to check if you have a power lust."

"I would have liked a warning about how that was going to go." Rubbing his neck free of the excess blood, he was confident his bite mark had healed and gone. "Did you get anything out of that?"

"Yes. Normal purebloods experience only pleasure when drinking another's blood, but for you and your mother, it becomes a struggle of life and death before allowing you the information that it holds." He grabbed a larger weapon off the wall and slid it open to check the blade. "There is a power lust within you, but it's not the kind that reflects our definition. You do not have any desire to chase down other purebloods. If you are going to go to war, you will need a stronger sword, though. Take this daito from the distant land in the east. I was there for some time, and you have the art written in your blood. You should know by instinct how to use this curved long sword fit for any daimyo or lord. May it protect you in the future, my grandson."

Taking the sword from him, Cedric could feel the information there; no different from his sword training he had spent years obtaining. Battles that he never fought gave him in-depth experience and visions of a strange place echoed in his mind. The daito was light, and the craftsmanship was astonishing as he admired the strength in its folded metal. Sheathing it, he bowed to Vladimir, thankful that he had been lucky enough to receive so much from him.

He turned to the doorway, where Angeline stood wide-eyed. He had failed to consider that she would have experienced the whiplash of his pain, especially since he had failed to pull all of it to himself. Their eyes connected and she ran to him, hugging him tight, trembling against his chest. Her hair was covered in sweat and she was cold to the touch. Somehow, she managed to hold back the tears and sobs, but there was no mistaking that she had felt every drop of pain. He could feel the waves of her anxiety, fighting it along with the fear and confusion of what she had witnessed and felt. Nodding at Vladimir, they returned to their room. She stayed silent as they lay in bed, falling asleep from exhaustion.

CHAPTER 17

THE HUNT

Waking from the tickling in his nose, Cedric found himself hugging the sleeping Angeline. His nose and mouth shoved into
the top of her head, he indulged in breathing in her scent with
a long, drawn-out inhale. Huffing into her hair, she shook her head away,
snuggling her face into his forearms. The thoughts that came to him
were foreign, and it took a moment to get them to slow down and in
one language. All that knowledge taken in so suddenly was almost too
much for him. He understood now what he was capable of and, more
importantly, knew how to use his powers effectively. It was clearer to him
about why he had been seen as nothing more than a lost puppy to the
rest of the demonic world. His pride and false sense of security were far
from the truth of where he sat on the totem pole of power. Compared
to those on the list, not only was he lacking in brute strength and abilities, but also he was nowhere near having the amount of knowledge
and experience needed to take anyone down on the top of the pyramid.

A wave of anxiety snuck out of Angeline and he merely shoved his
cheek against her head. It dissipated and nothing but a soothing calm
started in its place. The sounds of her blood and heartbeat had taken on
a surreal presence, which excited him in so many ways that it made him
tense. The moroi blood had infused itself with the incubine bloodline.
He would have to learn how to read it all over again, including what its
intentions were toward Angeline.

*I can hear every part of her, the blood whispering through her body, the
song of her heart, and with the sense of touch that sends my skin crawling,
it is uncanny. Will I be able to control this new blend? I know that I was
made complete last night when the mix of my bloodlines was purified with
the help of the blood of my elder. My mind screams the answers, but I have
my doubts.*

"Why did you not cry or scream? Why did you willingly take the pain?" Angeline shriveled in his arms, spooked that he had noticed she was awake. "I couldn't take the pain away and I barely handled it myself."

"I promised not to cry anymore." Angeline was mumbling, trying to pull herself out of his arms as waves of panic and fear leaked from her. "Let me up."

"No." Nothing she did could budge his arms. "Take off your shirt."

"What?" The flush of anger and humility flooded from her as she tried to shove his arms off of her. "No! You can't be serious?"

"Stop thinking that way, pet. I can still feel the ache of your ribs on my own side, so let me have a look." He released her, and she sat up, her back to him in a desperate act to hide her face. "I don't have all day."

Reluctantly, she removed her shirt. Exposing herself to him made her feel even more vulnerable. The deep red and black that painted her side looked cruel against her skin. Cedric's hand gently slid across it and she flinched for a moment, fearing any pressure on the mark. Every breath she took, he could feel the sharp pang that she was receiving in his own lung and side. Her injury was far more serious than she even realized and was lucky not to be coughing up any blood. He slid his hand down and across the top of her hip as goose bumps scattered across her skin. Grabbing the chimera hilt of her dagger, he pulled it free, earning a bewildered glance from Angeline.

Sitting next to her, he ran the blade across his palm, sending only pleasure her way and with it, slicing the edge off her panic. Encouraging his cut to bleed, and blood to pool in his palm, he quickly started rubbing it into her side. Shoving her down on the bed, he applied overwhelming pressure that came to Angeline as nothing more than pure bliss.

Her body was heating up under his hands as she moaned in pleasure. He ran the blade across the mark and she trembled in excitement as she screamed and panted in response. A grin crawled across his face as he worked his own blood into her cut. Sweat started pouring from her and his incubine side was drinking up every wave of arousal she was giving him. The more he worked her side, the smaller her mark grew. His newfound wealth of knowledge was already serving him with great assistance. If he had known that his blood was capable of healing others, her ring finger would not be crooked. The cut on her side was closing, the pain of the broken rib no longer existing. Rolling her to her back, he leaned down, licking her from her navel to her neck, allowing the incubus inside him to continue to soak in her ecstasy. Angeline shivered in excitement, her pulse racing as he began sucking on her neck, his fangs lightly catching her skin, but never going any further than that.

Cedric took a firm grip on her crooked finger as he worked his lips to her ear, suckling on her earlobe, making her hum. He could feel that each time his breath grazed her neck, it would cause a pulse of delight from her. She was shaking in her frenzy of exhilaration.

His whisper came to her, "I think I do love you after all, Angeline."

With a ragged motion, the loud crack flooded her eardrums, and she felt the eerie sensation of her bone breaking away in the finger he had been gripping so tightly. A gasp fled her lips, and she screamed as her back bowed from an orgasm like no other she had felt before. Straddling her, he jerked her hand and finger to his lips, his teeth skimming across her skin. Sitting there on top of her, Cedric's green eyes grabbed hers and she watched as he sank one of his fangs into her finger, the other piercing his own tongue. The sensation astounded her for a moment as she watched him work, never breaking their gaze. He sucked on her finger, keeping it as straight as possible in doing so, despite his animalistic manner. The bloods in his mouth mixed and did their work to correct what he had failed to fix before. Releasing her finger, she could see that it was healed and straight. He leaned forward, kissing her passionately as the taste of his blood invaded her mouth, causing her skin to quiver with delight as she clung to him.

Angeline woke, still clinging to Cedric's chest as he slept. She stared at her left ring finger, no longer crooked or discolored, as it lay across his skin. For the first time, she actually felt like his lover. Despite his lascivious manner, it was the first time that he allowed himself to openly love her without some emotional barrier in place. The passion and want that she felt flooding out of him came in every action he performed. It was tender and strong, and it took all she had to catch her breath at each turn.

Hugging him tighter, he stirred and rubbed her arm as he kissed the top of her head.

Daylight crept out of the crack of the thick curtain, casting its light across their naked bodies. Her fingers rubbed across some of his scars, curious as to why he had so many with the healing power he possessed. His hand covered hers, swamping it with its warmth as his eyes met hers with the softest stare she had ever received from him. The smirk that came to his lips only caused her to smile in response as waves of emotions blended together in a torrent between the two of them. They had found peace for the first time with one another, and the bond that had been created under forceful circumstances took a calmer stance.

"Why do you have so many scars?" She furrowed her brow as she lifted up her hand to expose the one she had been rubbing on his chest. "You heal so quickly, yet these seem like old wounds?"

"It's my way of remembering mistakes." Taking in a deep breath, he sat up, stretching his arms out. "I can choose not to heal and leave behind a mark. I suppose it is a form of self-punishment for making the wrong choices. That one was a cheap shot from Romasanta as he fled Williamsburg. Let's wash up, we have a lot to do still."

As they left Vladimir's manor, there had been no good byes or even another encounter with him or Charlotte. Barushka was happy to see Angeline as she walked out into the bright of day, her wounds healed and her shoulders free of burdens of the mind and heart. They traveled down the path, passing through the ruins of the village. The corpses were gone; not even a single bone to be found. The dirt even appeared cleansed of the blood that had soaked it during their battle. Cedric released an ear-shattering whistle as he brought Barushka to a halt. Two werewolves bounded out of the nearby trees, bowing before them and no longer behaving like animals. They panted, drool oozing from their doggish lips as they obediently waited for the next command, tails wagging.

"How can I find Romasanta?" Cedric glowered down at them, his jaw twitching at the thought. "Where is your creator hiding?"

"We do not know, Master." A whimper came from both of them as they looked at one another, ears flattened and tails tucked under. "But we can provide some information."

"Go on then, what do you have?" Barushka stifled as one of them barked back into the woods, signaling for a gray-colored werewolf to stagger out. "You know something about Romasanta's whereabouts?"

"Yes, Master." The gray one bowed deeply, exposing the knotted scars that ran across his back. "I unfortunately crossed into his territory once and received my fitting punishment. He travels with lepers, my lord. Find them, and you shall find him."

"Lepers, you say?" A frown crossed his face as he looked at his new servants. "Thank you for the information. I should be able to track him down on my own."

"Sire, I recommend you travel to the west. One of our smaller hunting packs caught wind of a large group of lepers and merchants traveling toward a large trader's village." They all wagged their tails excitedly and began panting once more. "We hope this makes up for our disrespect from the other night."

"It does. Thank you." Cedric sighed as he stared down at them. A wave of sympathy leaked into Angeline who shared the same feeling toward the werewolves. "You may continue what you were doing before."

It took Cedric and Angeline weeks before they managed to come across the sound of bells. Bandaged and wearing rags for clothes, the pack consisted of men, women, and even children, who all rang bells in a ritualistic way as Barushka approached them. It had been a law of the land for any leper or diseased person to warn other travelers of their condition. Many of them had been given their bells from their hometown friends and family before exiling them to this sad life of weathering the elements until their bodies and lives gave way to death. The sounds of rattling coughs and smells of decaying infectious flesh engulfed the air around the small group, making the rhythm of the ringing a more daunting sound. Angeline pulled her turtleneck up over her nose, trying to limit her exposure and hoping to drown the smell out. Barushka even gave a snort, but still took a moment to get a giggle out of one of the sickly children who looked up at him in awe.

"Greetings!" Cedric's voice boomed over the ringing, demanding a moment of silence. "I am looking for a man by the name of Romasanta."

After a few moments of whispering, a man with a cane responded in a coarse voice, "Yes, we know him. He is a merchant who often joins us in travels and supplies us with food and goods. I believe he is still in Cerdanya, but the town can be unfriendly if you do not speak Kerretes or Catalan. Not everyone has accepted English as the new trade language, you see."

"I can speak both. Thank you." Reaching into one of the satchels, Cedric pulled a small pouch of gold and tossed it to the man. "May this provide you some aid on your travels. Are you headed to the lepers' colony?"

"Aye! Bless you, my son!" The group groveled at Barushka's feet. Some looked as if they were not capable of standing again after doing so. "We bid you a safe journey!"

With a few taps of his heels, Barushka started into a gallop down the road. When they had managed to gain enough distance, Cedric finally snorted and rubbed his own nose, their scent numbing his sensitive sense of smell. The closer they came to Cerdanya, the larger the road grew as more and more side paths joined it like streams into the torrent waters of a river. More and more travelers and wagons started gathering until it became so crowded that Barushka had no other choice than to slow his canter and fall back into a walk. Angeline enjoyed seeing all the different people and outfits. The colors of the strange fabrics she saw were mind-blowing to her. Her ears struggled to catch the foreign languages whispered between merchants and travelers as they haggled over items and prices. The view she held of the world was expanding at every turn that Cedric took her down.

Passing through a heavily guarded gate, they came into the main street, where many wagons and shops were set up. Goods of all kinds lay across blankets and tables: Weapons, armor, food, and leathers of all types embellished the sides of the street as far as the eye could see. They both dismounted; nodding to one another, they each took a side of the street in hopes of finding information faster. Cedric switched languages with the greatest of ease as he pulled from his inherited knowledge. So far, they had shrugged and knew no one by that name, but suggested he ask a few of the other men deeper down the street. It wasn't uncommon to hear of a merchant traveling with lepers, but not very many admit it openly in fear of losing customers.

Angeline stood for several minutes in front of the first merchant, gawking at all the weaponry, lost in her own thoughts. Finally, the merchant spoke to her, but she did not understand anything he was saying. She lowered her turtleneck, trying her best to illustrate and say she did not speak his language. Looking her over and catching a glimpse of the bow and chimera hilt, he switched to English. Her ranger persona must have given her more acclaim than she realized, and the man greeted her in a heavy accent.

"Lady Ranger! Welcome! What is it that you look for?" A golden tooth glinted in the sunlight as he bowed his head to her. "A weapon, perhaps?"

"Yes." She was slow to respond as she turned her glare back to the display of items. "I was thinking of a special blade for my lord."

"Ah! I have many blades!" He made a sweeping motion with his arms. "What kind did you have in mind for your master and lord? A dagger? Short blade? Perhaps a new sword for tournament fights?"

"What kind of enchanted blades do you have?" His smile faded, and the scowl she received was not very comforting. "I did not mean to offend you. I'm so sorry."

"It is ok." Shouting in his strange language, he clearly asked an old man sitting on the ground behind him something. After a moment of back and forth, he turned back to her. "You are looking for magical items, yes? You should see the merchant farther down the street. Many of us fear to carry such dangerous items."

"Yes, thank you for the help." She pulled her turtleneck back up, bowing lightly to him as a form of thanks. "How will I know it's him?"

"He will have a large assortment of women's attire and jewelry. He is a tall, white man, broad shoulders and one of the tallest merchants I have ever seen. I believe he goes by the name Blanco." He pointed down the street to a back corner area, motioning with his hand that it was right where the street takes a slight bend to the left. "He usually sets up in that small outlet. Good luck, my Lady Ranger."

It took her a while to work her way through the crowded streets. Cedric had warned her that the busier the street, the more likely one's money would be lifted from their belongings. She was careful not to bump into other pedestrians for fear of being mistaken for a pickpocket, and dodged several shady characters with hungry eyes that seemed to lean toward her. Occasionally, she received a double look from the various men who made up the majority of the travelers here. It was hard to say if they were shocked to see a demon-hunting ranger, since no one else was dressed like her, or had realized she was female and not a young man. Shivering at the idea, she pulled her hood over her head a tad more to regain confidence that her face was hard to make out. Cedric had beaten it into her that she was to wear shades of black and green, insisting on certain types of attire, and had given her symbols to pin to her clothing. Her boots laced to just above her knees, a short hooded cape sat over her shoulders where she wore a long sleeve turtleneck accented with a laced-up vest that helped push her breast tight to her body. Its design optimized her abilities as an archer, and being a female, it was very important that men they came across in their travel could not tell so easily. It also allowed her breasts to be suppressed and not block her posture for a proper shot. She had seen huge improvements in her archery thanks to the outfit.

Reaching the nook just off the main street, she approached the blankets covered in merchandise. Jewelry, belts, and dresses filled them and the designs made her cousin's collection look like it belonged to a street sweeper's wife. Looking about, she saw no one, but took a moment to squat, taking a closer look at the assortment of rings. The variety of jewels and precious stones amazed her as she picked up one particular ring with its eye-catching deep blue gem. It was teardrop shaped with small pearls on either side as the gold braid band made its loop around. *I wonder if it would fit?*

"That one is cursed, they say." She dropped the ring as the deep voice snapped her out of her thoughts. "I'll sell it for half the price it's worth. I have had no luck with selling that one."

"Excuse me, are you Blanco?" Standing, Angeline brushed her knees off and looked up at the brown eyes of the man who easily beat Cedric by several inches. "I am looking for enchanted blades."

"I am Blanco, and that's a tall order you are asking for." He scratched his short beard for a moment as he stared at her, snorting for a moment. "But for you, Lady Ranger, I think I can oblige. I keep such wares in my wagon, you will have to follow me into the alley to the recently burned-out courtyard. It no longer bears signs of the plague, but many do not mess with me there. It has been a long while since I've seen a demon-hunting ranger in this area, but it was common to have them ask for such items."

"Do you have very many blades?" Angeline watched as he rolled and folded the blankets so that he could lug the merchandise over his shoulders. "I want to buy a blade for my lord."

"I have several enchanted and cursed blades. So Lady Ranger, who is your lord?" She followed him down the alley, feeling safe, seeing that his hands were full of his own merchandise. "I do not see rangers or ladies here in Cerdanya very much. I have traveled far and wide and it is pleasant to see people not from my homeland here."

"I am Lady to the Lord Romulus." It was awkward to say it, but it was the truth and the correct way of answering such a question. "Have you heard of him?"

"Lord Cedric de Romulus. The demonic knight from Williamsburg," He grunted as he repositioned the heavy blankets of goods on his shoulders. "Si, I've heard of him. Met him once before, in fact."

Cedric was growing more and more annoyed as he went from one merchant and the next. Bouncing between what felt like a dozen or more people, all of them reluctant to answer his questions. Mentioning anything about lepers was shutting down any further information, and he was running out of ways to ask. There were so many scents in the air in town, making it impossible for him to smell Romasanta out. His nose and senses had been flooded the moment they came within visual range of the lepers and their diseased flesh. Now in the busy commotion of Cerdanya, the smells were thicker, besides the smell of spices and foreign cured leathers, there was the pungent burned smell of wood and flesh from the recent fires to free a section of the town from the black plague.

He doubled back and started on Angeline's side. Looking around, he walked up the street, but could not see her in the crowds of people. Huffing, he knew she was fine. If she were in danger, he would have felt her signal, the same one she had managed to use when she ran into the chimeras. He approached the merchant that he had seen her first speak to before he got distracted by the reactions from the other merchants. His selection held a wide variety of weapons of Arabic design, but he spoke in the local tongue, Kerretes. It was still awkward to Cedric's ears and tongue to jump through languages in the blink of an eye. There was so much that his new abilities had to teach him and the knowing without experiencing firsthand was hard to comprehend. It was like trusting something he could not see or confirm that it really existed, but just needed to let it perform in the open for reassurance. His ears honed in on the private conversation as he stood there.

"*<Did you say something about blades of magic?>*" Cedric's Kerretes carried no accent, and he caught the attention of both the elderly man and the merchant as he eavesdropped into their conversation. "*<I am shocked to hear that someone would risk carrying that sort of merchandise.>*"

"*<Yes, the Lady Ranger was asking if I had any.>*" The merchant scratched the back of his head for a moment. "*<There is only one merchant in town who braves to sell those things.>*"

"*<Which way did the Lady Ranger go?>*" Cedric's instincts were turning and his blood rushed in response to the information, making him tense. "*<Where is this merchant that she went to?>*"

"*<Why are you looking for her?>*" The old man staggered to his feet with a look of concern. "*<Who are you and why would you to brave searching for a ranger of her caliber>?*"

"*<I am her lord and she is my lady.>*" The look he shot them sent their faces white. Cedric made it clear that they had made a mistake in questioning his business. "*<Who did you send my lady to?>*"

"*<The merchant down in the nook.>*" Shakily, they both pointed in the direction that Angeline had gone. "*<To the man named Blanco.>*"

"*<Blanco.>*" His jaw twitched as the heat of his anger seeped forward, his muscles becoming taut as he gripped the hilt of his daito. "*<Don't you mean Romasanta?>*"

"*<Yes, that's the one!>*"

They watched in confusion as Cedric took off down the street.

Shoving through the crowd, angry shouts echoed behind him from the sudden intrusion. Deeper down the street he went, as he looked for signs of Angeline. Nothing was giving him a clue as to where she had gone. The inability to sense where she physically was became a startling realization on his part. Their bond was limited and without the other one sending out some sort of emotional wave or a stab of pain or pleasure, it was like searching for a coin in the vast darkness. Grabbing up different men, they all pointed to the same back corner when asked if they saw a ranger pass through. Propelling himself free of the crowd, he stumbled into the abandoned nook. The only thing he had to go by was the narrow alley leading into the abandoned part of the town, which had two fresh sets of footprints.

Sweat crawled down his temple and cheek as he launched himself into another run. His nerves were overriding his senses and if he could calm down, he would have a chance to hear her beating heart, or at least over the sound of his own thudding against his chest. This was the worst place for him to be with his new abilities. Entering Romasanta's territory was a rash move to begin with. Surely, his scent was all over her, and with each stride, he felt more foolish for not taking the time to think this hunt for Romasanta through. Between his blood healing and the dagger, Angeline would have smelled identical to him. Cursing between pants, he could feel his incubine blood raging to be set free, making promises that the other blood knew it was incapable of achieving alone. This new awareness of his powers and demonic sides was like choosing between alternate versions of himself, yet they were still the same mind and heart.

I'm a fool! I should have kept her by my side! I know better than this. Why did I let myself fall in love again? Losing Yvette destroyed me. But Angeline, if I lose her—She's fine, she has to be. Wherever she is, she is not in pain and even if harm came to her, I can go as far as to take that from her no matter how far away he takes her. Damn it! Where are you?!

"ANGELINE!" His voice roared throughout the small courtyard as he came out the backside of the alleyway. "Angeline..."

"Cedric?" She was squatting over a selection of blades, but he saw no one else. "What's wrong?"

"Where is he?" Angeline's face paled as she stared into a face of pure rage. And she barely caught her own breath as the wave of emotions from him hit her. "Where is Romasanta?"

CHAPTER 18

ROMASANTA: FATHER OF WEREWOLVES

"Here." Blanco Romasanta walked out of the nearby wagon, his brown eyes turning yellow. "I could smell that she was yours. Seeing that you were able to find me, I assume that's why you have come so far. You were looking for me specifically."

"Roma...santa?" Stumbling to her feet, Angeline rushed herself behind Cedric as her nerves frayed. "Cedric, I—"

"Just stay back. This is between him and me." The tension between their stares had an unmistakable loathing. "It's been a very long time, Romasanta, since we last saw each other in Williamsburg."

"Maybe for you, but I must admit, you have grown since your days of pouting like a little girl." Romasanta was eerily calm as he took his time taking off his vest and shirt, and even sitting on the wagon wheel to pull his shoes off. "I can't believe you would willingly let your pet wander about in my territory without a more watchful eye. I could have picked her ribs clean with my teeth in the time I have spent with her. If it were not for the stench of your blood mixed with hers, of course, I would have indulged in doing so. No offense, Lady Ranger. However, it is shocking to see you bound to a magic user. I was hoping your hatred of their kind would keep you from searching for me, but here we all are."

"She can take care of herself." Cedric snarled at Romasanta, who stood up just wearing his pants, exposing the bare chest that had a burned rune down the center of it. "I owe you payment for what you did in Williamsburg! How dare you come to my town, dig up the graves, rob their dead bodies, and then dare to kill me with my own father's sword!"

"Well now, aren't we sour about that ordeal? I have learned there is no shame in gathering supplies from the dead, but you were so lost sulking in your own filth that I did not think it mattered that much. Survival takes precedence, and the dead are no longer actively surviving. Last I checked. As for the sword, it was on the top of the pile when I reached for a blade, nothing personal. Just reacting to an attacker. I was in the middle of digging when you came at me from behind." As he cracked his neck, he grew larger and taller. Fur exploded across his body as his face stretched and distorted into a large wolf-like head. He was far more humanoid than all the other werewolves they had encountered, and the bulk of his neck and shoulders made the fur look like a massive lion's mane. "Let's see if we learned any new tricks in the last seventy-eight years."

"I've learned plenty." Growling, Cedric willingly let his horns and claws come out in force. "You took something very important from me. Between that and the stunt you just pulled, you've earned a permanent spot on my shit list."

"Do you realize who or what you are challenging, pup?" Taking an offensive stance, Romasanta's voice was no longer humanistic. A rumbling demonic one with an eerie calm to it had taken its place as his yellow eyes flashed. "Does your moroi side tell you what the strigoi know about me? I am interested in knowing if that blood knowledge applies to something like you. I can smell Vladimir's touch on you, and trust me, he wouldn't dare to walk into my territory."

Cedric gritted his teeth and fangs as he stared up at Romasanta. The moroi in him shouted that he should not be attempting to challenge someone as old and ancient as the Father of Werewolves. His incubine instincts shivered with delight at being in the presence of a demon more powerful than King Boto. All he could do was beg his bloodlines to work together. Now that Romasanta knew about Angeline, he could not look weak. This was no longer a question of who had more brute force, but whose knowledge and experience could possibly serve them better. He tossed his daito to Angeline as he took an offensive stance as well. Nothing he could think of could make the knot in his gut reside. According to everything his mind knew about the cursed man before him, there was a very high chance that he might not be able to walk away from this fight.

Romasanta snorted as his lips curled into a coy smile, his sharp teeth showing. Cedric launched himself, taking a full swing at the demon. Much to his surprise, Romasanta had gripped his wrist and forearm, leading him around, and back in the direction he had come. With amazing force, he threw Cedric into the wall next to Angeline. Yelping from the sensations she was receiving from Cedric, she stumbled away from the explosion of cobblestone. A hole in the wall marked where he had hit. Angeline used her arms to block the debris that flew down on her as she tripped and fell to the ground. Kicking herself along the ground, she watched as a bloody hand gripped the lower part of the broken wall. The dust dissipated, revealing a panting Cedric. He was shocked by the unexpected feat of power and staggered over the crumbling wall, blood painting the ground under each step. Spitting at the ground, his green eyes flashed angrily as the black tips of his hair crept into place.

Romasanta shook his massive head, chortling as he rolled one of his shoulders, cracking the joint. Taking a deep breath, Cedric launched a second assault, dodging the counter swipe from Romasanta's massive claws. He managed to land a scratch across his backside, only to smack his own back into the wall that he sorely misjudged. Missing the sudden snap of Romasanta's wolf-like jaws, they found themselves staring nose to nose. Cedric could feel his skin crawl in fear for the first time in ages. Grinning wildly, the demon's breath swamped him as Romasanta hummed to Cedric in a questioning manner, as if asking, "What are you going to do now?" In a moment of desperation, Cedric kicked himself off the wall, ramming his horns into Romasanta and breaking himself out of the corner.

After gaining some distance, Cedric tried for another attack. Their claws met, both shaking from the force they placed against each slash. Claws dug in around Cedric's shoulder, spinning him around in a moment of confusion. Brown eyes of surprise locked with his own and before his senses could warn him, Romasanta rammed his head into the back of his left arm's elbow. The sound of snapping erupted and the cry of pain hit both Cedric and Angeline's faces. Releasing his shoulder, Romasanta let Cedric fall face forward onto the ground of the courtyard as Angeline dropped her bow and arrow. She was screaming as tears streamed down her face. The father of werewolves snorted as he walked away, back to his wagon as he shook off his demonic form. He sat once more on the wagon wheel, lighting his pipe. He took a few puffs as he waited for them to stop their cries of agony.

"Lady Ranger." Romasanta blew the smoke smoothly from his lips as his yellow eyes waited for hers to meet his. "You should have listened to your lord to stay out of the fight. His arm and your pain were an unwanted result because you thought you could assist by aiming your arrow at me. I have no patience for such tricks, and I am far too old to play with him after such a lack of respect on your part. Nonetheless, I respect your courage, and against some other opponent, I hope you do not hesitate to use that tactic."

"How did you do it?" Cedric's hair was turning black, sweat pouring across his body as he stared at his broken joint from where he lay with his face in the dirt still. A bone peeked through a tear in his skin; his blood pulsed past the obstruction, pouring across the ground. "What did you do to undo my control of our bond? How did you stop it from working?"

"Nothing." Grunting, he started to put his boots back on, clenching his pipe in his teeth. "A moment of confusion can be one of the most deadly weapons in a battle. Not only is that moment a break in thoughts and movements, but it is capable of interrupting abilities. You can thank me later for this essential life lesson. Remember it well; it may save your life one day."

"I see." Moaning as he pushed his bone back under the skin, he shuddered as he fought the incubine's want for more. "I should have never come. What do you plan to do with me, since I clearly have trespassed?"

"Nothing." Romasanta pulled his shirt back on and buttoned it quickly. "I merely wanted to show you your place. It seems no one has taken the time to do you this favor. You are welcome, pup. I admit it's been a while since I have had someone land a mark, so you get some merit for that accomplishment."

"You are setting me free?" Staggering to his feet, Cedric held on to his broken elbow, which was not healing as swiftly as he wanted. His body struggled to slow the bleeding and Cedric was failing to push his incubine blood into remission. "What makes you think I will willingly go?"

"That." Pausing, he nodded in Angeline's direction where she sat leaning against the wall, panting from the replaced sensation of pleasure Cedric was sending her from his own extreme injury. "That is why you will leave Cerdanya and give up this futile attempt at revenge. You came here over false pretenses, anyhow. Young, you failed to see the world does not revolve around you, Cedric. "

Cedric stared at Angeline as he watched a drop of sweat slide down her cheek. After a moment of fighting his own thoughts and feelings, he sighed heavily as he returned his gaze to Romasanta. "You're right."

"Si, I am always right, my friend." Romasanta took another puff of his pipe as he gave Cedric a pat on the back. "Come on, you look too pitiful in front of your lady. Perhaps I will cut you some slack for still being new to this world over the rest of the monsters, like myself."

Cedric leaned against the wagon as he watched Romasanta finish smoking his pipe. His yellow eyes lingered, but the rest of his werewolf features had disappeared quickly. Keeping some distance between him and Angeline, Cedric was struggling with getting the broken bone to set right. His skin was burning, blood rushing as the moroi inside him whispered notions of thirst for healing. The red in his hair had gone completely black, and from the corner of his eye, he could see that Angeline was watching him. Her hand shook as she kept a tight grip on the chimera hilt. It had been a while since they had to face this side of him and he had used that very dagger on himself in desperation to keep his actions in check. They both jerked as Romasanta stepped into his wagon and rummaged through his belongings.

Shuddering, Cedric took a seat on the wagon wheel a few more steps farther from Angeline, but it brought him no relief. The pain in his arm was still exciting him and the act of defeat had thrilled his incubine side. Unlike the time when he had desperately put his arm in Wylleam's fireplace, he was having an easier time keeping it at bay but still lacked trust that his vampiric teachings could handle the carnal side he possessed. Angeline, on the other hand, continued to sweat, her breaths short and quick as her body took each pang from his arm in the form of extreme arousal. The bond was exhausting her beyond measure as her dilated pupils looked at him under a furrowed brow. At least he had pushed back his horns and claws. *I am so sorry for this mess. If I had stayed beside you, you would have never had to experience this. Hate me if you need to, my Angel.*

"Ah, here you go. I believe this is what you were pissed about." Romasanta came out, grabbed Cedric's right hand, and placed something in it. "I see you two are missing this."

"But this is—" His green eyes were wide as he stared at the pair of rings in his hand, one with a blue gem between two pearls. "You never sold them?"

"I tried, but fate must have decided that you would earn these back. Today was your lucky day since out of the lot your Lady Ranger picked your rings out." Angeline's eyes glazed over and she was no longer reacting to the world around her. The extreme shock of pain and the choking wave of pleasure had been too much for her. "My, you may want to get yourselves taken care of. I will let Cerdanya's inn know you will be staying as my personal guests. Heal up and we will have a drink with one another for fun."

Romasanta stepped over Angeline as he walked away down the alleyway. Cedric stared at the rings with matching bands, one jeweled and the other simply sharing the same braided gold band design. He had chosen these rings for his marriage to Yvette, yet Angeline had found them by fate. Shoving them in his pocket, he choked back the old emotions as he looked at Angeline. The love he felt now was something so much more, not the foolish love he had chased so long ago. His arm still throbbed while his skin crawled in pleasure as he walked to where she leaned against the cobblestone wall. She was still breathing fast and her knuckles were white from the force of her grip on the dagger's hilt. He squatted before her, and slid the back of his fingers across her feverish cheek.

The point of the dagger dug into his neck as she struggled to hold her eyes open. It only excited him more, and another cruel wave hit her as she gasped in response. They stared at each other, both of them a complete wreck. Pushing her wrist down, he took the dagger from her and sheathed it. Her scent was intoxicating when he was like this, and he found himself paused there so close to her, taking in the smell as deeply as his lungs would allow him. Sighing, he pulled her onto his bad shoulder, since at least that arm was capable of holding her there for the walk to the inn.

"Stop." Her voice cracked as it came to his ears. "You're injured. I can walk. I just need some time."

"Don't say any more, pet." He tightened his grip on her as he walked down the alleyway. "We both know you are overwhelmed. Let's worry about getting behind a closed door."

No one questioned what had happened as they were pointed to the room at the end of the hall. Most of the town avoided stares, acknowledgment, or even speaking to them. There was a strong unspoken policy of minding one's business here in Cerdanya, which explained why Romasanta was comfortable being here. As he kicked the door to their room closed, Angeline wiggled to be let down. Kneeling, he slid her off his aching shoulder, failing to not move his arm and giving both of them a jolting reaction. He turned away from her, avoiding seeing her face at this point as he locked the door. Angry fists whammed him in the back, catching him by surprise as he felt her lay her forehead against his back. Frozen, he could hear her choking back her tears.

"Please don't turn around." Her fist pounded against his back once more and she clenched her teeth as she poured out her next words. "I don't want to care, but I don't want to hate—"

"Angeline." Another strike from her fist hit him. "It's okay."

"No. No, it's not ok." Her forehead rubbed against his spine as she shook her head, warm tears hitting his skin aroused his boiling incubine blood. "I don't want to hate you, and I hate it when I can feel you're so broken. I hate myself for not being stronger, for crying after I promised not to. Why do you destroy yourself like this?"

"I'm sorry." Closing his eyes, he sighed as she hugged her arms around him, sobbing. "This was all a mistake coming after Romasanta. Every instinct told me not to come. I never meant for this to go so sour, pet."

"Don't call me that." Her arms dropped, and she walked away.

After a moment, he turned to face the blotched face of Angeline, who sat on the bed. The fierce look in her eyes was captivating as he approached her. Staring up at him, she had managed to keep the tears back after struggling so hard. The bitter bite of the tone she carried was striking him hard, but it did nothing to belittle the fleshly wants that made his blood rush. Pulling her shirt off, she leaned her head and neck, as if offering it to him. The motion enraged him and he shoved her back on the bed, his left hand on her throat as he snarled at her. His left arm only sent the two of them into a heated pant. Trembling under his weight, fear took its place in her eyes as she realized how much more aggressive he was when the black hair of his incubus side was in full bloom. Despite the arousal from the touch of his skin, she couldn't stop the racing of her heart as panic seeped forward.

"I don't want your blood." Cedric growled, still holding her throat. "And I am in no mood for your tantrums."

She swallowed in response, and after a minute, she weakly replied, "It won't happen again."

"Good." Releasing his hold on her throat, he gave her a sorrowful look. "I don't want you to be afraid of me, but it can't be helped."

She opened her mouth, but was lost for any words to come out.

"I don't want you to hate me, but if it makes you feel better, you may do so. Yes, I am a broken creature, and that is just part of what I am. This thing you lay with, that you call your lord, is no man. I am your demon, and you, you are my angel." Leaning down, he gave her a kiss of longing and her lips returned the emotion without hesitation. "Forgive me for being so reckless with both our lives."

He tried to pull away, but she grabbed his arm, the pain pausing him in his movements. The look of hurt on her face caught his attention. Laying back beside her, he scooped her into his arms, ignoring the crackling of the bone that struggled to reconnect and heal. Nuzzling her neck, he kissed it gently, feeling the goosebumps flow across her skin. A smile crept across his face as a wave of arousal washed over him from her. She kissed his arms gently and rubbed her cheek against them, treasuring the security she felt. He was her shield, and she had failed to be anything for him. In her daze of thoughts, she felt his finger slide something onto her left ring finger. Pulling her hand into her line of sight, she looked in awe at the blue sapphire and shining pearls that fit too elegantly on her finger.

"You're the only one I want." His lips tickled her ear as he spoke. "I truly love you and want to live for only you."

Spinning in his arms, she rubbed his jaw, blood still staining his face from his collision into the wall. "I love you, Cedric. You are far better than any man I have ever met, and you have given me so much. I am your lady, and you are my lord."

Romasanta was in the tavern when Cedric finally made his way back downstairs. He had not vanished as he had feared, and as Cedric sat next to him, he ordered him some mead. After several minutes of sitting and drinking in silence, Romasanta spoke.

"I see you recovered rather quickly." He took down the last of his clear drink as he shot Cedric a side-glance. "Quite impressive. Did you drink from her?"

"No." Cedric paused from his mead and shot an angry glare. "I have other ways to absorb the energy needed to heal."

"Ah, I forgot about that." Speaking in Kerretes, he asked for a bottle of vodka and poured himself another glass. "Being an incubus has its perks, I would imagine. If I could hump anything and get some sort of nourishment from the act, I would never stop! Ha!"

"Speak for yourself. It's a troublesome talent if you ask me." He finished the mead and looked curiously at Romasanta's colorless drink. "What is this vodka that you drink?"

"Oh! This is a new drink. Have some." He generously poured some into Cedric's mug. "Go on! It's made by the lepers from the stores of potatoes they have."

"It barely has a smell to it and it looks like water." Cedric raised an eyebrow before taking a gulp, which resulted in a few rounds of coughing. "And it has a stout bite. This is most foul."

"Just watch. It'll stick for centuries to come." Romasanta grinned widely as he poured more for himself. "Now, I have been thinking, pup. You plan to go to war against Morrighan, si?"

"If I can pull together an army." He took in the vodka at a slower pace. "But I will need to find a lot more of your mutts to be able to get enough to have a slight chance of breaching the front lines and castle gates."

"I assumed you would take advantage of that trait." Leaning back, Romasanta scratched at his beard a moment. "Don't think this is to help you, but it's just convenient timing. There are a few things I have wanted to do, and this seems like a good time to invest my time for a change."

"You mean to tell me you have plans and wants?" Cedric gave him a smug smile. "I am curious to hear what these things are."

"Well, I can get you your army within the week." Cedric frowned and Romasanta saw the concerned look he wore on his face. "Being the Father of Werewolves, my call takes priority over their vampiric masters. A lot of strigoi these days have been collecting my offshoots like weeds and then encouraging their growth via breeding or ravaging towns. I am responsible for letting the curse boil over so much. I will call them to arms and lead the war efforts on your behalf in hopes of annihilating the cursed ones and the chimera abominations from the earth."

"Is that all? You only wish to wipe out chimeras, your cursed underlings, and make a clean slate again?" The tavern keep gave him another mug of mead as Cedric leaned back, staring at Romasanta. "Is there anything else?"

"Yes." He guzzled the last of the vodka from the bottle and slammed it on the table. "You must kill Boto."

"I hope to kill him and Morrighan." Cedric snorted as he washed the vodka flavor from his tongue with the mead. "It is the reason why I am going to war."

"You did not hear me, pup. *You* must kill Boto." His tone darkened as he leaned toward Cedric, the brown eyes faded to yellow. "That creature has crossed me one time too many, and if you dare to spare his life, I will devour your Lady Ranger. I have grown tired of Boto as the king incubus. It is long overdue for a new king to take his place."

"How do you suppose I assure his death, then?" Pissed at the threat, Cedric's jaw twitched as he stared into the eyes of a devil. "I have had no luck finding information on how to ensure I kill him."

"You are his offspring. That is all that is required in their caste for one to kill another. To be the strongest incubus, you simply have to hold some blood in your veins of being one and the ability to defeat the current king." Romasanta snorted, appalled and frustrated to have to explain so much. "You are too wet behind the ears. Perhaps I am putting too much faith in you."

"Then I should be fine. Boto will not live, if that's what it takes to keep your filthy teeth out of Angeline's ribs." Cedric earned a wicked grin from Romasanta. "This is a deal that stands for the rest of her lifetime, yes? That you and your mutts are to never to harm her as long as I hold up my end of the bargain."

"Si, it holds true." They both returned to leaning on the table, indulging in their drinks in silence.

CHAPTER 19

ARMY VERSUS THE PACK

Barushka shook his head as he and Angeline watched Cedric and Romasanta stand on a hilltop comparing a map to the landscape. It had been unsettling to be traveling with something like the father of werewolves. More disturbing was to hear the occasional werewolf running in the woods about them, or one appearing to make its report and vanishing again. After being overwhelmed in the small village by Vladimir's castle, it was unnerving to think she would soon be seeing the complete population of Romasanta's cursed ones. In smaller packs, they were easy to take down, but the larger the pack, the more impossible of a feat it becomes. Somewhere out of sight, just deep enough in the woods, was an army of werewolves awaiting the command to charge the field.

Chills ran across her skin at the realization, despite the heat of the sun that glared down at her. Spring was in full swing, and not even a chill on the breeze remained. It was so beautiful to watch the flowers sway in the wind down in the valley past the hillside from where they stood. Unfortunately, the black castle obstructed the peaceful scene. Morrighan's cathedral of dark magic looked like Death standing in the distance as dragon-sized, vulture-like creatures circled above it as if zeroing in on a corpse. This was where they would wage war. She had asked Cedric why he was continuing to chase after this suicidal attempt, but all he did was furrow his brow and keep silent as his jaw muscles tightened. He was no longer chasing the same vengeful emotion as before. Those breathtaking waves of emotion had subsided sometime after leaving Vladimir's estate. There was a new silence in any emotional reaction from him since his fight with Romasanta.

Behind her, she heard the rustling of the bushes and, much to her relief, she saw Wylleam. He nodded his dog-like head as he passed by and approached the two men. She watched as Romasanta and Wylleam shook hands, and the ruffling of Wylleam's hair and mane was hard not to take notice. Romasanta's power was visible, and it astonished her why she had not seen it that first moment she had met him. There was no mistaking that he was ancient, and that there was something in this fight for him. Otherwise, why would someone as smart and skillful as the father of werewolves bother to involve himself in a war? Looking over at Cedric, she caught his green eyes and he once more wore a look of concern. Seeing Cedric's distraction, Wylleam looked back at her and his long ears flattened as if he knew of what troubled his friend. All she could conclude was that he was going to war with Morrighan for her sake. A bargain or threat held Cedric in its strings, using her at the core.

"The spirits are in quite the uproar over this." Wylleam had turned back to Romasanta. "I cannot sleep, for their cries are so loud. Despite this, they understand the intentions and give you both their blessings to clean up the messes that have been made. One voice discourages this event, and that is the ancestor of Angeline. You both must watch her whereabouts in this battle; something may go wrong according to that one. That spirit knows too much about the things to come. I do not enjoy listening to either the old witch's ramblings or her anger."

"Tell her to show herself if she's got an issue with my ongoings. She chose me against my will for her descendant to bind with. It cannot be undone because what I do displeases the old hag." Scoffing Cedric looked over the map once more. "Should we follow one of the packs that will be providing an attack from the sidelines?"

"No, Morrighan and Boto will both be focused on your location above all else. I will provide a distraction in the heat of battle, east of the gates here. No one will be expecting me to join this fight. This should draw both their attention long enough for my elite pack members to open a line for Barushka to lead you swiftly through the gates. Reserve your strength; let the dogs do the fighting. If you are to succeed, you need all your energy for Boto." Sniffing the air for a moment, Romasanta then refocused on the map. "It seems the last pack just arrived within the territory. We will rest here tonight and ready ourselves for war tomorrow."

"Right, we will follow your lead, Romasanta." Cedric rolled up the map and handed it to him. Exchanging stern looks, they guaranteed one another of the verbal contract made in Cerdanya. "Now, if you don't mind, I would like to catch up with my friend."

"Understood." Romasanta shook Wylleam's hand once more, showing the utmost respect for the shaman. "I regret meeting you under such circumstances. Take care, Shaman."

"Same here." Shuddering off the weight of Romasanta's aura, Wylleam returned to where Barushka stood. "Good to see you well, Angeline."

"Same to you, Wylleam." It was clear there would not be any answers to why she was the center of attention. "Am I staying in camp for the battle or riding with you, Cedric?"

"You will ride with me." Cedric rubbed the bridge of Barushka's nose, avoiding eye contact with Angeline. "I want you close, where I can see and protect you best."

"I wouldn't want to be anywhere else." After watching Cedric for a moment, she nodded to Wylleam. "Let me get back to camp then. I have a lot of preparing to do and gear to mend. Farewell."

Cedric watched as she disappeared down the backside of the hill before turning to Wylleam. "Thank you for coming."

"You are my close friend." Walking over to an old fallen log, he took a seat, laying his shaman's staff across his lap. "My place is to come to your aid and support. Though, I must ask you something, and though the spirits tell me, I would like to hear the truth from you. Why are you still chasing after Morrighan? Angeline has become quite the woman. Nothing of the naïve girl she was before seems to be there when I first met her."

"I have been given no choice." Cedric flopped onto the grass, lying out on his back, staring at the passing clouds. "Romasanta has made it clear that if I fail to kill Boto, then he will kill Angeline. I am doing this for her. It is no longer about me. I am a mere bug in comparison to the mountain of power that Romasanta truly is."

"Then you will succeed." Cedric looked over at his doggish friend in confusion. "Revenge never ends well for anyone, but you are in the position of protecting something you love. Nothing can beat the strength of the heart and soul."

"You have been against this all this time, yet you flip so easily despite the bad news." He rubbed his face with the palms of his hand. "Before I die tomorrow, I wish to hear what it was that the spirits in Williamsburg told you. Can you do this for a friend staring at his future grave?"

"If it would ease your mind, I will tell you. They had a wish for you in the end."

"What kind of wish would a town that I destroyed have in store for me?"

"They hoped for you to find love again, and a reason to live with it."

Cedric took a deep and unsteady breath as he returned his gaze to the stream of clouds above. Emotions and thoughts flooded his mind as he mulled over Wylleam's words. Clenching his teeth, he did not know whether to be upset, angry, or happy.

Did you all really forgive me so quickly? Why?! I destroyed everyone, everything was taken from them, and I was to blame. Who forgives a murderer, a demon that lived under false pretenses? Whether I knew it at the time was irrelevant. I don't deserve to be forgiven, let alone wished to have happiness and a prosperous life. Father, my dear Yvette, I don't understand...

He crushed his palms in his eyes, demanding the tears not to come. Desperately, he pushed them back, begging his emotions to stay away. It all hurt so much. *It wounded me so deeply to lose everything I had the first time, and if I lost it all again—*

"You should have a reason to live." Wylleam's voice cut through his thoughts. "Is that not what your father told you? That the day he found you, he found life again?"

"Why do you torture me so!" Hiding his face under his hands, he could not hold the tears back. "Damn you, Shaman. You hear the spirits too well."

"It's a gift and a curse, my friend." Wylleam looked up at the sky to watch a few finches fly by. "Life is a fleeting thing that we all strive to chase and hold in our hands. To think you can protect it with just your own two hands is foolish. It is something the earth gifts us before taking it back when she sees fit. In the end, life was never ours to own or hold. We can only cherish what is given to us. Whether it is sour or sweet, it is a blessing to experience the chance to walk the earth before retiring into her arms again."

"Thank you..." Wiping away the last of the tears, he regained his composure. "I could not imagine hearing the whispers of so many spirits. I should be thankful that my family and friends from that time loved me enough to bless me instead of bestowing a curse."

"Speaking of which, I wanted to also ask of the curse you bear."

There was a moment of silence as Cedric pounded his fist against the ground from where he lay. "I know. It has not left my thoughts, either. It is the reason why I am hating myself so much for falling for her. A curse for someone to experience the worst heartbreak ever is a dangerous curse. Whatever end I receive will have to surpass what I have already experienced, and that only doubles for Angeline in her recoil for cursing a demon, or technically, a demonic creature of magic."

Angeline's words echoed through Cedric's mind from that night at the fire when they met Barushka. *"If I knew how to curse someone, I hope that you experience the worst heartbreak ever."*

"So you are aware of it?" Wylleam scratched under his long and massive jaw as he pondered his friend's way of thinking. "And does she know?"

"I don't think she even realizes what she has done." Sighing in exasperation, Cedric sat up and looked his friend in the eye. "There was no mistaking the sensation when she spoke the words. If you are still seeing it there, then the curse has not come to pass for either of us. The question is which of the two will strike first, the one she bestowed or her own recoil for laying it on me?"

"Have you told her?" His jaws opened as he panted like a dog from the heat of the day. "Or is this one of those times that you see it best that the girl enjoy what little of a normal life remains?"

"It's been a while since I have thought about the matter of the curse and telling her." He rubbed the side of his jaw before continuing. "I decided that it is best for her sake to not know. If I had known of my existence, I would have missed some of my best memories. She will have to learn a hard lesson about cursing those of the magical sorts."

"It is your issue, and if she had been aware of her bloodline's dangers, it would have been prevented." Standing up, Wylleam walked over to Cedric, lending him a hand to stand. "I pray that it does not end with either of your lives being shortened. Good luck tomorrow, and sorry I am not in the position to help you in your battle, both the war and curse."

"You're a shaman, a peaceful Cynocephali, and one of the last of your kind." Hugging Wylleam, he gave him a few hearty pats on the back. "I'd prefer my friends not to be in battle. Otherwise, there would be no one to clean my sorry carcass off the field in the end. Goodbye, Wylleam."

After Wylleam had vanished from sight into the woods, Cedric started the long walk back to camp. His shoulders were heavy from the burdens he faced. All he could do was try to dig deep into his new well of knowledge to see what he knew of curses. None of his past vampiric relatives had survived or avoided their curses from what he could gather. There were instances of overcoming a curse for a short time, but in the end, not one had outlived their curse. Walking into his tent, he rubbed the back of his neck as he stopped to watch Angeline stitching some leatherwork in her hands. Her brown eyes looked up at his, and he returned his stare to the ground, ashamed of himself. *She doesn't need to know. When it happens, perhaps I will be blessed enough to tell her then.*

The pungent scent of dog and slobber filled the air in the field as Cedric and Angeline marveled over the sea of fur and muscle that lay before them. Barushka stifled and snorted, nervous of the pack he found himself standing in. This was the army. No, this was Romasanta's pack in its entirety. Romasanta approached them and after a nod with Cedric, he made a loud whistle that rang like a teakettle. A large, golden-brown werewolf appeared out of the grays and blacks. This one had several brandings burned into his skin and fur, like that on a knight's flag or the bishop's robe. Unlike the common werewolves that made the bulk of the pack, this one walked on his hind legs and, like his master, held a more humanoid look. He bowed to Romasanta as if he were royalty and awaited his command.

"This one will lead the group that will break a line to the gates for Barushka." Shooting a glance at the elite werewolf, it responded with a wagging of his tail. "Are you both ready?"

"As ready as one can be for war." Angeline tightened her hold on Cedric's waist as he shifted in the saddle. "On your command."

"Excellent." A wild grin crossed Romasanta's face as he transformed before them. "Remember our bargain well, pup."

He broke into a deep and massive howl that knocked the wind out of the lungs of those near him. Barking and howling rang out in response as the ground shook from the massive shudder of the pack moving toward Morrighan's castle. Angeline could not cover her ears hard enough to keep the noise from deafening her. She felt the nerves in her body tighten and twist across her spine and joints as she looked out over the surges of fur. The sight was unholy and picking up speed. Breaking her eyes off the pack beside them, she looked across the ever-shortening gap to the horde of Morrighan's army and castle. The chimeras of hundreds of years of magically made monsters stood firm, waiting to meet their onslaught.

One of the vulture-like creatures with features of a lion and the size of a dragon, called a heliodromos, broke from its circling above the castle. It dove across a section of the pack. The screeching thudded through their chests as it ran its jaws and claws in a line before them, like plowing a field. A fountain of blood sprayed up into the air, a red curtain waving in the wind. Angeline watched in horror as the other heliodromos followed suit. Blood misted the air all around them. She could feel spots of cold and warm speckle across her skin as they passed the devastated areas. Burying her face into Cedric's leather tunic, she hid from the gore that painted the sunny skies like a million sparkling rubies. Feeling no fear from him was the only comfort she had in the chaos; her shield against all the monsters of life.

Her fingers still ached from working so hard on the tunic he was wearing. It had been damaged a while back during his fight with the chimeras. It was one he had brought from Williamsburg and held the seal for the House of Romulus. She wanted to give him something knightly to wear in the war since she had failed to find him a blade. Barushka leaped over a row of mangled werewolves, and Angeline groped at the front of Cedric's shirt in surprise. After landing, Cedric pulled her hands off and repositioned them in a more secure spot around his midsection. He had made it clear that she was to do nothing about attackers until they got within the castle walls. All she could do was hang on and pray she could stay on the saddle before hitting their destination.

When she pried her face from Cedric's back, she was astonished to see how much of a gap they had covered in such little time. The brown wolf and his pack were cutting down all manner of creatures. Ravenous in their work, they went as far as taking down their own. They took the task of clearing Barushka a path as top priority and all in their path were as good as dead, werewolf or chimera. Morrighan's castle walls cast a wicked shadow over them. The blackened stones were tall, and it was difficult to see the very top of them at the short distance they were from the gates.

Another howl rang out to their right, and there was no mistaking it; that was Romasanta's signal. It was amazing to watch all the monsters around them halt in their actions and pause in admiration of feeling such a powerful aura. Barushka and the pack that led them forward increased their gaits, now free of conflicts. The sea of chaos shifted, the torrents of chimeran creatures fought to seek out Romasanta. Morrighan's interest had indeed shifted to this rare appearance of the father of werewolves. There was a crashing sound up ahead as part of the pack had run ahead in the moment of relief and taken out the castle gates. They could feel the ground shake from the weight of the massive iron doors through even Barushka's bulk and gallop. The flames in Barushka's eyes and hocks flared taller as he ran over a plantlike creature.

They left the demons in the courtyard for the pack, and Barushka slammed through the castle's front doors. Angeline yelped as fiery splinters of wood skipped across the black marble floors. It was a massive corridor, long and tall, as they cantered down its length toward the black throne in the distance. Laughter and giggles echoed off its walls and ceiling, sending Angeline's skin crawling. Snorting, Barushka stopped before the black throne, where Morrighan and a man flirted and fondled one another. Their playful behavior misplaced with the sounds of the war echoing in from the fight that was now spilling into the castle.

The man she sat in the lap of was far more massive than even Romasanta. His long black hair was wild and the dark red eyes stared at Cedric, amused. Morrighan released her suckling of this man's neck to see who had interrupted them in their moment of lustful play. The gown she wore was straps upon straps, all buckled with garnet jewels and gold. The front skirt piece held the largest of the garnet-colored ovals, and there was no denying that the items all held magic within them. Shiny and slick, her black hair was pulled back into braids with a bun to one side, sporting more gold and garnet ornaments. She was shorter than Angeline was, but her lips of black were sharp and held a deep red glare to them as they curled into a wicked smile.

"Welcome, my dear Cedric." Her tone was clear and melodious. "Have you met your father?"

"Morrighan, stop teasing the poor boy," The man's voice was deep-toned and the cunning sensation behind the way he spoke made even Cedric uneasy. "He's come a long way to visit us, dear. Show some care and concern, or he might think wrong of us."

CHAPTER 20

King Incubus Boto

"I am here to challenge Boto for the right to be the incubus king." Cedric's voice was firm and unwavering as the words flowed from his mouth. "As a half-blood, I am entitled to challenge the current king anytime I wish to do so."

"What?" Angeline's mind filled with questions. None of the words that came to her matched anything she had known as to why they were conducting this war. "What do you mean—"

Cedric yanked her arms off him, dismounting. "Do you decline the challenge?"

"No, I am not allowed to decline any challenge. So, you have finally taken an interest in the idea of becoming the king incubus? Following in your old man's path?" Shoving Morrighan off his lap, he stood, exposing his unnatural height and size. "The question is, are you sure you don't want to decline, my little bastard? Do you know how many things like you I have killed for my own enjoyment?"

"I've heard the stories." Spitting at the ground, Cedric's jaw twitched as they stared at one another. "I was curious to know if you lost count of your bastards and that's why you forgot to clean me out with the rest. It's hard to get any challenges if there are no challengers left alive, you know?"

"Feh, I wish I had known Lamashtu allowed you to live." Boto's grin faded to a look of anger. "That bitch of a Babylonian demigoddess waltzed in here and indulged in the act of snatching you from the womb. She laid burden across the body of that already half-dead moroi, spoiling any chance for another try. That one fought harder than Lillith when I mounted her. She tasted so sweet."

"That explains a lot as to how one would be able to escape a fortress as a newborn." Cedric thumbed the sheath of the daito that Vladimir had given him. Feeling his grandfather's grief and fury made him clench his teeth. "So do we battle it out right here, or is there some place special you want to be put to death at?"

"Here is fine, you little cocksucker." Boto's grin grew wide, exposing the dual set of fangs that were larger than Cedric's own. "It's about time I stopped for a moment to wipe the last of my bastards off the earth before Lillith's new clutch hatches."

Angeline watched in terror as Boto's skin grayed and the muscles about his scarred body exploded into existence, making the towering man into a wall of strength. Horns curled wildly from the sides of his head, the same black ram-like horns that Cedric had, yet larger and more aggressive in appearance. Wings stretched out from behind him, like a second pair of muscular arms with clawed fingers spreading wide. Lillith's wingspan seemed miniature as Cedric stood in the Incubine King's shadow. A tail whipped side to side as a monstrous laugh flowed from Boto.

"What's the matter, boy? Didn't expect the old man to be so massive?"

"Don't worry, I'll be cutting you down to size soon enough." Pulling the daito free of its sheath, Cedric took an offensive stance, relying on the knowledge given to him by his vampiric relatives of the fighting styles from the Far East. "You've been sitting in that position far too long, Boto. It's time for someone new to rule over the incubine scum."

With a glint of his red eyes, Boto launched forward with amazing speed, claws clashing against the curved blade of Cedric's sword. His feet were sliding backward on the slick marble as he received the force from the attack. Furious, Cedric stared into Boto's fanged grin and reluctantly he allowed his own horns and strength to come out. This was enough of a boost to allow him to stop his feet from slipping. With one quick motion, Cedric spit into Boto's face, causing him to leap back in a growling rage. As Boto wiped his eyes clear of the insult, Cedric managed to run his blade across Boto's shoulder.

The only reaction from Boto was a shudder and wave of arousal that hit everyone in the room. Being the king incubus, and having lived so long, his powers had everyone taking a second to catch their breath from the intrusion of sexual excitement. A bead of sweat ran down Cedric's cheek, as he already knew all too well that this was going to be a fight much like the one with Lillith. Everyone had concluded that Cedric had something no one else possessed in order to beat Boto, but what this special thing was was not clear. Despite the moment of painful pleasure given to him, Boto was fuming from the motion of Cedric's spitting on him. With a roar, he came at Cedric again, who did his best to dodge the incoming assault. Disregarding the claws that scraped open his side, Cedric managed to land a wide cut across Boto's back. Boto's wings reached back with uncanny speed and gripped Cedric's ankles, yanking him to the ground. He had failed to consider Boto using his wings as a fighting tool.

"How fucking annoying can you be?" Grunting, Boto released Cedric as he shook off the arousal that was crawling across his own skin from his cuts. "I am impressed. It's been a while since one of my bastards has been this feisty."

Leaping back to his feet, Cedric wiped the blood from his nostrils from hitting the floor nose first. "You should have kept your grip on me."

Running at Boto, Cedric ran his blade across Boto's side and ducked under the counterattack from the spiked elbows of the wings. Sweat was pouring across Boto's skin as he panted in the ecstasy that fueled him. The same drunken grin that Cedric had worn in the past was now on the king's face as he folded his wings. Like a bull, Boto rushed in, horns down. Cedric landed a foot on the back of Boto's head as he launched himself over. A tail sideswiped Cedric midair, sending him skipping across the hard marble floor. His daito spinning far out of reach and stopped in front of Morrighan's feet. Coughing and shuddering from the painful impact, Cedric was trying to stop his head from spinning while his eyes struggled for a moment to refocus properly. Unlike Boto, he was receiving only the pain of each hit, protecting Angeline from the waves that might render her incapable of fleeing.

"Oh! What a shiny piece this is!" Morrighan picked up the sword, turning the blade in her hand. "I think I will keep this."

Picking himself off the floor, Cedric panted as his body ached from skipping across the ground like a rock on a pond. His head throbbed from smacking against the cold floor, and looking over at Angeline, he received a knowing nod. They both knew deep down if Cedric had any chance of winning, it would have to be Angeline feeling the pain. Their bond was keeping him from his true nature when he forced the reversal of the sensations they felt. Her eyes were firm, her expression grave, and the nod confirmed that she was ready to do whatever it took to ensure he made it out alive. Sighing, his skin crawled as the pleasure from his injuries flooded his body, warming his blood, making his heart rush. Angeline paled. Her grip on Barushka's reins tightened and her knuckles went white. Cedric's skin crawled as the drunken sensation started to take hold faster than he could assess it. It was overwhelmingly distracting, receiving the solid wave of ecstasy.

Boto grinned wildly as he felt this shift within Cedric; stretching his wings wide, he flew forward with a powerful flap. There was a deafening clack as they locked horns. Boto was shoving Cedric backward with the force of the impact. Face to face, they both gritted their fanged teeth. The red glow of Boto's eyes taunted Cedric, further thrilling the incubine excitement within them both. Calling forth all his strength, he knew this was not the time to hold all his demonic intentions at bay. He would have to take the risk of setting free all that resided deep within him. Heat surged through him, mixing in with the poignant sensations that now overwhelmed him. Tingling erupted across his body as he too formed incubine wings and tail. His horns pulled further out, his fangs larger, as his overall bulk and size closed most of the gap between him and Boto. It became clear that there was no mistaking that he was the offspring of the incubus king.

His hair held onto its red color with the black tips. This was not like the incubine takeovers he had experienced in the past where his hair had given way to the solid black. Everything flooded his senses, his sense of smell, touch, taste, and hearing all changed. So much was making him feel excited as he managed to push Boto back a few steps. Shivers ran across his spine as the salty smell of Angeline's sweating body hit his nose. The sound of her heart pounded in his ears, the grinding vibrations that tickled his skull as their horns shoved against each other. The taste of his own iron-filled blood in his mouth made the whole event seem surreal. Cedric was struggling to stay focused in all the waves of arousal, all the excitement coming from his actions and surroundings. Incubi were truly animalistic, indeed inferior demons.

With a flap of his newfound wings, Cedric was pushing Boto across the black marble floors. A look of surprise and excitement lit Boto's face as he broke away from their locking of horns. Cedric's heart was racing; every thought was exciting in this state, whether it was for fear of receiving a hit or giving one, it did not matter. Whipping a tail side to side added to his pleasure as his blood boiled through his veins. A gasp escaped Angeline's lips from where she still sat on Barushka. This new form brought forward waves of desire, unlike anything either of them had felt before. More shivers washed over him. Looking back at Angeline made it very clear to him why Boto had fully changed. The whole fight Boto's arousal increased with every injury, and Morrighan reflected the same sensation, not one of pain but pleasure. After allowing himself his full demonic form was the only time that the bond between him and Angeline shifted so they both received positive sensations. She felt only desire with each impact, and this removed the last of his ties to stay tame. Cedric could once more afford to be as reckless as needed to get himself that much closer to bringing Boto down.

In his moment of distraction, Boto lunged forward, ripping his claws across Cedric's chest and shoulder. Ecstasy flooded every part of him as the violent pain turned into a frenzy of longing. His thoughts and body begged for more. Arousal flowed out of Angeline, which added to the drowning flow of feelings Cedric was experiencing. Both of them felt the lascivious manner of the ability an incubus held and its condescending effects. Boto's horns rammed Cedric square in the back, slamming him to the ground. Growling came from Cedric as his cheek felt the bite of the marble floor once more.

Catching his focus again, Cedric jerked to his feet and leaped forward. His claws slid across Boto's cheek and chest with effortlessness. More excitement seeped out of the king as he laughed. Cedric was still moving too slowly, hindered by the unfamiliar form. Boto's claws gripped the hair on the top of his head, lifting Cedric off the floor with the greatest of ease. With a wicked smirk, Cedric went flying into the closest column. Orgasmic pleasure erupted across his body from the impact, and he landed on his feet, barely able to catch his breath. Angeline moaned in response, sweat pouring across her as she watched in horror as the fight continued. Shaking the sensations down, he was starting to get the hang of manipulating all his new feelings.

Both the king and Cedric took a great leap into the air, their wings wide. They slammed into one another with a sickening thud. Surely, bones were broken as a cracking sound echoed over the sounds of the war that was spilling farther down the great hall. Falling to the floor, Boto was on top of Cedric, one claw gripping Cedric's throat, the other held high, ready to strike. Cedric was struggling to concentrate as amazing pleasure flooded his body from the broken ribs he had received that lay under the weight of the king. His new bulk was still not enough to give Boto's size a challenge in a head-on collision. Angeline could feel the extreme arousal from Cedric, but pushed the distraction back. She readied her bow and struggled to keep her aim focused and her shaking arms were frustrating. Cedric needed her.

Barushka reared up into the air, knocking Angeline to the ground. Gasping from the awkward pleasure of the pain she should have felt, her eyes locked with Cedric's green ones. They both looked back in time to see Barushka fall to the ground, the daito buried deep in his chest. In the commotion, they had failed to keep watch on Morrighan. Barushka had taken the sword in order to save Angeline and lay gasping on the cold ground, his flames disappearing. Crawling to his side, tears streamed down Angeline's face as she hugged his massive horse's head. Whispering her gratitude and apologies, she choked on her tears. Barushka exhaled, his massive eyes rolled back, and the warmth faded from him.

Morrighan's laughter echoed about them as she sat on her throne. "Oh my, I missed."

Cedric tried to sit up, but Boto's grip on his neck tightened and slammed his head back against the hard floor. His blood was no longer heated by pleasure, but rage. He felt toyed with, but his strength could not surpass the incubus king's hold. The air was being cut from his lungs. Fear was starting to take hold of Cedric, as all he felt was the sickening excitement of his death coming closer. His vision was blurring as he fought for his eyes to stop their attempts at rolling back in their sockets. His gasping did nothing, no air would come in his attempts. He had failed. Angeline would be dead, whether by Boto, Morrighan, or Romasanta... she would follow close behind his own death.

A great roar brought his focus forward, Boto's grip failing, Cedric rushed to his feet. He wheezed as he engulfed air, hungry to breathe again. The pain and arousal that Boto allowed to wave out of him and into all in the room imploded back into him. The sensations Cedric had been receiving from the king became eerily silent and empty. The great king was clawing to reach something in his back, clearly in pain. His red eyes were white as he twisted and turned, his cries harrowing. Cedric caught the gasping face of Angeline as she stumbled back, away from the incubine king as he swung about wildly. Returning his bewilderment to the great demon, Boto wrenched and twisted himself on the ground now, a chimera hilt protruding from his back.

Screeching came from Morrighan as she twisted in her chair. The pain Boto was experiencing was reaching her body as well. Their bond was taking a toll on the both of them as their pain fed into each other. Breaking out of his shock, Cedric scrambled to put himself between Boto and Angeline. Clawing at the floor, the incubus king managed to wrench his arm-like wing behind him and grip the chimera hilt of the black-bladed dagger. With another round of howling, they watched the blade burn and sizzle as it pulled free of his flesh.

Cedric leaped forward, scrambling for the dagger that inflicted such a large blow. Boto swung his massive tail, sending the dagger spiraling down the hall and too far out of reach to chance chasing after it. Angeline was still sobbing, while Morrighan gasped for air, leaning against her throne. The great incubus looked like a maddened beast, his eyes still white and foam dripping from his fanged mouth. Boto crawled toward Cedric on all fours, toppling over him with all his weight. Feeling crushed beneath him, Cedric was struggling to hold back the wrists of angry claws that yearned deeply to rip at his flesh. Blood from Cedric's injuries seeped into his mouth and fueled his frustration. Spitting into Boto's face once more, he was met with more howling of pain from the incubus. His bloodied spit sizzled as it seared Boto's cheek.

Boto lashed out wildly, landing a strike across Cedric's abdomen. Stumbling back, pissed at his dumbfound moment of standing still, Cedric lunged forward in retaliation. Boto's tail swung violently, desperate to keep all the attacks at bay. Dodging, Cedric was given no choice but to back off and wait for another opening. Boto had given himself to the incubine animal within. He was no longer coherent or aware of anything. This was what Vladimir meant and the more it raged on, the more pitiful and belittled Boto seemed. His cries and roars were mixtures of rage, frustration, and constant pain. Turning to face Cedric, Boto had clawed his face and neck open. The loose flaps of fileted skin were grotesque enough to make Cedric's stomach turn. It was an insane reaction to both his spit and the dagger, but the logic and reasons seemed so distant still.

The answer to the great puzzle exploded in Cedric's mind: *That's it! My blood is the key! Incubi are weak to the invasion of another incubus's blood! And considering Boto's hunting off his offspring, the closer to the king's lineage one is, the more poisonous it is to him. Even my dried blood has devastating reactions, which means—*Biting into his tongue, Cedric coated his fangs red with his blood, the flavor of iron igniting his excitement. Predatorily, he leaped onto Boto, staring down into the white eyes of an incubus ravaged with pain. Cedric's fangs dug deep, savaging Boto's neck further. He pulled all the power and strength from centuries of experience from him. Every gulp held immense energy as Cedric devoured Boto's soul. Morrighan's cries wailed as she twisted to the floor in front of her black throne. Cedric could feel with each sip of the king's blood, the unstitching of their bond. The process was beyond painful as Boto roared and squirmed under his weight.

Boto stopped moving, going cold and limp. Cedric broke away from him and gasped for a breath of air. Stepping backward, Cedric moved away from the large gray heap that was no longer with the living. Morrighan crawled to her king, her face painted with black streaks from her tears and makeup. She nuzzled his cold face for a moment before kissing Boto deeply. Sobs of pain and sorrow engulfed the sorceress as she hugged the once-great incubus. All Cedric and Angeline could do was watch in silence. It was clear that breaking one's bond was like destroying the soul. They watched as Morrighan's body shook. Her grip on the dead Boto left marks from her nails as her pain continued to take hold.

"No, no. This can't be!" Morrighan's voice was cracked as she struggled to speak. "Boto, my love, why have you left me all alone?! Why does it hurt so?!"

"What do we do now?" Angeline was leaning against the blood-stained column that Cedric had hit earlier. "What do you plan on doing with her?"

"I... I don't know." Cedric was at a complete loss. "This is not how I had imagined it. I have played this moment out in my head so much that I did not take into account how heavy a binding could break. I have finished the deal made with Romasanta with Boto's death, but what to do with Morrighan..."

"Is, is this what will happen to you when I—" Cedric's sharp glance at Angeline stopped her.

"Let's go." Cedric turned his back to the sorceress, who sat on the ground drowning in her grief, walking away from his vengeance, once and for all. "I think I have done efficient damage."

"You're so much weaker than him." The bitter tone of Morrighan's words stopped Cedric. "Go ahead, my little chimera. Kill me. Did you not wish to destroy the one that created you? To take down your god?"

"I think death would be too soft of a punishment for you, Morrighan." He refused to look back into the broken eyes that burned at his back. "You have made me and so many others suffer similar emotions of loss that it is only fitting I leave you like this. This is the plague you have drowned many in, and it is natural you drink from the cup of sorrow as well."

"He wasn't as horrible as you think." She stumbled to her feet. Her voice rumbled as she demanded Cedric's attention. "You have no idea what drives me to do the dark arts that I practice. Boto knew, and he loved me despite knowing the true motive behind it all."

"Normally I would feel sorry for someone's loss, but you have taken so much from me, Vladimir, and many more that the idea is numb." He glanced over his shoulder at the broken girl before him, no longer seeing his creator, his vengeance, or even the menacing sorceress. "Morrighan, you know the dangers of practicing magic on demons and magical creatures. What made you think you were immune to the recoils? I am shocked this did not happen sooner. You were lucky to be able to get this far before it struck."

"You twat!" Suddenly, laughter came from her, mixing into a deeper tone still. "You have no clue! I am immune to recoils thanks to the Amulet of Avalon that I wear. Do you not understand that something far larger is in play?! Do you not realize there are Morrighan and me inside this putrid body?"

"Morrighan and me?" Cedric turned around as his senses started to push past the pleasure that was still haunting his body, making him aware of the other danger that had been in the room with them. "Badbh had mentioned a possession, but this is the first sign of your existence, demon."

"My name is Beelzebub." Her voice took on a demonic sound as her eyes rolled back into a solid black color. "How else do you think this sorceress was capable of mixing and controlling such powerful demons of old? The poor thing summoned me and here I am trapped in this disgusting human flesh. It is time I possess something far more appealing. Perhaps you shall do."

"I refuse your offer." Cedric's jaw muscles tightened as he looked for any aid within his mind. "You should go back to the depths of hell. There is not much else Morrighan can do for you in her current state."

"And I have you to thank for her worthlessness." She spat on Boto's corpse with a look of disdain. "This thing was far too affectionate to her, unlike the reputation he held. Incubi have always had soft spots for the heart. You're all laughable to the fallen, such as me."

"At least we don't spend eternity roasting in hell." His gut was twisting as he looked into the black eyes of Beelzebub. "Doesn't one have to willingly accept or make a deal with your kind in order to gain access to your powers and be possessed?"

"Technically, yes." A wicked grin crawled across her face as a reptilian forked tongue glided across her upper lip. "But we have our ways around that annoyance."

"I refuse to allow you access to my body." The wealth of knowledge stirred in him, and he avoided saying the demon's name, in fear this was all that was needed to leave him the tiniest crack to seep into. "You have no place here. Go back to your fiery home. I think the devil misses his bitch."

"Watch your mouth!" The demonic tone dropped deeper as it blasted him backward into the column with an unseen force. "How dare you speak to a superior with such filth!"

"Struck a nerve, I see." A grin crept across Cedric's face as he kneeled at the base of the column. "I would have thought you were used to hearing such talk."

"You are toying with the wrong power, maggot." Snarling, she stretched her hands out, black flames whipping out of her palms. "Let me share the searing pain that Hell's fire brings!"

CHAPTER 21

THE CURSE

The heat and smell of death engulfed the great hall as the flames from hell crawled farther from Morrighan's hands. Cedric tensed, unsure of what pain the black fire held, but the waves of knowledge within him told him enough that his goal was to keep away from its venomous touch. Looking behind him, Angeline shook, unable to move in her fear. As she drew closer, the heat from the flames sent unnerving chills across Cedric's skin. This heat surpassed any he had encountered. The chimera's and hellhounds' flames were nothing by comparison. Shaking off the last of his nervousness, he readied himself for the fight that was approaching.

A great wind blew through the hall, swirling about the three of them; it extinguished the black flames with ease. Cedric watched as a look of surprise hit the possessed Morrighan's face. This was not the doing of Beelzebub or her. Something far more powerful was making itself known. A figure began to materialize behind Morrighan as it reached around and pulled the larger enchantment stone from the front of her skirt. Howls erupted from Morrighan as the ornament broke free of her dress. Her body twisted and contorted, the smaller stones cracking and shattering as her body shifted and deformed. All the recoils from her magical attempts at creating chimera hit her at once, changing her, mashing the chimera species into her body.

The figure stood back as he stroked his long, white beard, staring at the large amulet, the Amulet of Avalon. He paid no attention to the commotion of Morrighan and Beelzebub's cries that spilled from the same mouth. The wind had dissipated as Angeline and Cedric watched the shifting of claws, spikes, snouts, and more come into existence, then shift and fade away again. It was unclear who took the most recoil, Morrighan or the demon within her. Falling to her knees, she collapsed onto Boto's corpse. Her final transformation left her with a wolf's head and the skin of a snake. Large fur covered her arms and claws, and her legs were the hocks of a massive goat. No longer conscious, it lai panting from its pain in silence now.

"Hmm, so that's what centuries of chimera recoils look like." He paused from stroking his white beard. "Sorry, my dear, but I need my amulet back. Thank you for finding it for me. Now, to tend to the next piece I need."

The white-haired man turned his attention to Cedric and Angeline. His pale blue eyes were icy as they looked the both of them over. Humming to himself, he slid the amulet into one of his robe-like jacket sleeves. Pulling up on his belt, tugging at his satchel, he took a step toward them but paused at seeing Cedric's defensive reaction. He leaned to the side, catching a better glance at Angeline before returning a look back at Cedric. Removing his pointed cap, the old man scratched his bald head for a moment. Stretching his wings out to hide Angeline from sight, Cedric took an aggressive step toward this unknown figure. His instincts were reeling. Something was not right. If the only thing he needed from this place was the amulet, he would have left as swiftly as he had entered. He wanted something from them, but at what cost?

"Who are you?" It came out as a growl and Cedric whipped his tail from side to side. "What do you want from us?"

"Merlin." Placing his cap back on his head, he took in a deep breath. "And you are in my way, demon."

"The girl belongs to me." Once more, his wings flared wider. "We have no business with you, wizard, nor do we have anything of interest to you."

"On the contrary." A coy smile slithered across his thin lips, and he began stroking his beard again. "You are responsible for devouring my Coinn Iotair, or hellhounds as you call them here, and behind you is the item I sent them here to look for."

"Leave her be." His heart thudded hard against his chest as the sensation of magic nipped at every nerve in his body. *No, not now! Don't let this be the moment you come into existence, curse!*

"You see, I have been digging through a century's worth of time and resources trying to find that particular bloodline, but I see you have spoiled it with your own blood." A frown crossed his pale, elderly face. "This is going to delay my work. I will have to find a way to undo the damage you have done to her witch's blood. I despise demons and the work they do on the human body. Worse off, you have gone as far as binding yourself to her. It's degrading."

"Don't touch her." Heat radiated off Cedric as waves of Angeline's fear hit him. "You will not take her!" *You'll have to kill me first. I will not let her go without a fight, wizard. She's mine!*

"Ah, but I will. Demons are such poor thinkers, tsk." The thin smile returned, and a sparkle shone in his eyes. "She will be making her new home on Avalon, without you, of course. It never shocks me to see how easily demons fall for humans. The wolf never sleeps with the sheep for a reason."

"What do you want from her?" Behind Cedric, Angeline shakily picked up her bow and readied an arrow. "Her magic is dormant; there is nothing you can get from her." *Angeline run, you fool, this is not the time to get brave!*

"Ah, but you see, I have been pulling such deep magic into my own blood's magic to gain immortality. With the ancient line she holds, I will be able to achieve this as well as the power to clean the rest of the demon powerhouses off this earth. I will become supreme ruler of mankind, not Beelzebub, or any creature of such spoiled lineage." A look of disgust crossed his face. "Feh, but unfortunately, I got here far too late and now will have to cleanse her of your filth. Without killing her in the process of doing so. Binds and transformations are difficult filths you hellish dogs have plagued mankind with."

The wizard took another step forward and Cedric charged. Inches away from Merlin, Cedric only swiped a swirl of wind. Catching his balance, he spun around, searching for the wizard. When his green glare caught the ghostly form of Merlin, it was too late.

"CEDRIC!" Angeline's shriek unraveled his nerves as their eyes met. "LET HER GO!"

Merlin had materialized behind Angeline and held her by a fist full of her hair. Cedric was frozen where he stood, his mind reeling at what he should do, fearing to take any rash actions. Her brown eyes were wide as the tears poured from them. A dagger pressed into her neck drew a small drop of blood that slid down her pale neck. The scent of it hit his nose, and he clenched his teeth. Glaring at the pale eyes of Merlin, he struggled to keep his fears in check. Smiling, Merlin's eyes grew wilder seeing the panic growing on Cedric's face. Angeline's racing heart filled Cedric's ears. There was nothing he could say to calm her. The weight of the curse pulled at him. There was no mistaking the sensation. *You fucking curse, why? Not like this!*

"Oh, what do I see there?" Merlin's eyes drifted their focus to Cedric's left hand. "You can't be serious? A wedding band on a demon's hand is improper and insulting. Let me fix that."

The pale blue in his eyes brightened to an azure blue. Pain erupted across Cedric's left ring finger as the gold band turned red with unnatural heat. Melting and burning, it flowed through his finger and bone like a hot knife. Screaming from the horrid pain from the wizard's heat, his finger dropped to the floor as the golden ring melted into the black marble, sparking and sputtering as it seeped out of sight. Angeline paled as she only felt extreme pleasure from the tormenting scene. Despite the agony, Cedric could sense the fears from Angeline, and choking back the tears, he gathered what words he could. *This damn curse is taking her from me, but I will not let it win!*

"Angeline, remember that sensation well!" His tears flowed heavier as she watched in shock. "I promise you that no matter what, you will never feel pain again! And as long as you feel my touch through our bond, know that I am still searching for you!"

Grunting, Merlin pulled her tighter to him, and in a rush of wind, they both vanished.

Cedric sank to his knees, despair swallowing him completely as his reason for living was gone. Left in his mind was her horrified face, at feeling electrifying ecstasy from his ring melting through his finger. Slinking forward, he punched the marble floor in anger, staring woefully down at his own finger where it lay. Guilt came crushing down on him. *Why didn't I try? I should have made a dash for her. Merlin needed her alive. Why did I stop thinking? Was my fear and panic that overwhelming that it cost me everything I ever wanted, ever needed? I am so sorry; I failed you, my angel. Demon is a worthy name for a creature as pitiful as me. I will find you, this I will promise you. As long as you breathe, and I feel your pain, I will spend every second of my miserable existence to undo this curse and save you from your torture.*

"You're a pitiful sight." Morrighan's melodious voice was trying to break through, but the new body she controlled made it difficult. "First off, I have no more quarrels with you. I just desire to be free of my own curse and I am pleading for you to help me expel Beelzebub."

"Sorceress, you will have to ask elsewhere." The dripping of his tears against the floor rang out over the yelping and roars of the war that was still raging on down the hall. "I am neither a miracle worker nor a priest of any kind. Seek help elsewhere and leave me to my mourning."

"Are you not a vampire?"

"What of it?"

"Vampires can expel possessions with a single bite."

After a moment, he looked back at the disfigured creature that looked at him with desperate eyes. He could hear her sister Badbh's words echoing in his mind. *If you figure out a way to set Morrighan free, I would owe you for the rest of my life.* Climbing to his feet again, he towered over her; tears no longer came to his eyes. His mind flew with thoughts and ideas, plans were already forming within him. With extreme force, he jerked her monstrous head to the side. His fangs dug angrily into her. The heat from Beelzebub's being was burning his mouth as he pulled the demon's soul apart from Morrighan's body. Cedric's eyes opened wide as his instincts kicked in and he began drinking heavily. The immense power that Beelzebub had contained was still carrying the weight of the binding of Boto. In his mind, he could hear the shouts of anger from the prince of demons as his soul sank back into hell, lacking the power it once carried. This was enough power to put him closer to the strength of Romasanta, but if he was planning to take Merlin on, he would have to acquire more than the strength of the father of werewolves.

Releasing her when the last of the burning liquid was swallowed; Morrighan fell to the ground, her human form pulling itself back to normal before his eyes. She was panting while gripping the ravaged bite on her neck. Cedric wiped the blood off his mouth and chin, a look of disgust on his face. There was so much he had to do before he could get Angeline back. He knew nothing of who this wizard Merlin was.

"I... I owe you my life, Cedric." Morrighan was pale, and sweat covered her shivering body. "I didn't think any creature could handle absorbing him out of me, but you were capable. Ha, his own creation sent him back to hell after all."

"Merlin, who is he?"

"He is a wizard who strives for immortality. When magic users like him, or us, fully devote themselves to a specific school of magic to the point of obsession without distraction, we can obtain immortality or god status. It rarely happens anymore. Though his practice is with manipulating time, he fails to devote himself to the art completely. He has too many desires to destroy demons and other magic wielders as well as wanting to rule over men. Mankind is his highest priority since they pose no threat or challenge to him." She lay mournfully on Boto's cold chest as she spoke, "But there is no telling where in time he is hidden, and Avalon is impossible to visit without being allowed access by Merlin or having a blood relation to the same line. You may never—"

"I will find a way, and when I do, you and your sisters will be called upon. Be ready."

Walking over to the large black heap of Barushka's cold body, he kneeled. After a moment of frowning down at the large shag foal, he gently slid his sword from his hairy chest. Sheathing his sword, he began walking down the hall. His thoughts were working out every move he would need to make, every task that would need completing in order to secure Angeline's rescue. The war was starting to die off, with dead piles of werewolves and monstrous creations lying on the floor. Halfway to this lifeless pile, he paused, looking back at Barushka where he still lay. "We don't have all day, Barushka Matushka."

The great horse erupted into flames once more as he stood. Cantering up beside him, Barushka shook his head, snorting and huffing, as Cedric mounted him. With a few clicks from Cedric, they took off, riding past the castle gates and raced by Romasanta. The father of werewolves was killing off the last of both his cursed ones and the chimera. He paused in his activities as he watched them ride by at great speed, knowing all too well the look Cedric wore on his face. He had completed their deal, but Angeline was not with him. Something grave had happened inside that black castle, and Cedric would call many to aid the battle that would ensue.

CHAPTER 22

RUSTY'S BAR, PRESENT DAY

"And that was the last time I saw her." Cedric's green eyes were dull under his baseball cap as they stared far off to another time and place. He rubbed the nub of his left ring finger for a moment before returning a glance to the bartender, Tony. "That's how I lost the love of my life and my finger."

"Wow." Tony scratched the back of his head, unsure how to take in such a wild tale. "That's some story, Cedric. I couldn't imagine how you must have felt just seeing her disappear like that."

"Well, I am getting closer these days to getting her back." Cedric took a sip of his drink, a smile gracing his lips. "Thank you for letting me share my story with you in the last several weeks. Sorry to be a bother."

"None at all. After the first few Thursdays, I looked forward to hearing you share more of it." Tony was doing his routine of cleaning the shelves as he idly chatted with his red-haired regular. "The only other guy who comes in is the homeless man in the back corner over there. He never orders anything and the boss told me to leave him be. Rusty seems terrified of the guy."

"I noticed that." Gulping down the rest of his glass, he slid it toward Tony. "In fact, can you put that bottle of top-shelf vodka on my tab and send it his way?"

"Really?" Picking up the bottle of vodka and an empty glass, Tony gave him a quizzical look. "That's a first for you. Are you feeling well? I don't think I have ever seen you buy anyone a drink?"

"Much better than normal, to be honest." Cedric leaned back on the stool and shot a glance at the back booth. "A lonely soul deserves a good drink, if you ask me."

Tony walked the bottle back and the large homeless man looked back at Cedric with an accepting nod. He was a broad-shouldered man, with big brown eyes, and a scruffy beard. He remained silent as Tony left to return behind the bar. Refilling Cedric's glass, he went back to taking inventory and continuing the conversation.

"So what does a guy do over so many centuries?" He shot a look back, expecting a smirk, but found that sad, distant look in Cedric's green eyes. "I'm sorry. I didn't mean to upset you."

"No, you are right. What does a man or demon do with so much time?" He downed the glass and flicked his finger for more. Sorrow in his voice as he continued. "I wish I could say I was very productive, but there were centuries of sulking or dedicating myself to research and further knowledge. There were battles fought, and many friends and family lost in that time. Not to mention the pain I felt and knew she was going through..."

There was a moment of silence as Cedric's voice failed him. Tony waited for him to come back to the present, setting down his clipboard. He could not help but wonder if the wild tale he had been hearing from the regular had some truth to it. Cedric's green eyes shot up, startling Tony, as they demanded his attention. A smirk came back to his face, and a hint of a fang sent Tony's hair on end. Perhaps he had been serving a demon over these several months.

"Tony, let me tell you about the fall of Vladimir. Perhaps a story about how I indefinitely became the last of my family for quite some time might help you understand the depths of the loneliness I have felt." He leaned back onto the bar top, his usual stance in telling his stories. "When I left Morrighan's castle, I had managed a huge growth in power, but it was not enough to challenge a wizard as old and clever as Merlin. The years that followed, I had used new and old connections to shift my focus on ancient tomes and folklore about the man who stole what was mine. I even joined a monastery for some time, to gain access to unimaginable libraries that still lay hidden today. Strangely enough, I was able to find some peace for once in my life there. Some of the monks feared me, as I would pale and sweat at any given moment. I was struggling with those moments of pain I received from Angeline, so it was one of my better decisions in life going there."

The bell on the door called both of them to take a glance, interrupting the story.

"Ugh, it's a shitty time for a blizzard." The girl was tall, and she had shoulders like a gymnast. Agitated, she shook snow flurries from the wild curls of her deep, purplish-toned hair. "Couldn't you have rescheduled this, Cedric?"

"Weather is weather. You've been around long enough to not be bothered by it." Cedric sat up as he smirked at the woman. "Where's your sisters?"

"No worries, they are on their way, but it seems it may be a few weeks." Flopping on the stool next to him, she huffed, her lips and chin looking awkward to Tony with such a horrific scar across them. "Gimme some Jonnie! Make it a double neat, no, a triple. Why the hell not?"

"You two know each other?" Tony looked confused as he poured the triple shot of Jonnie Walker and slid it over to the woman, who tossed her thick, black coat off on another stool. "From your story, Cedric?"

A coy smile crossed Cedric's face as he pulled his hood down and placed his cap on the bar top, revealing his hair, pulled back into a pony-tail, red with its black tips. "Yes, that's correct. Tony, meet Badbh. Badbh, this is Tony, that bartender I was telling you about."

"Badbh?" He watched in amazement as she took the triple down all at once, her cheeks reddening from the feat as she exhaled, slamming the glass on the table. "The battle goddess?"

"AH! That's one way to warm your ass up!" She was obnoxiously loud as she hugged Cedric. "When was the last time you and I sat down for a drink like this?"

"Not long enough, if you ask me." A lonesome sigh escaped Cedric's lips before he leaned back, looking over his shoulder at the ever-silent homeless man in the back. "Anyhow, I was about to tell Tony about what happened to Vladimir."

"Oh?" Badbh's voice went soft as she looked on in curiosity. "I haven't heard this story either. Do not let me stop you. I've been wondering about what happened myself."

"Yes, please tell me what happened to your ... grandfather, was it?" Tony poured more Jonnie for Badbh as he turned his attention back to Cedric. "I thought he was a vampire. Don't they live forever?"

"A strigoi, the pureblood, does have a lifespan nearing immortality." Cedric looked pleased that Tony was paying attention to the retelling of his life as he wet his throat once more with the burning liquor. "And yes, Vladimir was my grandfather by blood. Unfortunately, he lost himself when Charlotte passed and is written in history as several people. Vlad the Great was the man I met, but he then became Vlad the Impaler in the 1400s."

"Wait." Tony pulled a stool behind the bar and took a seat as he mulled the name over. "Isn't that who Dracula is based on?"

"Yes, he was also known as Dracula." Pushing the empty glass away, Cedric paused a moment while Tony topped it off. "That name was given to him by the strigoi and then it was Sultan Mehmed the Second who sent word to me about my responsibilities to take him down."

"He was killing people and devastating the Romanians and the Turks." This was a history that Tony was intrigued and knew something about. For once, he could carry some of the conversation. "Isn't his death a mystery? Or the whereabouts of his body?"

"No, far from it, kid." Badbh leaned back as she, too, indulged in the information. "The purebloods reserve the first wave of bringing their own kind down for family. Last I heard, Vladimir had been hunting down his own kind and sucking them dry. He was begging to be put down."

"Yeah, he was shrinking the vampire society drastically and with uncanny speed. I was a monk at the time when the Ottoman soldiers showed up at our doors looking for me..." Cedric rubbed his neck a moment as he continued with his life's story.

CHAPTER 23

THE SULTAN'S REQUEST

Cedric had agreed to leave the monastery with the sultan's guard. It was clear he had already stayed among the monks for far too long, and whispers of his ageless complexion were starting to scare some of his fellow brothers. He traveled far across Europe and farther east to an area called Anatolia with the guardsmen. This was a place with a harsh history, and in the current state of the world, the Ottomans were not a power to oppose. Brought before the sultan, he looked misplaced and pale compared to the people who lived in that hot, dry land.

With a wave of Sultan Mehmed the Second's hand, everyone left the throne room. The doors thudded closed, echoing throughout the white and golden hall. After a moment of exchanging stares in silence, the sultan spoke.

"Stand Cedric." He motioned for Cedric to stand on his feet. "I know who and what you are, unlike the blind that we live among."

"My reputation still holds after all this time, keh." Cedric gave him a scowl as he shifted to a more relaxed stance. "And I am surprised that a strigoi would be living in a place so full of light."

"Ah, you are no fool. Vladimir's grandson is as clever as they have said you would be." There was a chuckle before he continued. "Do you know why I have brought you here?"

"Honestly, no." Sighing, he looked over the short, plump vampire. His skin strange with its dark skin and the brown eyes he held did not show any of the customary signs of a strigoi. It was only the scent and the moroi within Cedric that had told him what the sultan was. "Why have you brought me here?"

"You have a responsibility to tend to." A grave look crossed the sultan's face as he sat down on his throne. "Vladimir has vowed to wipe out the world of strigoi, but he has also killed many innocents in his lustful hunt for gaining powers from the others. Are you familiar with our customs?"

"Of course I am." Cedric's jaw twitched as he confirmed what he knew. "Being the closest blood relative, it is my duty to hunt and kill Vladimir. This is due to the higher possibility of knowing his skills, matching his abilities, and even possibly being immune to more lethal attacks."

"Yes, yes." He stroked his chin a moment, noting the tension Cedric held. "It is a horrible task, but if he is not stopped…"

"I will leave at once. Where may I find my grandfather?" Cedric was growing irritated with the situation.

"Being a monk, I would consult his private monastery at Lake Snagov." Turning on his heels, Cedric left the sultan alone on his throne.

Barushka huffed as the blizzard blew hard against them. The mountain paths during the peak of winter were treacherous, but Cedric had no patience to wait out the weather. His thoughts trailed on about the task at hand. He had his assumptions as to why Vladimir would go on such a path of destruction, but this was the only blood family he had. It had been a comforting thought to know that Vladimir was out there in the world with him. Wylleam had died of old age and he had traveled far to devote himself as a monk to gain access to libraries that were unknown to even the pureblood's knowledge. If he had to kill Vladimir, then he would be alone, with only the comforts of the pain he felt from Angeline's never-ending torment.

That was the single sensation they could exchange at the distance they were. Searing, bloodletting, and unspeakable sensations plagued him. All he could assume was that Merlin had continued to fail at breaking their bond. His binding was too strong for the magic and techniques he had access to. Never had Cedric thought that Angeline would still be alive after so long, but Morrighan had explained that the island of Avalon knows no time. He just needed a ticket onto the island. Hunting the lineage of possible relatives to the ancient wizard was proving to be difficult.

Stomping and bopping his head, Barushka neighed with excitement to see the monastery's tower through the darkened skies of the blizzard.

It sat on an isle on the frozen lake and a small stable hugged it to one side. Crunching their way through the snow and ice, they managed to reach the shelter of the warm stable. Cedric took a moment to unsaddle and brush Barushka down. Since Angeline was gone, the two of them had grown closer. A smile crossed his lips as he imagined this must have been the comforting sensation that Angeline had found in the shag foal before they...

The monastery's front doors opened, and a monk waved for him to come in. Patting Barushka, he pushed through the snow to the door and entered the heat of the front hall. Another monk approached, and they both welcomed their fellow brother, blessing Cedric that he had made it through such deadly weather. The elder monk was standing at an altar, reviewing scripture in silence. In great tradition, Cedric visited the holy water fountain and blessed himself. Being an abomination had its advantages. He had no known reactions to holy items, but knowing Vladimir, he would have invested in a small place like this to find sanction. He kneeled before the altar and hummed the customary prayer and when he looked up, the elder had stopped his reading. He stared deep into Cedric's eyes with a knowing nod and left the room.

Vladimir was there, or at least not far. His presence had disturbed the elder, which was a good sign that he was very aware of who had walked into his monastery. Patient, Cedric sat on a pew, soaking in the silence and solitude. Living the life of a monk had been a welcomed change, and it had given him time to adjust to the painful sensations that were slowly becoming a feeling of comfort. It was a reminder that he still had a chance to save Angeline and break the curse that had ripped them apart. The elder returned, handing him a map. He opened it to see that it showed paths from the monastery to a castle deeper in the mountains.

"May God have mercy on you for seeking out such a demon." Nervous, the elder blessed himself and Cedric. "This is where he resides for now. I beg you, if you are here to end this madness, do so swiftly."

Barushka was not pleased to be back in the blizzard so soon. Night had fallen and so had the temperature. A normal man and horse would have frozen to death in the temperatures and elements they pushed through. The thin rocky path was almost impassible, with unsettled snow and blinding sleet. Finally, it became clear that Barushka was far too large to chance going any farther. Leaving his friend behind, Cedric took only his grandfather's daito for company.

It was not long before he stumbled across the broken castle that lay in the darkness of the snowstorm. Blood and decay filled his nostrils as he worked his way past the frozen bodies and impaled innocence. His blood boiled as he stepped over and walked by not only soldiers, but also women and children. This was not the Vladimir he knew, but something more demonic in nature. The sultan was right to send him to take care of the matter. The front doors were falling off the hinges as he weaseled past them. Someone had downed them in an attack and seeing that he kept no being alive, no one was left breathing long enough to make the proper repairs.

It seemed like hours of wandering the desolate place of lavish ornaments before he came to a grand bedroom. It was dirty and broken as he entered and greeted him with an old sensation as his foot passed the doorway. He had failed to use his vampiric senses to locate Vladimir, but being within the same room was enough to trigger them forward. The vibrations he received from his grandfather were not the same comforting ones he had experienced in the past. These screamed of unforeseen ambitions and it became very clear why it had become customary for blood to chase blood.

"Cedric?" A broken man sat in a chair under ripped curtains, his long black hair now joined with a mustache and beard. His eyes were no longer the elegant yellow, but were large black iris framed with blood-colored eyes from overfeeding. Vladimir's clawed hands gripped the chair arms nervously. "I was wondering when they would call on you."

"What you have done is unforgivable." Cedric's jaw twitched, his senses telling him of the overwhelming power he had gained since their last encounter. "You have gone beyond killing other strigoi to killing humans for enjoyment. This is not the man I once met who was capable of being gifted a moroi—"

"You know nothing!" Vladimir's shout echoed throughout the castle of death. Gritting his fangs, his face distorted as his voice took on a demonic tone. "You do not know what it is to lose a child! And lose your soulmate! How dare you question who I am!"

"You have no idea." Cedric could feel the heat of his own anger seeping forward. "You lost them to death. Do you know what it is like to feel your soulmate's pain from torture? And I may have never conceived a child, but I lost my first love to my own animalistic instincts and acts. If this was what drove you to your madness, then I was wrong to have seen you as strong!"

Bloody tears rolled down Vladimir's eyes as he watched Cedric pale and sweat. Another wave of Angeline's torture had come. It was still difficult to keep himself from showing it outward, as invisible knives filleted his skin. Tears came against his will as Cedric's next wave of sensations made his heart ache. The sting and pull of threads worked their way through his skin. Unseen stitches were sewing his lips closed as the scraping of shackles tore at his wrists and feet. Merlin had grown tired of her mouth and now, standing before Vladimir, he had to endure what would have crippled him emotionally if he had been some place in solitude.

"That pain..." Vladimir's voice was soft as he looked on. "Is this the torture you speak of?"

Cedric's breath was racing, his words failing him as he felt the struggles Angeline fought against; each pull of the twain brought knots to his stomach. He felt the aches and pains from her pulling on her constraints. His hope was that it was from the pleasure, the ecstasy of knowing he was still out there looking for her.

"I can almost feel it, the stitches, and the struggle." He stood, wiping the tears from his cheeks. "But I do not care for your troubles..."

"Then we shall end this here." Cedric pulled the daito; a symbol of the good Vladimir, it would soon cut down the demon he had become. "It only seemed fitting that you would die by your own weapon."

"You're a fool." The room distorted about them, shadows swelling in size as Vladimir sunk into one. "I have been waiting here to absorb your power..."

Pushing his emotions down, ignoring the sensation of the tightening of the last stitch, he called on the moroi within him. If he had any chances in this battle, he would need his ancestors to do him well. Movement around him was starting to come to his eyes as Vladimir's corrupted laughter bounced in on him from all directions. His arm reacted on its own at the very second his eyes had sensed another glimmer of movement. The daito returned bloodied, though Vladimir's laughter grew wilder. Gaining focus was difficult with his binding pulling him out of the ability he was attempting to use.

Claws dug deep into his back, and turning, Cedric found nothing. Another slash across his abdomen caused him to stifle back, but much to his horror, this was a strike from Angeline's torture. A firm hand gripped his jaw from behind as Vladimir hissed into his ears, clawing his face and fading away as Cedric swung at him. The technique Vladimir was using was taking advantage of his current state. Once more, Cedric begged himself to focus. Another glimmer and he swung. Blood sprayed across his face, cold and black. An angry wail came from Vladimir as another strike hit Cedric's shoulders. It was hard to say through all the pains he was feeling how many times the two of them took turns taking another slice out of the other.

Covered in sweat, Cedric was painting the floor under him red. Black blood smeared the floor around him, but he could not get a clear visual on Vladimir. There was no way for him to gauge who had the worst injuries, but he was not going to be able to keep the game up much longer. Once more, his senses shouted for him to swing. With a great roar, Cedric hammered the blade toward the ground. Screaming erupted from Vladimir as the blade pierced through his thigh and locked itself into the wooden floor beneath it. His game of cat and mouse had ended, and Cedric had a chance to see what damage he had managed with such blind swings. The deep cuts that crossed Vladimir's body were far more devastating than his own. He was somehow winning with luck.

"I will suck you dry, you hot-blooded halfling!" Ripping his thigh free, he toppled the weakened Cedric to the floor. "You are nothing to me!"

"Then the feelings mutual!" A flash of rage struck Cedric, a wrath shared by unseen forces that he had required from Vladimir so long ago. "I will not let you kill me as long as she's still alive, Vladimir!"

"You have no choice in the matter!" Hissing, claws dug into Cedric's throat.

The shredding of his veins popped as the sharp nails took hold. The sensation of Vladimir's tongue brought a sense of fear, and Cedric's heart raced. His strength was failing. Perhaps he had grown too weak as a monk all these years. Studying and not using his abilities, denying himself the pleasures he once indulged in before losing Angeline. Perhaps he had done the opposite of his grandfather and simply hid from his loss where Vladimir was lashing out against the world. Many times, his anger had brought him such thoughts. Those painful nights full of Angeline's torture, he lay crippled in his room at the monastery hating the world and his existence. The agony had done more damage than he thought, and he was losing the strength to struggle to save his own life, let alone live long enough to save her.

Vladimir was feeding, gaining power while he was dying, growing colder. Another wet scrap of his tongue sent chills across Cedric's spine. Painful stitches tugged at his lips and with uncanny speed, he snapped himself out of the trance Vladimir had induced. It had been so subtle that Cedric failed to consider he would use such a low-level skill on him. His green eyes flashed with fury as his own blood spilled down his chest, his hand gripping Vladimir's throat. The strength Cedric pulled from baffled both of them, but as the incubine horns pulled forward and wings shadowed the both of them, it became clear. This was not a fight between vampires, but the king incubus and an overfed strigoi. Pleasure replaced his pain in his full form, a monstrous embodiment Cedric had not felt since the day he lost Angeline. His skin crawled with pleasure once more, his size equal to that of the Boto.

"I do not have time to die," Cedric growled as he slammed Vladimir to the ground. Grabbing the daito, he pinned his grandfather to the floor through his chest. "But, once more, I will need you to give me the strength and knowledge I need in order to survive."

A chuckle gurgled out of Vladimir. "You are no different from me if you feed from your elder against their will. They will send many to hunt you down!"

A smirk crawled across Cedric's face and fear took its place on Vladimir's face. "Oh, but you forget. I am not a strigoi, or even a vampire. I am an exception to your rule. Thriving on feeding on other demons, including your kind, has always been my way. This executioner has the right to claim the power held within."

Screaming and struggling, Vladimir was no match for the bulk of the incubine Cedric. Ravaging his grandfather's throat, he drank for the first time in hundreds of years. Claws ripped and ravaged his shoulders and back as the thrashing grew more desperate. Waves of pleasure washed over Cedric. His skin crawled in excitement as it welcomed the old sensations back home. Once more, as with the ceremony from so long ago, the foul filth had ended with one sweet drop. Releasing the ever-colder body of Vladimir, he roared his anger and grief to the sky. Tears flowed down his cheeks as the pang of loneliness mixed with the grappling of his body absorbing powers and knowledge. Life and death rattled him as he relieved himself of his incubus form and scuffled to a chair nearby. Holding his still-bleeding neck, he watched as Vladimir's body shifted to ash and collapsed. His body was too weak to move any farther. Satisfied that Vlad the Impaler no longer existed, he let the exhaustion take its hold on him.

"Well, you are up here, after all!"

A loud female voice interrupted his sleep, and he shifted his stiff, frozen body. Rubbing his neck resulted in finding a crusted material across it. His attempt to sit up failed for a moment, and panicking, he realized he could not back away. Hands rubbed across his forehead and cheek, and for a moment, his blurred eyes saw Angeline. "Angeline?"

"Oh, no! Wrong girl, lover boy." A chuckle came through as they placed a cold, wet cloth across his neck. Burning heat greeted his wounds as they began to scrub the hardened blood that covered him. "Looks like I missed a hell of a battle!"

"What are you doing?" Cedric hissed, his wounds failing to close in the time he had slept, each open crevice aching and burning under the cloth. "Who are you?"

"For crying out loud, it's me, Badbh!" Huffing, she continued with her rough nursing of cleaning so she could better see the damage done. "We found you out here bleeding to death! Who the hell did you get in a fight with?"

"Vladimir." Blinking several times, Cedric's eyes focused enough for him to see the customary bronze mask sitting on the floor next to where Badbh kneeled. Badbh's familiar scarred lip and chin framed the bottom of her pale face as she waited for his answer. "I was sent to end his tyranny by the strigoi and..."

"Ah, I keep forgetting the strigoi like to clean up after themselves." Cedric hissed as she moved on to the slashes across his shoulder. "Shame I missed this one, though. I was in the area after I had gotten word of some nasty battles. I was hoping to participate and give those Turks a boost of morale. It tends to keep the wars motivated for my entertainment."

"Wait." Sitting up with great effort, Cedric pushed her back a moment. "What did you mean by, 'we found you?'"

Badbh shuffled to the side, clearing his visual range to the bulk of fur that stood in the doorway. Yellow eyes peered back, a brand etched into the werewolf's chest. Romasanta sat patiently, awaiting Badbh to finish cleaning Cedric up. The unnerving sensation that crawled up Cedric's spine added to his worries. The room was icing over. It was hard to say how long he had been sleeping, or how long Romasanta had been in the area. Shaking off a cold chill, Romasanta smirked and turned his attention back to watching the doorway.

"Romasanta found you, and then called on me." Badbh stood up, sighing. "How he even knew I was in the area, I have no idea."

"How did you find me?" Leaning forward brought more pain as he broke his bloodied back from where it had attached itself to the fabric of the chair. "What are you doing out here?"

"You spilled so much blood that the smell was making me sick." Romasanta huffed. "And like you, I am always searching for information on the matters that concern me. My research led me here, but instead, I found you, pup. It seems we were meant to cross paths again."

Cedric sighed, staring at Badbh and Romasanta. It was strange seeing those faces again after so long. Feeling his destroyed neck, he realized how lucky he was to be breathing somehow. Something within Vladimir wasn't mixing with the magic that kept him as one being. Covering his face, he mulled over what to do. He had no Angeline to drink from, and he was far too weak to push himself. Romasanta huffed once more and left him alone with Badbh, as if in a silent gesture to the answer. He needed someone of a magical bloodline to reconnect his bloodlines, and in the current world, most had been slaughtered, watered down, and would not do him any good. Looking back up, Badbh nodded.

"I told you my life was yours for saving my sister from Beelzebub. Romasanta is fully aware of what you were in need of; otherwise, he would have brought someone else to this place." She kneeled before him, pulling her hair to the side, her nerves calm and solid. "Whenever you are ready, Cedric."

A look of dread crossed his face as he stared at her neck. It already bore several scars where blades had attempted to free her of her head. Anxiety and regret were haunting him as he felt his thirst encourage him to give in. Reluctantly, he took her neck, his fangs pushing firm against her flesh as he drank. Warmth was flowing back into his body, confirming how close to death he had come. Eyes tight, his thoughts stayed focused on Angeline and the need to survive in order to save her from Merlin. He would have to make many sacrifices in order to accomplish the impossible. The moment he felt the last broken tie within him fixed, he jerked away.

Badbh had been shoved back onto the floor. Grasping her neck, sweat sparkled across her skin as she smirked at him. "Wow, never thought it would feel so exciting-"

"I don't want to know." Wiping his mouth, his scowl made it clear he was not pleased with having to depend on her, or anyone. "But, thank you."

Managing to scavenge some clothes, they regrouped where Romasanta and Barushka stood in the snow. The blizzard had passed long before they had found him. Barushka trotted about them, happy to see Cedric once more, alive. Badbh wasted no time to leave, seeing the discomfort the experience had been for Cedric. Romasanta shook snow and ice from his fur as he smirked at him. Once more, the father of werewolves wanted something.

"What sort of deal do you want out of me this time?" Cedric leaned his forehead against Barushka's as he gave the shag foal hearty pats on his muscled neck. "I know that look, and we both know you do not save others unless there is something in it for you. What will you ask of me now?"

"Well, let's just get to business." Steam rolled out from his massive nostrils as his yellow eyes shined. "I believe we are chasing the same foe."

Pausing a moment, Cedric shot the old werewolf a glare. "And what has Merlin done to you?"

"You are looking at it." The smirk faded from his massive jaws, and his lips curled in disgust. "Merlin is the one who did this to me ages ago. I am immortal and tortured to live as a disease upon humankind for his own enjoyment."

"Then, are we to work together to get both our hands on the bastard wizard?" Cracking his neck, Cedric grinned at the idea of having such a powerful ally. "Is that the deal? Free exchange of information between the two of us?"

"That is essentially the deal." Standing, Romasanta offered one of his massive claws as a moment to shake in agreement. "I want the killing blow when we find him."

"I just want Angeline safe." Shaking, it was agreed. "But what makes you think I can locate someone that an old dog like you has failed to do so?"

"Let's just say, I have a gut feeling that you already have a plan and just need time."

CHAPTER 24

THE SISTERS ARRIVE

"Whoa, so Merlin is the one that cursed Romasanta?" Tony was wiping down a few tables on the floor as Cedric finished the new installment of the story. "Man, this wizard really likes to piss people off."

"He's a clever one." Badbh scoffed. She had been coming in with Cedric the last few Thursdays. "But I was wondering what the deal was and why you two became buddy-buddy."

A smirk crawled across Cedric's face as he finished sipping his drink. "By the way, would you like something to drink with Badbh and me, Romasanta?"

"No, thank you." Tony stood in bewilderment as the homeless man's, Romasanta's, yellow eyes flashed for a moment before going back to looking out the wintry window at the back of the bar. "Badbh is far too much for me these days."

"What is going on?" Tony's body shivered, not from the cold, but from the alarming feeling that was taking over his instincts. He returned behind the bar, the only barrier he found some comfort in. "These are the people from your fairy tale? This is insane. I must be dreaming. Is this some sort of prank?"

"We have much to discuss with you, Tony." Cedric met Tony's panicked face with a stern look. "But just wait a moment longer; we have more on their way. When they get here, I will explain what is going on. Please, do not be startled. No harm will come to you."

"Harm?" Tony's back hit the shelf of bottles, all of them clanking and wobbling in protest from his intrusion. "Are you crazy?"

"What a mess." The door rang as two more women walked in from the snowstorm that painted the streets white. The one who was talking met the description of Morrighan as she shivered in her black fur coat while the other huddled deep into her similar white coat. "You were never good at being diplomatic, Cedric."

"It has nothing to do with my lack of diplomacy." Cedric's jaw muscle twitched as he glared at Morrighan and Nemaine, who walked over to greet their sister. "I blame your sister."

"Stop knocking your knees together, boy, and pour me another round of Jonnie." Badbh crossed her arms. "Or just hand me the bottle."

Tony shook as he gave the bottle up to the sorceress and her two giggling sisters. He found himself lost in his own flood of fearful thoughts as he stared into the glowing green eyes of Cedric. The story he had spent weeks listening so deeply to was becoming more and more tangible, but his mind and heart were conflicted with one another. His elbow knocked into a bottle, it rolled on its heel for a moment before falling to the tiled floor. The crashing and shattering of the glass sent everyone silent. The eyes that stared at him were all strange and inhuman as he stood paling in the moment. The door to Rusty's office swung open and the bar owner stomped out, his face reddened. He paused a moment, surveying the room as he scratched his large gut through his stained, button-up shirt. Snorting to himself, he shoved past Tony, leaning over the counter, staring down Cedric. His ploy for intimidating him was failing as smirks crawled across the sisters' faces at the move.

Clearing his throat, Rusty's green tooth grin added to his scummy demeanor. "What's with all the ruckus?!"

"I have no clue what you are talking about." Cedric's tone was smooth. "I invited some friends over, that's all."

"I know who you are, and you are going to cause me more trouble than what it's worth." Badbh laughed some before taking another thirsty swig from her bottle of Jonnie. "Leave here and don't come back. You and your friends are no longer welcome. It's bad enough you have my girls spooked."

"No. We are staying. I have business with Tony." A fang was peeking out from under Cedric's lips as he spoke.

Looking back at the startled Tony, Rusty snorted again. "What do you want with a partial blood like that? The kid knows nothing."

"Step aside, Rusty." Cedric stood, towering over all in the room in size. "This has nothing to do with you, your girls, or your kind. If you stand in my way, it will bring unwanted attention in your direction, Himeros. I know exactly who you are."

"Hah, I haven't heard that name in centuries." Crossing his massive arms, he huffed. "Shocked to see something like you is capable of identifying someone of my power so easily in today's time. What gave me away?"

"I am the king incubus, head of the vampiric order, the hero Ilya Muromets, Bringer of Death, Slayer of Demons, and more importantly, Lord Romulus." A wicked grin snaked across Cedric's face, his pupils catlike as he leaned over the bar top, fingers breaking through the wood with ease. "I am the all-knowing, you godling of the Greeks!"

Tension filled the room and no one dared to intervene. The sounds of the snapping of wood were interrupted by the whistling wind of the blizzard. A bell cried out from the front door and a hard snow-filled wind blew across everyone. A tall, voluptuous woman walked in, her dress lacking winter protection, and her long, white hair fell behind her as the door shut. The licking of her tongue graced her dark red lips and her red eyes fell upon Cedric and Himeros. Her heels clicked as she walked toward the commotion. Rubbing herself against Cedric, she provocatively nibbled his ear. There was no reaction or movement from Cedric to her obscene behavior. She turned her glare to Himeros and a wicked grin crawled across her face as she groped her breasts that lay loosely under the covering of her black dress, bringing his stare to them.

"Well now! Since I can't get what I want from the incubus king, I shall settle for the son of Aphrodite and Ares!" Himeros paled as she pulled herself to sit on the bar top, leaning over to him. "I don't recall ever laying with you. Let's see how much you actually inherited from your father, godling."

"Li-Lillith." It came out as a gasp before she gripped the hair on the back of his greasy head. "This can't be."

"Did your daddy ever recover?" She licked Himeros from his neck to his cheek and temple. "Mmm, not completely, I see. No worries, Cedric, baby, leave this one to me."

"Enjoy your new toy, Lillith." Pulling his fingers from the bar top, he turned his back to her, his tautness toward her overpowering the atmosphere prior. "Come join us at the table, Tony."

Desperate to add distance from Lillith, Tony scrambled out from behind the bar to catch up with Cedric. Himeros screamed as Lillith dragged him to the back office, his face white with horror. They stopped at Romasanta's table where Cedric gestured he slide in first. Being between the vagabond-dressed Romasanta and Cedric was like sitting between two prison walls that could destroy you if touched. Tony shook, unable to control the fear that drowned every thought, muscle, and beat of his heart. All he could hang on to was Cedric's words, "No harm will come to you."

He watched as the three sorceress sisters cleared the center of the room from its tables and chairs. Badbh put a foot to the pool table, and with an effortless motion, kicked it into the bar where they all had been sitting earlier with an ear-shattering clash. Bottles tumbled to the floor, and with each hit, Tony jerked where he sat, wincing uncontrollably. Laughing as she downed the last drop of her Jonnie Walker, she tossed it into the remaining bottles that had miraculously survived her first assault. Candles were marked and laid out in particular orders as Morrighan consulted a large tome. Nemaine danced about as she lined the floor with salts and other herbs and items.

"Tony." Cedric's voice jolted his attention back to them. "Let me explain what is really happening."

"O-Okay." Swallowing, he braved to look Cedric in the face.

"I apologize for the intrusion into your life, but you hold a very important key that I need in order to locate Merlin."

"Merlin?" Tony's confusion was growing. "What do I have to do with Merlin?"

"I am afraid, more than you realize. And you even have something to do with me." A sheepish grin came across Cedric's face, but the look in his eyes was soft. "I hope you were paying attention to my story, because what I am about to explain might seem confusing otherwise."

"I think I can recall a good amount." Tony's heart was pounding in his ear, his stomach turning into tighter knots. "Go ahead; explain it to me, please."

"You are a blood-relative to both Merlin and me."

It took several minutes for this to soak in, before Tony came up with his next question. "Ok, and how is that possible?"

"Well, there was one element I had failed to consider in my hundred-year youth, and that was the responsibilities of the king incubus. As much as it sickens me to admit, I am responsible for replenishing the world with succubi and incubi. I took advantage of this fact and have taken a different route than Boto. It is rare that I have to kill one of my offspring, but they are all very aware of my search for Merlin and Angeline. By some bizarre turn of fate, along some point over the hundreds of years, one of my children slept with someone from Merlin's original bloodline, or even Merlin himself, perhaps. That line moved forward for at least 200 more years before someone was born with at least some essence of holding the magic in their veins." Cedric paused a moment to receive a nod from Morrighan, clearly a motion to signify they were ready. "You carry a strong bond and connection to Merlin. All I need is one drop so that I can launch my attack on him. This keeping and torturing of Angeline has gone on too long."

"How?" Tony paused, his mind chewing over the information, and, out of need, he continued the next harrowing question. "How do you know if she's even alive after all this time?"

"I feel her pain." Cedric's eye dulled and his complexion paled. "Every burn, cut, broken bone, and magical torture I have felt in full force. In doing so, she has felt the love and pleasure of which I can only give her, letting her know I am still here looking for her. She has had all her fingers broken, her ribs cracked, healed, and cracked again. Legs smashed with the weight of hammers and the cuttings of a dull blade that snags one's flesh in such a way that it is more like being torn open. Magic has seeped deep within her body and soul, but with the pain going to me, Merlin has failed to cleanse me from her body or break our bond."

Tony stared at the broken man before him, realizing that all this time, his only reason to keep living was for a chance like this. Despite such a tiny spark of hope, he chose not to take it with force. Holding out his arm, Tony pushed back his fright as he spoke his shaken words. "My blood is yours."

Morrighan wasted no time to rip his hand open with her blade, gathering the blood in a copper goblet. The three sisters took their places on their ornamental floor pattern. They hummed and swayed, facing the center of the pattern where the goblet sat. Tony watched as he held his throbbing hand close as the blood in the goblet spilled upward. It snaked in the air, forming a large spiral design before starting its rotation, spinning like a coin. It made a popping sound as it burst into a blinding light, as if someone had taken a picture in the darkness of the bar.

Tony sat bewildered in the shattered bar, alone.

CHAPTER 25

MERLIN'S DEMISE

Cedric's ears hummed and the darkness he saw took a moment to fade away to light as his eyes adjusted. A damp, putrid smell hit his nose as he wobbled to his feet. He found himself standing alone on the foggy shoreline, freckled with black rocks. Before him was the faint sight of a castle. It was hard to say how tall the building was, drowning in the haze that filled the sky that even hid the sun from sight. Magic engulfed the air here, and there was no sense of time and whether it passed at all here was questionable.

His ears were met by the lapping of the waves against rocks, but no sounds of seagulls could be heard. No creature in their right mind would set foot near Avalon. This was a cursed place where terrible magic had stained its very nature. Distorted and filthy, Cedric rubbed his nose, wishing he was not so sensitive to such things. His sensations for Angeline had heightened. She was here, but Merlin's magic was sending the compass spinning. There was no clear sense of direction in this place.

He made his way over the rocks and seagrass-covered slopes of sand. Reaching the granite outer walls, he picked a direction and began to follow it. After a moment, he could see a large bulky shadow on the path up ahead. Romasanta was in his full form; his muscles were tense and he wore a hard look. Nodding to Cedric as he drew closer, he sniffed the air with his large, doglike nose. His ears pricked forward and his fur ruffled. He had managed to find some sort of scent to follow among all the magical distortions and barriers. Without Romasanta, there would have been a high risk of being forever lost in one of the many magical barriers that protected the castle from intruders.

"What is the full story behind you agreeing to chase Merlin?" It was a question that had been dodged more times than Cedric could count as he followed behind Romasanta. "What history do you have with the old wizard? Besides the fact that he cursed you? I assume you had something he wanted."

"More than you would want to know." His yellow eyes flashed back at Cedric. In that look, there was a similar pain shared. "Let's just say he is to blame for my form and my own heartache. He is a greedy man, and deserves what is coming to him. I pray to the Ancient Ones that I am the one who rightfully serves him with the punishment that he has been avoiding."

"I see this is the sort of story that dates farther back than any man who was capable of writing his own history to paper." Cedric sighed, recognizing that he was treading on dangerous ground with Romasanta. "I just wanted to know that this was not one of your backdoor deals, again."

Scoffing, Romasanta managed a toothy grin. "Fortunate for you, this is a personal reason that requires my direct dealings to satisfy the wants and needs I feel. Perhaps later on in life, I will reveal my story to you, but not today, pup."

Surprisingly, they stumbled across a crevice in the castle walls. It was becoming clear now that Merlin's obsessions with wards and his own greed had distracted his ability to physically maintain the castle and surrounding area. Perhaps at one time this was truly a place of good and provided safe harbor to many, but the smell of rot was heavy as they tore away more bricks to gain access into the hallway that lay on the other side. Nodding to one another, they split ways. Both were capable of covering a vast amount of ground and holding their own until the other could catch up.

Once more, Cedric struggled to gain a sense of direction. Without Romasanta's uncanny sense of smell, he felt lost. Angeline's bond tugged at him. Having been nearly severed for so long made the sensation feel savage and desperate. Shaking it off, he wandered halls that seemed to lead to dead ends, with no doors or even spiraling stairways. Time did not exist inside the castle, and worse off, it made the air thick and choking. His own magical stitching was reeling from the contact with such spoiled magic.

By pure chance, he came across the old broken hallway. It looked heavily used and at the end of the hall, two heavily used oak doors stood tall. Walking up to them, his nerves tightened, his skin crawled excitedly. There was no mistake; Merlin was on the other side. The muscles in his jaws tightened as he pondered waiting for his comrade. Taking in a deep breath, he swung the doors open with great force. Merlin swung around, bottles from his alchemist's table shattering against the stone floor as they dropped from the old wizard's hands. The look of surprise turned to anger as his pale eyes met the demonic green ones.

"Where is she?" Cedric's voice was stern as he marched closer to the wizard, fearless. "Your time with her ends here, Merlin."

"This is not right!" Disbelief filled Merlin's voice as he jerked up a large book from the table, thumbing through it. "You cannot be here, demon. What manner of trickery is this?! No magic in the world could have brought you here! Why have I not received warning? How were you brought here to my doors so quickly?!"

"Why, of course not." Cedric smirked, seeing the confusion on the wizard's face as he consulted his tome for an answer. "It was not magic, but our grandson that brought me here. Was that not generous of him?"

"Filth! A blood relative of mine has to willingly give the blood to you in order for Avalon's calling spell to work." Outraged, he threw the book to the ground and threw a ball of wizard's fire at Cedric's feet, who failed to flinch. "They have to declare their blood to be yours and no spell has to be cast on them when they do so! Only those given the blood blessing can pass through Avalon without fear of her wards and spells!"

"Do not be surprised, Merlin." Crossing his arms, Cedric enjoyed seeing the panic and bewilderment Merlin was drowning in as the wizard rubbed his forehead. The wizard had engulfed himself in his work so much over the centuries that he had driven himself mad. "I am fully aware of the stipulations that you have put in place. You have given me plenty of time to figure this out, and I took my time to gain my grandson's respect. However, being the demon that I am, it would have been far quicker to snatch him off his feet and sacrifice him to the cause, if that would have worked for the spell."

"Impossible! This cannot be!" Ravaged in his rage, Merlin swiped his arms across his table, sending all of his alchemy gear and bottles smashing to the floor. A fog of panic was taking its hold of the old wizard's mind, now facing a demon he had no time to deal with as he was running out of time to achieve immortality. "Outwitted by a demon, a mixed blood abomination made by magic itself is unforgivable! I have been too careless in dawdling in spells on breaking that blasted bond of yours!"

Cedric watched as Merlin cursed gods of names he had never heard of and pulled at his hair, mumbling about how his own spells had betrayed him. This was not the same wizard that Cedric had faced before. He was older, his time fleeting, a panicked old man who had run out of time. The investment in Angeline had failed him. His torture of her had come to trickle in the last few centuries, and now the once coy and clever Merlin was nothing more than a senile old man. Fear was swallowing him, destroying the great rival he had once been. This did not mean he was any less powerful, but simply not as focused. There might be a chance after all.

"Don't worry, Merlin. We'll help put you out of your misery." Merlin turned, his eyes locking onto the dual set of fangs that mockingly grinned at his distraught. "Your time here has ended."

"We?!" Merlin huffed as he leaned on his table, glaring at Cedric over his shoulder. "You brought more demons to my dear Avalon? How dare you defile this place!"

"No, I am the only demon standing on this hallowed ground." Cedric held up his left hand, the missing finger left an unsettling gap in his large hand. "I came to cash in my payback for this and take back what is rightfully mine, wizard."

Merlin's stare with Cedric broke as something slithered across his hand. He paled as a two-headed cobra sneered up at him. Its red eyes flashed. The speed with which it struck left him little time to react. Stinging pain crawled up from his hand where the two heads gnawed at his flesh. Veins were blackening as they snaked up his flesh. Tossing the snake to Cedric's feet, more panic flooded the wizard. Trembling, Merlin fell to his knees, chanting desperately in order to slow the progress of the poison. His eyes glowed a deep azure blue as he worked his magic. Slowing the venom to almost a stop, he gave a smug grin to Cedric.

Nemaine appeared from thin air; her snake slithered and coiled around her leg as she stood behind Cedric. Wrapping tightly around her ankle to the top of her shin, the snake turned to gold, its ruby eyes the only hint of life left. Her insane smile expressed her love for the ways venom worked. Pain waved through Merlin, the black veins breaking into a run and stopping again. His magic was failing him as he stared up at the wild eyes of the venom sorceress. Nemaine looked like a Greek goddess staring down at the feeble old wizard, whose expression shifted to hatred at how easy it was for her to belittle him.

Tossing more balls of magic at them, Cedric and Nemaine dodged them. The heat and spark of the impact on the floor sent chills across Cedric's skin. An injury from one of them meant instant death as he watched one more sink and melt into the stone floor. Another wave of Nemaine's venom slowed Merlin down as he gripped the aching hand. Coughing up black ooze, he raged on, muttering more healing spells. Nemaine once more let out one of her wicked laughs, seeing that she had managed to best a high wizard as ancient as Merlin. Unlike the foolish wizard, Nemaine had been granted immortality for her devotion to her love of toxins. Merlin could only slow the bite of the venom goddess's snake. No magic could undo the damage done. Feeling the godlike magic tearing him apart, Merlin stood once more, casting more spells and an onslaught toward them. His aim was skewed as his vision blurred.

Arms wrapped around Merlin from behind, one hand gripping the Amulet of Avalon as lips tickled his ear. "It's my turn to have this again."

Morrighan jerked the Amulet of Avalon free of Merlin's neck, his eyes wide in terror. Nothing happened as Morrighan stepped back, attaching the amulet to her skirt. He laughed as he stumbled on his feet, still chanting under his breath. The azure glow was flickering in and out of his eyes, like a candle fighting gusts of wind. The two sisters looked at one another, neither of them sure as to why there had been no recoil. Merlin was building a ball of wizard's fire in his hand, fuming in Morrighan's direction. He reached his hand back, ready to launch the oversized fireball. Pain exploded across his hand again. Merlin looked back to watch his fingers fall to the ground and his wizard's fire with it. The air filled with the smell of smoldering flesh as his own fireball devoured his fingers. A blade had sailed through his flesh; Merlin's lack of focus had been a grave mistake.

"I don't think so." Cedric's green eyes were wild as he sheathed his sword. "Let's all play fair now."

The point of a blade brought his attention to Cedric and the three sorceress sisters. Badbh's brass raven mask greeted him, her dagger drawing blood as Nemaine's poison snaked up the wizard's neck. Fear was taking its toll on Merlin as he stood there, bleeding, poisoned, and caught between the vengeance of, not one, but four powerful beings. Gritting his teeth, Merlin began chanting loudly, the air about them vacuuming into him. As the glow in his eyes grew brighter, the black marks of the poison retreated, and his fingers were coming back into existence and bouncing off the ground to rejoin the hand they had fallen from, making all normal again. Merlin was turning time back on himself, and the shield around him had pushed everyone back.

Cedric's jaw twitched as he spat on the ground. Nodding to the girls, they vanished. They had done what they could, but now it fell back to him. Merlin's winds died down and he glared at him through glowing eyes. Wizard's fire was building in both hands as the two of them now stood alone. Laughter erupted from Cedric's mouth at the sight of the raging wizard. Sneering, Merlin threw the first fireball. Leaning sheepishly to the side, Cedric dodged it. He watched, amused, as Merlin's face reddened at the notion. Rage was blinding the old man before him, and he continued to pull it out of Merlin.

"Are you forgetting something?" Cedric stroked his chin, closing one eye as he continued his nonchalant mannerisms. "You've been around long enough. Do you recall how a curse and recoils work?"

"That is of no concern—" A loud sucking of wind muted all sounds.

Surprised, Merlin turned about to face the direction from where this commotion originated. A small black hole circled about, pulling the wizard in, showing no interest in the other items in the room. Merlin struggled, stepping backward, casting spells to slow its pull and gain any inch he could away from his recoil's fate. The thud and cracking of ribs jolted his body, his feet losing their touch on the stone floor as the black hole sucked the wizard in. As he spun and twisted in the air, his eyes met the unmistakable yellow stare of Romasanta. The stern look on the father of werewolves's wolf-like face was the last thing he saw before the black hole collapsed.

"You ok?" Cedric walked up behind Romasanta, who stood staring at where he had last seen Merlin. "I know it doesn't fix things but—"

Huffing, Romasanta walked past Cedric. "You're the only one who knows the truth about my curse and Merlin's involvement. Let's keep it that way."

Changing back to his human form, Romasanta walked out into the hall. Rubbing the back of his neck, Cedric sighed. Merlin was gone and the weights of promises made in the last several centuries were repaid. His skin crawled with excitement; Merlin's spells were breaking as they had thought. Smells were revealing themselves for the first time and one sent him in a run. The unforgettable smell of her salty skin sent excitement waving through him. As he instinctually ran through hallways, doors, and stairs, she was sending mixed waves of fear and excitement. It was clear she was aware he was there on Avalon, but the wards had fallen and the compass had stopped spinning. He was coming for her.

Landing a shoulder into a steel door, its hinges shattered. Thudding onto the dirt and stone, the weight of the block of metal vibrated the ground. The room was dark and chains rattled from the center of the dampness. There was an eerie silence as Angeline's fear waved to him, followed by more clanking of her chains. Cedric's eyes dulled as his eyes adjusted to the cold blackness of the dungeon. Slowly, he walked to where she sat. Her dress, once white, was torn and stained. The walls trickled with water; the floor splashed under his feet as he sank to his knees beside her, tears racing down his face. Her fear washing over him was choking, and all he wished was to take it all away from her.

Gently, he took her pale face into his warm hands. Her brown eyes watered at his touch, their bond electrifying every sensation after going so many centuries without touching one another. He thumbed her broken lips, stitched closed. Memories of that painful moment flooded through him. He had felt every needle jab and the ungodly sensation of the coarse twine pulling through each hole. She nuzzled her face into the warmth of his hand, ashamed of all the years of feeling nothing but pleasure for such ruthless torture. Pulling her chimera-hilted dagger from his belt, he cut the strings, softly pulling each strand free of her skin and flesh. When the last of them hit the ground, he leaned forward and kissed her cracked lips. She pressed harder into his lips, her chains scraping across the stone floor.

It took a few moments before he broke her wrists and ankles free of their iron homes. Scars littered her pale skin, serving as reminders to him of every moment he had felt them. Her hair was far longer than he had remembered and it lay tangled and damp all around them, like a gothic form of Rapunzel. Throwing her chains against the wall, he hugged her hard against his chest. Kissing her damp hair, the smell of mildew and filth filled his nose. She was dirty, cold, and broken. Clenching his teeth, his tears fell harder as she trembled from the waves of regret and sorrow that came from him. No words could come to him, but the emotions they exchanged were overwhelming. How she had lived through such torture and in such a place all this time was beyond him.

Angeline nuzzled his neck. Her tender kisses and waves of arousal pulled him farther away from his drowning in grief. Fangs scrapped across his neck, both of them excited from the sensation. His eyes grew wide as Angeline's fangs popped through the skin of his neck. Hungrily, she drank his blood, her warm tears sliding down her cheeks and meeting his skin only aroused him further. With a sigh of pleasure, he let her regain her strength through him. A wicked smile crossed his face as she bit down hard. His thoughts returned to the day she had been taken as Merlin's words echoed in his mind, *"I got here far too late and now will have to cleanse her of your filth."* This is why she had survived. The bonding had changed more of her than either of them had realized so long ago.

Shoving herself away, she had let go of her bite, panic erupting from her. Her mouth opened to form words, but her voice was still missing from having gone too long without using it. She was panting, confused and aroused, afraid and excited. Cedric pulled her back to him, shoving her on her back on the wet ground. Drunk from the excitement, his incubine instincts were reeling at the sight of his blood on her lips and chin. The pale color in her skin was fading away as warmth returned to her body. Scars were fading ever faster and her lips were returning to their rose petal softness before his eyes. Leaning down, he began kissing at her neck, chills crawling across her skin as his fangs teased her with every slight touch. Suckling on her earlobe for a moment, the warmth of his breath on her only added to her ecstasy.

"Don't be afraid, my angel." Kissing her cheek, he wiped the tears from her face and kissed her blood-covered chin. "With this, we can be together forever. I need you as much as you need me. We crave to drink from one another's blood. Embrace what you have become, pet."

"I—" Her voice failed her, but she swallowed and opened her mouth once more. "I love you, my Demon, my Savior, my Lord, my Cedric."

Passionately kissing, he ran a hand down her thigh. Her body trembled in excitement, no longer cold from the water that covered her. With every touch, every kiss and lick, their bond was reconnecting, remembering what it had once been. Cedric's horns and wings came out, adding to the stimulation that was overwhelming them. Angeline's memories of the night she had first lain with Cedric, where they had been bound to one another, flooded back to her. The compassion and tenderness of every touch and move from him focused on pleasing her.

Moaning and gasping escaped her lips with each gesture from him as her hands gripped his incubine horns. The ridges on his black horns felt like the handle to her dagger, making her release arousing waves through him from her own excitement at the thought. His green eyes locked on to her brown ones, and she shuddered under the shadow of his wings. The motion and the overwhelming strength he held onto her let her know that he would never let her go ever again.

CHAPTER 26

A Curse Broken

Tony was wiping off the new bar counter as he sighed. Stopping a moment, he rubbed the scar on his palm where Morrighan had ripped it open with her dagger. Rusty had sent him the deed to the bar, making the establishment his, and he hadn't seen him since Lillith had taken him to his office the night the place was destroyed. A mysterious check had also come to his personal address with an insane amount of money. He had invested most of it getting the bar in better shape than it had been before. It was now named The Lion's Den and he couldn't help but laugh to himself. He had definitely felt like Daniel that night with so many inhuman customers. The bell on the door called his attention to it, but he did not see anyone there as it slowly closed again.

"You'll never catch me actually walking in, you know." It was his Thursday regulars.

Stopping a moment, he smiled, pouring two vodkas on ice. "Here you go. Same as always, I see."

"I owe you the world, Tony." Cedric's green eyes flashed, grabbing the drinks up, no longer missing a finger. "How's business?"

"Booming since Rusty left." Waving at the short, brown-haired girl, he sighed. "And how are you doing today, Angeline?"

"Perfect."

To Be Continued...

READY FOR BOOK TWO?

ROMASANTA:
FATHER OF WEREWOLVES
IS WAITING FOR YOU.

If you enjoyed the book, or something really nagged you about the story, I encourage you to speak your mind about my book in the form of an honest book review. Both authors and readers depend on them to know if they will like the story and characters within the pages.

Where can you leave the reviews? There are a lot of places! Amazon and GoodReads are great places to leave them. But feel free to visit your favorite online venues and leave them there. Whether it's a one-liner that sums up how you feel, an in-depth review breaking down the book and characters, or a spoiler warning of a rant to follow—

ALL ARE ENCOURAGED.

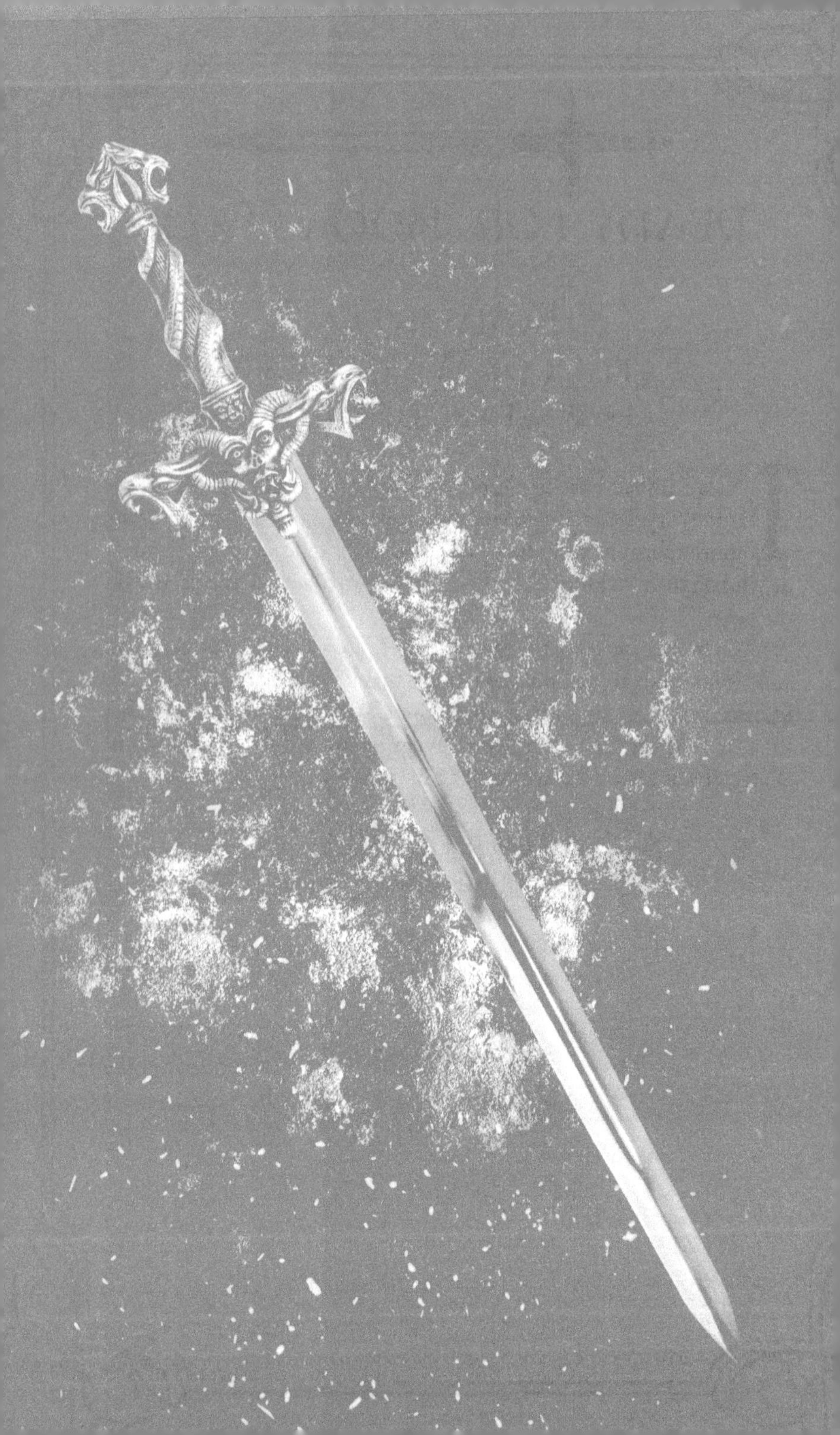

About the Author

Valerie Willis is the Chief Operating Officer for 4 Horsemen Publications, Inc., an expert digital typesetter, and a fantasy romance author based out of Central Florida. When writing, she loves crafting novels with elements inspired by mythology, legends, folklore, fairy tales, and history. As COO, she oversees the design of all books including covers, typesets, and author branding where she pulls in creative print design while making versatile eBooks.

You can find her hosting workshops or attending as a guest speaker at many events (MegaCon, DragonCon, OCLS Writers Conference, Florida Writers Conference, SavvyAuthors, Women in Publishing Summit, etc.). She's been on panels with best-selling authors from Peter David to Delilah Dawson sharing her expertise in writing, research, worldbuilding, character development, book design, reader immersion, and more. You can also find her co-hosting on the Drinking with Authors Podcast speaking with Jonathan Maberry, Heather Graham, Charles Gannon, and many more on their own journeys as an author! Or talking about the spooky stuff over on Eerie Travels with topics such as big foots, mermaids, and even Bloody Mary!

Her award-winning dark fantasy paranormal romance, *The Cedric Series*, is a blend of genres that appeals to a wide range of readers who describe it as "dramatic, lustful, and fantasy fulfilling." The motto here is: "No immortal is beyond the ailments of man" that includes powerful creatures, demons, witches, and deities! Many of the monsters are derived from Medieval Bestiaries adding a fun flavor of new yet deeply-rooted assortment such as Coin Iotair, Shag Foal, Cynocephali, and more.

Like many authors, her writing journey started in grade school and carried her through high school. Many who grew up with her talk often of the traveling binders that were often kept safe in their lockers. This was the precursor to the now complete young adult dark urban fantasy of the *Tattooed Angels Trilogy* starting with *Rebirth*. This alternative historic piece about immortals and a failed reincarnation Hotan covers a wide variety of life lessons such as whether to follow your own lifepath or the one chosen for you, breaking toxic traditions, and the obligations of cleaning up our family's mistakes and destruction. Inspired by her own life tribulations, it has been the beacon to keep her moving toward the world of books and writing even now.

For readers of fantasy MM romance, check out her pen name V.C. Willis with the Traibon Family Saga starting with books *The Prince's Priest* and *The Priest's Assassin*. If you are looking for steamy paranormal erotica, chase down Urban Legends and modern retellings of fairy tales with Honey Cummings. Many have found themselves laughing out loud and fanning themselves while reading *Sleeping with Sasquatch* and *Wanton Woman in White*.

In 2021, she left her day job to join 4 Horsemen Publications, Inc. full time to bring over a decade of typesetting skills and industry knowledge to the table. Nothing is more rewarding for her than making fellow author's dreams come to life in physical format so they may share them with readers. Designing and writing books has been a longtime passion since childhood of hers and she continues to inspire and encourage authors around the world whenever possible, indulging whenever she can to chat about the books folks are reading and writing.

Keep in touch and keep reading!

WWW.WILLISAUTHOR.COM

LINKTR.EE/WILLISAUTHOR

MORE BOOKS BY VALERIE WILLIS

Cedric: The Demonic Knight
Romasanta: Father of Werewolves
The Oracle: Keeper of the Gaea's Gate
Artemis: Eye of Gaea
King Incubus: A New Reign
Queen Succubus: Holder of the Crown

Val's House of Musings: A Mixed Genre Short Story Collection

Rebirth   Writer's Bane: Research 101
Judgment   Writer's Bane: Formatting
Death

ANTHOLOGIES & COLLECTIONS

A World of Their Own
Work of Hearts Magazine Release
How I Met My Other: True Stories, True Love
It Was Always You: A Thrill of the Heart Anthology

Demonic Wildlife: A Fantastically Funny Adventure
Demonic Household: See Owner's Manual
Demonic Carnival: First Ticket's Free

The Hunted—Thrill of the Hunt 3
Urban Legends Reimagined—Thrill of the Hunt 4
Buried Alive—Thrill of the Hunt 5

PUBLIC DOMAIN REMAKES

Bulfinch's Mythology with Illustrations
Book of Werewolves
The Fairy Faith of Celtic Countries

WRITING MM ROMANCE AS VC WILLIS

The Prince's Priest
The Priest's Assassin
The Assassin's Saint

The Champion's Lord: YONDER webnovel
Champion's Love: KU short story

WRITING AS HONEY CUMMINGS

Sleeping with Sasquatch
Cuddling with Chupacabra
Naked with New Jersey Devil
The Erotic Cryptid Collection

Laying with the Lady in Blue
Wanton Woman in White
Beating it with Bloody Mary
The Erotic Ghosts Collection

Beau and Professor Bestialora
The Goat's Gruff
Goldie and Her Three Beards
Pied Piper's Pipe
Princess Pea's Bed
Pinocchio and the Blow Up Doll
Jack's Beanstalk
Pulling Rapunzel's Hair
The Urban Erotica Fairy Tale
Collection

Curses & Crushes: KU short story

Queen's Incubus: YONDER webnovel

Book Club Discussion Questions

1. What character growth is seen in Cedric? Angeline?

2. At which point do you feel the two characters finally accept each other?

3. How does their love story differ from other stories?

4. After being bound to one another, what is a permanent after-effect? How does Cedric use this? How does this change him?

5. Chapter 12 reveals Cedric's past to the Angeline. How does this change your views on him? How does this change Angeline's views?

6. After finishing the book, was there any foreshadowing in the first chapter?

7. During the first half of the story, do you believe Cedric's attraction to Angeline was solely physical, emotional, or both?

8. During chapters 17 and 18, what does Cedric realize he wants to do with his life?

9. What is Merlin trying to do? Which of the characters seem to have been victims of Merlin?

10. In chapter 8, how significant were Angeline's words, "If I knew how to curse someone—I hope that you experience the worst heartbreak ever?" How did this come true? How was her recoil worse?

11. Who is responsible for resupplying the world with incubi and succubi? How does this affect Cedric after defeating Boto?

12. Barushka was feared to be dead. What did Cedric do to awaken him again?

13. The author was inspired by medieval period myths, lore, legends, and history. How much of this can you find evidence of within the reading? People, places, events, culture, or other means?

14. In chapter 24, what is the significance of Cedric stating the title "hero Ilya Muromets"? Why do you think the author placed this here?

15. Throughout history, Morrighan has been in many stories in several different cultures as well as portrayed in various roles. The author chooses to include her sisters. Why is this important? Does this help readers think of her as a different entity than what they have been introduced to prior to the reading?

16. What new creatures, myths, or other paranormal aspects were you introduced to?

17. If Cedric had known that Angeline had magic in her blood, how do you think he would have handled the situation?

18. Which characters are based on actual historical figures?

19. What events and elements of the story are based on medieval history and culture?

20. Out of all the opponents Cedric faces, which one, or fight, had the greatest influence on him? Why?